SPIRIT
OF THE
SEASON

Books by Fern Michaels

FEARLESS
SPIRIT OF THE
SEASON
DEEP HARBOR
FATE & FORTUNE
SWEET VENGEANCE
HOLLY AND IVY
FANCY DANCER
NO SAFE SECRET
WISHES FOR
CHRISTMAS
ABOUT FACE
PERFECT MATCH
A FAMILY AFFAIR
FORGET ME NOT
THE BLOSSOM
SISTERS
BALANCING ACT
TUESDAY'S CHILD
BETRAYAL
SOUTHERN COMFORT
TO TASTE THE WINE
SINS OF THE FLESH
SINS OF OMISSION
RETURN TO SENDER
MR. AND MISS
ANONYMOUS
UP CLOSE AND
PERSONAL
FOOL ME ONCE
PICTURE PERFECT
THE FUTURE SCROLLS
KENTUCKY SUNRISE

KENTUCKY HEAT
KENTUCKY RICH
PLAIN JANE
CHARMING LILY
WHAT YOU WISH FOR
THE GUEST LIST
LISTEN TO YOUR
HEART
CELEBRATION
YESTERDAY
FINDERS KEEPERS
ANNIE'S RAINBOW
SARA'S SONG
VEGAS SUNRISE
VEGAS HEAT
VEGAS RICH
WHITEFIRE
WISH LIST
DEAR EMILY
CHRISTMAS AT
TIMBERWOODS

The Sisterhood Novels
BITTER PILL
TRUTH AND JUSTICE
CUT AND RUN
SAFE AND SOUND
NEED TO KNOW
CRASH AND BURN
POINT BLANK
IN PLAIN SIGHT
EYES ONLY

Books by Fern Michaels (*Cont.*)

KISS AND TELL
BLINDSIDED
GOTCHA!
HOME FREE
DÉJÀ VU
CROSS ROADS
GAME OVER
DEADLY DEALS
VANISHING ACT
RAZOR SHARP
UNDER THE RADAR
FINAL JUSTICE
COLLATERAL
DAMAGE
FAST TRACK
HOKUS POKUS
HIDE AND SEEK
FREE FALL
LETHAL JUSTICE
SWEET REVENGE
THE JURY
VENDETTA
PAYBACK
WEEKEND WARRIORS

The Men of the Sisterhood Novels
HOT SHOT
TRUTH OR DARE
HIGH STAKES
FAST AND LOOSE
DOUBLE DOWN

The Godmothers Series
FAR AND AWAY
CLASSIFIED
BREAKING NEWS
DEADLINE
LATE EDITION
EXCLUSIVE
THE SCOOP

eBook Exclusives
DESPERATE
MEASURES
SEASONS OF HER LIFE
TO HAVE AND TO
HOLD
SERENDIPITY
CAPTIVE INNOCENCE
CAPTIVE EMBRACES
CAPTIVE PASSIONS
CAPTIVE SECRETS
CAPTIVE SPLENDORS
CINDERS TO SATIN
FOR ALL THEIR LIVES
TEXAS HEAT
TEXAS RICH
TEXAS FURY
TEXAS SUNRISE

Anthologies
HOME SWEET HOME
A SNOWY LITTLE
CHRISTMAS

Books by Fern Michaels (*Cont.*)

Published by Kensington Publishing Corp.

FERN MICHAELS

SPIRIT OF THE SEASON

ZEBRA BOOKS
KENSINGTON PUBLISHING CORP.
www.kensingtonbooks.com

ZEBRA BOOKS are published by

Kensington Publishing Corp.
119 West 40th Street
New York, NY 10018

All Kensington titles, imprints, and distributed lines are available at special quantity discounts for bulk purchases for sales promotion, premiums, fund-raising, educational, or institutional use.

Special book excerpts or customized printings can also be created to fit specific needs. For details, write or phone the office of the Kensington Sales Manager: Attn.: Sales Department. Kensington Publishing Corp., 119 West 40th Street, New York, NY 10018. Phone: 1-800-221-2647.

Zebra and the Z logo Reg. U.S. Pat. & TM Off.

First Kensington Books Hardcover Printing: October 2019
First Zebra Books Mass-Market Paperback Printing: November 2020
ISBN-13: 978-1-4201-4885-5
ISBN-10: 1-4201-4885-0

ISBN-13: 978-1-4201-4886-2 (eBook)
ISBN-10: 1-4201-4886-9 (eBook)

10 9 8 7 6 5 4 3 2 1

Printed in the United States of America

Prologue

Thursday, November 1, 2018

Anna Rose Huntley, all ninety-two pounds of her, took the last pan of orange-cranberry-nut muffins from the Sub-Zero oven, then checked the clock on the oven, caught her snow-white hair in the oven's reflection, and sighed. Who cared about hair at five-fifteen in the morning? Not her, for sure.

At Heart and Soul, breakfast was served promptly at six o'clock every day during the week and at seven on the weekend. Most guests liked to sleep in a bit on the weekends, and if they didn't, Anna always offered a bowl of fruit and several varieties of freshly baked loaves of bread, delivered promptly at 5:00 A.M. by Delirious Delights Bakery. Early-rising guests would never go hungry in her establishment.

Mary Jane Mosler, Anna's dearest friend from high school,

who had keys to Anna's famous bed-and-breakfast, sent her grandson, Kyle, to deliver the goodies every Saturday and Sunday. Sitting on a side table in the dining room, along with homemade jams and jellies and dozens of RealCup single-serve coffees, teas, and hot chocolates, were a twenty-four-carat-gold-plated Dualit toaster and a Grindmaster RealCup RC400 Black and Stainless Steel Single Cup Coffee Brewer for the convenience of early risers.

On weekdays, Anna insisted on preparing enormous breakfasts for her guests. After all, it was a bed-and-breakfast, and as the proprietor, it was her duty, and one she cherished. At seventy-one, she still had her health, pretty much, and her daughter, Elizabeth Preston, who'd recently turned fifty. Elizabeth had been widowed three years ago and seemed to be enjoying life cruising the world with her new friends. Her granddaughter, Joy, was a very successful businesswoman in her own right, a long-established tradition in the Huntley and Preston families. Though Anna had been disappointed when Joy chose the University of Colorado over Duke University or North Carolina State University, Anna reluctantly supported her choice, reminding herself that it gave her a reason to travel west once a year to witness her granddaughter's enterprising business, and it also allowed her to visit her friend Sophie Blevins, who occasionally stayed at that lovely beach house in California with her wacky but endearing group of friends. She'd send Sophie an e-mail this afternoon to catch up.

In keeping with the upcoming Thanksgiving theme, today's menu consisted of sweet-potato-honey biscuits, a turkey-bacon frittata, hand-rolled apple-raisin crescent rolls with a brown-sugar glaze, thick-sliced hickory-smoked bacon, freshly ground sage sausage patties, and hot buttered biscuits, along with her famous sausage gravy. French toast served with a pear compote and omelets made to order would keep her and Izzie, her assistant chef extraordinaire and honorary adopted daughter in mind only, busy for the next few hours. But she wasn't complaining, as this was her life, and had been the life of her parents, though back in their day, Heart and Soul had been known simply as Huntley's Boardinghouse.

When her husband, Samuel Huntley, had died thirty years ago, she'd completely restored the old boardinghouse, which had quite a rich history. Since the house was located in the Spruce City historic district and listed on the National Register of Historic Places, visiting it was noted throughout the state as one of the highlights of the Christmas season, owing to the extensive holiday decorations, both inside and out. And then there was the annual Christmas Parade of Homes competition, which she'd won for the last fifteen years. Heart and Soul was also very well-known for its Christmas cakes, cookies, pies, and other baked delights, which were provided to visitors attending the many festivities during the month of December she'd become so passionate about. She liked to think that Heart and Soul was a mini version of the Biltmore Estate in Asheville, though physically it was certainly nothing like the grand and lavish architectural marvel that George Washington Vanderbilt II had built and furnished late in the nineteenth century.

Anna heard Izzie singing at the top of her lungs in the prep kitchen. "Izz, quiet down back there; you're going to wake the dead." She heard Izzie laugh.

"Right," Izzie called back to her in a lower tone. "Don't need my singing to wake the dead around here."

Anna rolled her eyes. It wasn't a topic she wanted to delve into at this hour of the morning. "Just lower it a bit, okay? You know I enjoy your singing." She did. Izzie had a beautiful and powerful voice; she just sometimes forgot the time. Anna thought that Izzie, who was in her early fifties, was an exceptionally beautiful woman, with light brown skin and amazing butterscotch-colored eyes that sparkled like deep golden rays of sunshine. Today, she'd tied her long black-spiraled hair in a braid that reached her waist, cinching it at the bottom with an old piece of leather. Izzie had been divorced for twenty years and had never had the slightest desire to date or marry again—or so she said. Anna had hoped for years that Izzie would meet someone, but she hadn't and seemed as happy to be on her own as was her own widowed daughter, Elizabeth. Izzie had no family other than Caroline and Carl, her twins, who were living in Seattle. Anna always thought of Izzie and her children as the second family she'd wanted so badly all those years ago after Sam died. She was sure Izzie felt the same.

Currently, Heart and Soul had six guest rooms and two cottages for those who needed a larger space. The cottages were equipped with a small kitchen, Jacuzzi tubs, washers and dryers, and two bedrooms. These rooms were mostly used by families, whose visits were much longer in December than the average guests'.

During the Christmas season, she changed the names of the guest suites to something a bit more suitable for the holiday season. Each year, she did this, and each year, she delighted in doing so a bit more elaborately than she had the year before. While she hired professional decorators to do much of the work, she always assisted them with the minor details, making sure each suite was unique. They started in late July, as the planning and designing were quite an undertaking.

This year, the first suite they'd completed was the Santa Suite. It was perfect for couples with one or two children, as there were twin beds in one bedroom and a king-size bed in the master bedroom. The rooms were decked out in rich reds and dark green draperies with matching bed coverings, and throughout the years she'd collected every shape and size of Santa Claus she could find. This was one of her favorite rooms, as it personified what she thought of as the perfect Christmas guest suite. Her very own perfect Santa land. Given that Christmas was synonymous with Santa Claus, Saint Nicholas, Kris Kringle, and Father Christmas—to name just a few of the old man's many names around the world—it was only fitting that she have a suite decorated accordingly.

According to Western Christian culture, Santa Claus was a jolly older man who visits the homes of all well-behaved children. From her personal experience when Elizabeth was a child, Anna knew for a fact that her "Santa" also delivered to those who might be a tad on the ornery side. Just thinking about those days made her grin.

The Santa Suite had all different styles of the legendary old guy. Saint Nicholas, portrayed as a bearded bishop, wore his canonical robes. Father Christmas, his scarlet robes lined with white fur, was a personal favorite of hers. She'd picked this particular Santa up on a trip to

England. She'd collected many different examples of Santa, and they each had a special spot in this special suite.

Her second-favorite of the guest accommodations was the Teddy Bear Suite. A variety of bears—some new, some old, different colors, shapes, and sizes—decorated these rooms. Anna kept her favorite childhood teddy bear here but had had it encased in glass for the guests' viewing pleasure; it was too delicate and sentimental for her simply to place it in the room for touching. The material for the drapes in this suite featured replicas of all the teddy bears in the room. When guests realized this, they were always surprised. Anna loved this part most. What she hoped for was that her guests would take away memories they would cherish forever.

Nor did it escape her notice that, yet again, this made Heart and Soul the favorite holiday business in Spruce City. There were four other bed-and-breakfasts in Spruce City, and she'd been voted the favorite holiday business yearly since the inception of the award eight years ago.

Realizing that dwelling in the past wasn't going to accomplish a single thing, she went to the giant walk-in refrigerator in the prep kitchen, grabbed several cartons of eggs for the morning omelet lovers, and took them to an area set up for preparing, as the guests always seemed to ask for something different omelet-wise.

Back in the walk-in, she took out miscellaneous cheeses, mushrooms, spinach, onions, red and green peppers, tomatoes, jalapeños for those who liked a bit of heat in their omelets, and a bowlful of kale in case she had a guest on a health kick. She placed each item in a decorative dish and returned to the refrigerator for her special blend of half-and-half from Mrs. Moo, her favorite dairy cow from

Castle's Creamery in Siler City, North Carolina, located smack-dab in the center of the state. Other than having one of the best dairy farms in North Carolina, in Anna's opinion—one that was shared by many others—it was also notable as the city next door to the home of Frances Bavier, commonly known as Aunt Bee from the 1960s hit TV show *The Andy Griffith Show*. The farm's owners, Brenda and Norm Castle, made a weekly trip to Spruce City to deliver the coveted half-and-half. The Castles prided themselves on healthy, well-fed cows, and their diet proved to make a huge difference; it was their mixture of cream and milk that made her omelets as light and fluffy as a summer cloud.

Anna was reaching for the glass bottle of half-and-half when she felt a searing, intense pain in her left arm, unlike anything she'd ever experienced. She took a deep breath and felt a heaviness in her chest. She sat down on top of several boxes stacked in the corner of the freezer. As she took another deep breath, the pain from her arm radiated to her chest, and she felt as though she was going to pass out. "Izzie," she struggled to call out. The pain was so intense, she knew this wasn't indigestion or overexertion. She was seventy-one years old, not ready for . . . *this*. Again, she called out, "Izzie, help," but her words came out in a whisper. Hard to breathe, couldn't speak. Needed help.

Not. Going. To. Make it.

"Anna, what the heck are you doing, taking a nap in the freezer? For Pete's sake, we have guests ready for their breakfast," Izzie said when she entered the freezer and saw Anna sitting on the stack of boxes. Her head had drooped to her chest, and both arms were hanging loosely at her side.

"Anna," Izzie screamed, and grabbed her arms. "Anna?" she said, shaking her. "Wake up!" Realizing this wasn't Anna's version of a silly joke and that she wasn't napping in the freezer—something she'd never do—Izzie screamed as loud as she could.

"Someone call nine one one!"

Chapter 1

"I don't care how long it takes, just get it done, Hayley, please. We don't have a boatload of time!" Joy shouted into the phone, frustrated that she'd had to play boss. She did not like to play boss. At Simply Joy, she, Hayley, and Jessica were a team. They worked together and were great friends, but Hayley had worked on the new label for six weeks and still hadn't come up with an appropriate design for the Valentine's Day launch. Yes, it was closer to Thanksgiving and Christmas, and thank goodness, those polishes had been shipped to retailers across the world already.

Simply Joy was a successful nail polish company, her baby. Joy knew it sounded like a frivolous occupation to some, but nail salons, spas, and women across the globe used her products, and she was not going to settle for anything less than perfection.

"You said you didn't want hearts, Joy. That's what Valentine's Day is about. Falling in love, Cupid, pinks and reds, you know this," Hayley replied, then added sheepishly, "and chocolate."

Joy heard the desperation in Hayley's voice. They were down to the wire. "We need a totally different conception than our competitors have. OPT, Lacquer Lovers, Tammy's Talons . . . you know they're just dying to beat our sales this year. Do what you have to do, but do it fast, Hayley. We have exactly one week before we have to send our designs to the labeling department, and they'll rake us over the coals if we're late." Joy paused and softened her voice. "I'm really counting on you, Hayley."

"Sure thing, boss," Hayley said, then hung up.

Joy stared at the phone for a couple of seconds, then replaced it in its cradle. She hated being the boss sometimes, and now was one of those times. Hayley hadn't given this campaign her best, and now they were wading in deep water. She did not want her labels to look like those of all the other polishes out there in the land of lacquers. She wanted Simply Joy to stand out, to catch the consumer's eye with a color, a Valentine's Day label so original they wouldn't so much as glance at her competitors' products. That's what made her company unique. She'd almost cornered the market. But to her way of thinking, "almost" wasn't quite good enough.

A knock on the door interrupted her train of thought. "Come in," she said, not bothering to see who was at her door. She had a small staff of six, counting Hayley and Jessica, her best friends, webmaster, and graphic designer. All were welcome inside her office; her open-door policy applied to everyone.

Standing in the doorway, Hayley said, "I'll stay all

night if I have to. I know how important this is to the Valentine's Day launch. My brain just doesn't want to co-operate for some strange reason," she finished.

"I know you're trying your best," Joy said calmly, hoping to take the sting out of her earlier words.

"I am, and I'm on it. Really," Hayley replied. "I won't let you down. I promise," she said, then left.

Joy tried to focus her attention on the Christmas display that had been shipped across the globe in October. She'd worked tirelessly on this year's campaign and needed it to succeed to put her firmly at the top, once and for all. Again, almost wasn't quite good enough.

When she'd first come up with the idea to start her own nail polish company, she'd been in college studying business and marketing. Her marketing strategy and man-agement professor, Dr. Baines, told them that the simplest ideas were almost always the most successful. He'd then asked them to write down five simple ideas that made them respond in a positive and triumphant way. She re-membered at the time thinking her professor was crazy, but when she'd started the assignment, it hadn't been quite as easy as she'd thought.

While she'd had a few ideas for different types of busi-nesses, the one that wouldn't stop nagging her was now, as she looked back, pure genius. There was one little lux-ury that she completely enjoyed, and she knew that most women did as well—having beautifully painted finger-nails. Of all the indulgent, pampering services she'd had in her life, the one that brought her the most joy was sim-ple. She absolutely adored having her nails polished.

And that idea became Simply Joy.

Her product was presented in a classic square bottle with a square lid, the initials SJ etched on the front of the bottle and on the top of the lid. She'd chosen pigments that were different enough to make her colors stand out among dozens of others, and her company became known for being slightly different and edgy enough to stand out from the competition. And it had. Joy liked to think Simply Joy would continue to thrive as long as she and her staff were willing to work hard and never give up.

In the seven years since Dr. Baines had given his students that assignment, Joy had completed it and built the resulting company into one of the fastest-growing nail polish brands in the industry. Their overseas sales were at a record high this year, too, and she wanted next year to be even better.

She spent the next hour looking through dozens of new shades for her spring line and decided on a palette of pastel shades that gradually deepened in color for those who preferred a darker shade. Joy would personally try out all the colors before sending them to the lab for the final pigmenting process. She would check for color match, wear time, and ease of application. Simply Joy brand brushes were known for their long stems and rounded, flat brushes. This style made application easy for anyone, and professionals loved it because of its thin, accurate strokes. Fewer mistakes meant fast client turnover.

It was getting late, and there was no word yet from Hayley, so Joy decided she'd do an all-nighter herself. If Hayley couldn't come up with something on her own, maybe they could if they put their heads together. First, she needed to get the polish on her nails and start gauging the wear time for the spring collection. She usually did this several times before giving her final approval. Using the samples from the lab, she painted the nails on her left hand one color and those on her right hand another. She kicked off her Uggs and heavy wool socks, then polished her toes different colors, too. She found her sandals and slipped them on before heading to Hayley's tiny office down the hall from her own, which wasn't really all that much larger. She knew, when it came down to the wire, that ultimately it was she who had to come up with all the ideas, no matter how many employees she had. Yes, Hayley was a graphic designer, but in the end, none of those details were relevant. In the end, she needed results, and she could make them happen. She *would* make them happen. She tapped on Hayley's door.

"It's open," Hayley called out.

Joy entered the tiny workspace. "Any new ideas?"

"Actually, I think I've come up with a few designs that might salvage my pride." Hayley handed her a sheet of paper with three drawings sketched on the page.

Joy held the paper under the small desk lamp for a better view. "These are fantastic!"

"You sure?" Hayley asked.

"Yes, I am. You did us proud," Joy said, smiling. "Why don't you head home? It's after three in the morning, in case you haven't looked at the clock. You need some sleep."

"Dang, I didn't realize how late it was. Do I look that bad?" Hayley joked. "Though I'll go if you're sure?"

Joy laughed. "You're as gorgeous as ever. Now get some rest, and I'll see you later."

"Thanks for not giving up on me," Hayley said as she straightened her desk. "I don't know what's gotten into me lately."

"Give up on you? Never! Remember, we are a team, and I don't give up easily. I really like these, too." She fanned the paper out in front of her. Hayley had gone with simplicity. "We'll use the black letters, with a small heart dotting the 'I' in *Simply*."

"That's my favorite," Hayley said as she walked toward the door.

"Okay, now go home and get some sleep while you can."

Joy switched off the lights and returned to her own office. She should go home, too, but she had a few more items to check off her "get them done" list. She never referred to her lists as "to do lists." It was just a thing with her. She'd always been a doer and hated wasting time.

She spent the next half hour answering business e-mails and responding to messages from all of her social media groups. That in itself was becoming a full-time job. After the holidays, she'd look into hiring a company or maybe a freelancer to take care of that end of the business. Doing social media was great advertising, but it was tremendously time-consuming. They'd reached half a million followers on their Instagram page, and almost one million on Facebook. Many required a reply of some kind, even if it was nothing more than a like or a heart or a thumbs-up. She jotted this on her "get them done" list. Also, she would check into starting a YouTube channel. All of her competitors had one. She jotted this down on the list, too.

Joy shut her computer down and went to the office kitchen to make herself a cup of tea. She liked this quiet time to herself. Reflecting on her life, she decided that, right at this moment, she was totally content. Even though her father had died three years ago of an unexpected heart attack, she had accepted this as a part of life. As sad as it was, it had happened. She still had her mother, and her grandmother. She didn't see either as often as she would have liked to, but again, it was all part of being an adult. Or didn't they call it *adulting* these days?

The microwave dinged, and she took her cup of hot water and placed it on the counter. She rummaged through the canister of tea bags, found her favorite, orange spice, and dropped the tea bag into her mug. She added a splash of honey before heading back to her office. She'd rest on the futon for a while, then go home as soon as it was daylight. It had been snowing most of the day. While she knew the roads would be clear, the thought of driving now made her a bit edgy. Usually, she didn't mind the drive—heavy traffic didn't bother her—but for some reason, she felt as though she needed to stay in her office.

She sipped her tea, allowing her thoughts to wander. Most of her college friends were married now; some were expecting their first child. She had been so busy building her business, any thought of having a serious relationship was just that—a thought. Joy had always wanted a family of her own and knew age would be a factor a few years down the road. She was twenty-nine. Not too old yet, she thought. There would be time, just not in her immediate future. Her cell phone buzzed, jolting her from her reverie.

"Who in the world?" she thought, as she reached for her phone. This had better be good. It was after four in the morning. Late-night and early-morning phone calls didn't usually bring good news.

"Hello."

"Joy, it's Izzie."

"Izzie, I hope there's a good reason for your calling at this ungodly hour." The words were out of her mouth before she had a chance to filter them. It was after six on the East Coast. Still, too early to make phone calls unless there was bad news.

"Hey, kiddo, I know what time it is. It's your grandmother," Izzie said.

"What do you mean, it's my grandmother? Is she okay?" Joy stood up and began pacing across the small space. Definitely not a good-morning call. Immediately, she felt an intense sense of loss, knowing the news she was about to receive was not going to be good.

"They did everything they could, but they couldn't save her," Izzie explained.

Joy stopped pacing.

"Does this mean what I think it means?"

"I'm afraid so, sweetheart."

Chapter 2

Denver International Airport was filled with holiday travelers from all over the world. The colors, accents, and smells almost suffocated Joy. It was the last place she wanted to be. To be sure, she wasn't traveling to a location to take advantage of sand, surf, and sea. Nonetheless, where she was going had all of those, sort of. Spruce City did have sand and the sea, and there were surfers. It was just that this was the wrong time of year to take advantage of those amenities.

In a daze, she pushed her way through the throngs of people and headed toward her gate. She hadn't planned on returning to North Carolina for the upcoming Thanksgiving holiday, and if she were honest with herself, she had had no plans to return for Christmas either. Could this be her grandmother's way of getting her home for the holidays? No, Nana wasn't that cruel. And she really wasn't that old ei-

ther. To the best of Joy's knowledge, she hadn't even
been sick. If she had, she'd kept it to herself. Tears filled
her eyes. Nana Anna is, *was*, the best. She'd certainly
picked a heck of a time to . . . *die*. Feeling guilty for even
having such thoughts, Joy looked up and realized she had
arrived at her gate. She saw that she still had an hour before they were due to board, so she located a seat next to
a woman with a baby and a toddler.

The woman, probably close to her own age, held her
baby in one of those sling things, while she watched the
toddler, a little boy, run in small circles in the aisle in
front of them. Joy gave her a quick smile. "Cute," she
said, nodding toward the little boy. "How old?" she asked
the woman.

"He's almost three, and this little bug is only five
weeks old."

Joy sneaked a peek at the infant. Girl. Pink clothes.
Tiny pink bow taped to her downy blond hair. A pink
pacifier clipped to her pink clothes. *Pink overload*, Joy
thought. Maybe a new nail polish color? Before she forgot, she took her phone out of her pocket and typed the
name in under "Miscellaneous" in her notes app. Business was business.

"So is this their first airplane trip?" Joy asked, not
really caring one way or the other. She was making conversation, avoiding thinking about what she had to face
back home in Spruce City. It was home, but not home.
She'd moved to Denver as soon as she'd graduated from
high school. Colorado had been her home her entire adult
life. "Back home" and "Spruce City" didn't belong in the
same sentence, she thought.

"It's Betsy's first trip. Ben has been on a few. We're

from Spruce City. It's my home," the young woman said, a smile lighting up her hazel-colored eyes.

Joy nodded. "Mine, too. A long time ago."

The woman adjusted the infant in her sling. "Going home for the holidays . . . it's the best trip ever, don't you think?" she stated in a dreamy voice.

What in the world had she gotten herself into? A talkative young woman and two little ones. Praying she wasn't seated close to them, Joy said, "Uh, yes." She hated to tell a half-truth, but she didn't feel like answering any probing questions.

The past three days were a blur. She didn't remember much after Izzie's early-morning call. Her mother was somewhere out in the Pacific and hadn't a clue she'd lost her only remaining parent. Joy dreaded breaking the news to her, but there was no one else to do it. According to Izzie, her mother was due to arrive soon in Tampa, Florida, where she'd catch a return flight to Spruce City tomorrow evening. Tears filled her eyes. Her mom was great, and she had suffered so much when her father died. She didn't deserve this. Taking a tissue from her tote bag, she blotted her eyes.

"Are you okay, sweetheart?" the young mom asked. Joy nodded and felt a fresh wash of tears fill her eyes.

"You sure don't seem okay to me, hon," she said, her Southern accent more noticeable now. "You want to talk about it?"

She shook her head. "I'm . . . fine. Really." She was anything but fine and felt silly for her public display of tears, but she was grieving in so many ways. She wiped the tears from her cheeks, then blew her nose. "Thanks," Joy added, not wanting to appear rude.

A male voice came over the loudspeaker, announcing that her flight was ready to board and asking that all passengers with a disability board first, followed by anyone with small children. Joy gave a silent prayer of thanks as the woman secured the sling and baby on her shoulder, picked up a rather large bag, draping it over her other shoulder, then reached for Ben's hand. "Maybe we'll be seated close together?" she said, smiling.

Joy nodded. "Maybe."

"Well, have a nice flight if we're not," the woman added.

"Sure," Joy said. "You, too."

Taking a deep breath, Joy checked her cell phone for any messages from Hayley or Izzie. Nothing. She put the phone on airplane mode when her seating assignment was called. Taking her boarding pass from her bag, she went to stand in line with the other passengers.

Joy was seated at the very back of the plane, several aisles away from the woman and her small children. "Grateful" didn't begin to describe how she felt, though she did feel a slight tinge of guilt for having such a thought.

She had almost five hours to work on several business-related issues. She had been hoping that would keep her mind occupied with relatively trivial things, but it wasn't working. She couldn't focus; there were just too many other more important issues now.

Giving her mother the news of Nana's death was probably going to be the most difficult thing she would ever have to do. Her mother was a very tough woman. She'd survived the loss of her husband at a relatively young age and continued to move forward in life, going on a variety of cruises around the world and making new friends, and

Joy hoped that someday her mother would meet some-one. She was only fifty years old, way too young to spend the rest of her life alone. These thoughts ran through her mind as she tried to stay focused on her work-related matters, which, truth be told, were nothing more than minor details about nail polish colors. In the scheme of things, certainly none of them were as important as family. She'd been away for so long, she'd forgotten what life was like back in Spruce City. Her hometown was a place where the entire town seemed to know every detail possible about the lives of its citizens. In Denver, Joy was relatively anonymous, running into people all the time who had no clue about her life.

One thing that she was sure of: she could never live in a small town again, certainly not Spruce City. It was too personal, too invasive. The local pharmacy knew what medications you took; the postmaster knew how much mail you received and, when it arrived, most likely knew what was being delivered. You couldn't call to get out of work for a sick day because the entire town would know about it; then they'd come to your house to offer advice, food, or stories that were so long that you'd recover from the illness that kept you home in the first place. No, she was too citified to go back to that lifestyle. And why would she? She had her own life in Colorado. She planned to stay for a week—two at the most—just until things were settled. Nana had run the bed-and-breakfast, a very thriving one, but she was sure her mother would step in and take over. She knew the business almost as well as Nana. And there was Izzie, who'd been with them so long, she'd become family. Maybe her mom and Izzie could run the place together. Maybe they could turn it into a B&B for singles only. Maybe they'd each find someone to love, and she could return to her life in Denver guilt-free.

Why, she asked herself, *am I having such thoughts? There's no reason for me to feel guilty. Mother is my biggest, staunchest supporter. She would never ask me to give up my life and my business.*

Her Nana had wanted her to stay in North Carolina and attend one of the many colleges in the state, but Joy had been adamant about Colorado. The winter before her high school graduation, they'd taken a family vacation to Vail during her Christmas break, a rare trip for her family. They'd skied nonstop for a week, and Joy felt as if she were leaving part of herself behind when they'd returned to Spruce City. Something about all those mountains, the snow, the lifestyle, the people had made her feel as if she belonged in Colorado. It was all she talked about, though at the time, she really hadn't given a lot of thought to how it would affect her family. A week after she graduated from high school, she was gone, and to this very day, she'd never looked back. Now, she remembered how sad her Nana had been, how she'd offered her the moon to stay in Spruce City. In hindsight, maybe she should have given more thought to her family, especially Nana, but it is what it is. Once Nana saw how happy she was, she'd been elated at her graduation from college, and even more so when she'd started Simply Joy. Nana's friend Sophie Blevins lived in California. When Nana came out west for a visit, she'd always spend a few days in California. Had anyone called her friends? Izzie probably had everything under control, as usual. They were so blessed to have her in their lives.

In the past, before a new nail polish was released, Joy always made sure Nana, Mom, and Izzie received a big care package of her latest colors before they arrived in the stores. Naturally, her family was quite proud of her success and always encouraged her to be the best she could be, no matter what her profession. There was no reason for her to feel guilty for wanting to leave Spruce City. Yet it was only natural for her to feel this way under the circumstances, to think about the time she could have been with Nana, the time she could have spent with her father. They were her family, and she loved them. She closed her eyes and, much to her surprise, drifted off. And when she woke up, the flight attendants were giving their usual spiel: tray tables needed to be put in the upright position and seat belts tightly fastened as they prepared to land.

After she got off the plane, she quickly located her suitcase at baggage claim, rented a car, and prepared herself for her stay at Heart and Soul. Izzie would be waiting for her. The B&B was at full capacity this time of year and would remain so until after the New Year. Many of Spruce City's festivities were centered on Heart and Soul. Joy always enjoyed the extravagant Christmas trees, the rooms that were decorated in a different theme every year. It was the best place to be during the holiday season, but this year, she had her doubts that this would be the case.

She was unsure whether her mother would continue with Heart and Soul's elaborate Christmas extravaganza; she wouldn't blame her if she chose not to. However, if Joy knew Nana as well as she thought she did, she would want them to continue the tradition. The question was, would her mother be up for the task? Would *she*? It wouldn't matter, because she didn't plan to stay around that long. As she told Hayley, one week, two max, and she would be home—she had a business to run. If her mother was unable, surely Izzie could handle the Christmas festivities?

In the parking garage, Joy located her rental car and clicked the key fob to open the trunk. She hefted her luggage inside, then settled into the driver's seat. Giving herself a few minutes to familiarize herself with the workings of the new vehicle, she pushed the START button, and the car's engine hummed to life. Catching a glance of herself in the rearview mirror, she was surprised at how ragged she looked. Her reddish-blond hair could use a wash and a blow-dry; she hadn't bothered with makeup. Purplish half-moon shadows emphasized her deep blue eyes, which were bloodshot from crying. She was a mess but didn't care. All she wanted right now was to see Izzie, take a hot shower, and figure out how she was going to tell her mother the sad news.

She could have literally walked from the airport to the bed-and-breakfast; it was only about two and a half miles, but she couldn't see herself dragging her suitcase that far, not to mention how silly it would be.

As she drove the short distance, she admired the Neuse River, which paralleled the main road leading into the heart of downtown Spruce City, where Heart and Soul was located. She gave a half-hearted smile as memories of small-town life flooded her mind as she drove down Main Street. She remembered how friendly, how Southern, many of the shops and business owners were. Unique boutiques, restaurants, and a variety of locally owned shops dotted the small city. Bells chimed from the old clock, which was part of the local history. The City Hall Clock Tower made up half of the city's skyline, yet it was certainly nothing compared to the Mile High City she called home. But the redbrick buildings around Main Street were part of what gave off that friendly, small-town vibe.

Part of the downtown's history was the old pharmacy where the soft drink Cherry Crush was born. If you weren't a Cherry Crush drinker, you'd best hide your drink label if you had a soda in public. Joy had always been a Diet Coke person herself but would never let this fact about herself become known. Joy realized she *did* miss small details like this. Not that it was relevant to her life in Colorado; it was just a good memory. Most of all, her memories of living in Spruce City were good. Any negative thoughts came only from her teenage imagination. At times, she'd thought the place a little backward, and not quite as fast-paced as Raleigh or Charlotte. As an adult, Joy had come to realize that the quiet pace was part of the town's charm.

The B&B was at the end of Main Street, and guest parking was behind the giant structure where her grandparents had lived, and their parents as well. She found an open space, then maneuvered the rental between an SUV and Izzie's old silver Cadillac.

The ancient, three-story mansion reminded her of something out of a Thomas Kinkade painting. Even though it was November, the shamrock-colored grass remained as vibrant as it was in the summer. Heart and Soul was stunning all the year round, and at Christmastime, people from across the state of North Carolina, as well as other Southern states, came to view the elaborate decorations, both inside and out. The Parade of Homes was just one of the many holiday activities for which Spruce City was famous.

Each guest room had a different theme every year. Joy

could not wait to see how Nana and Izzie, along with a full staff of interior designers, had created another year of new designs. They had managed to keep them fresh and unique for almost thirty years. A work of love, Nana always said.

The grand porch wrapped around the entire structure. Tables and comfortable chairs of all kinds, a swing, and dozens of potted plants and ferns hung in various places, creating a look of comfort and old Southern charm. The entrance to Heart and Soul was as homey and inviting as the inside.

Joy tapped on the back door leading into the prep kitchen. She didn't want to startle anyone. Izzie herself opened the door. As was the norm, Izzie looked beautiful, even though she wore an apron and had tied a bright red scarf around her hair. "Oh, sweet girl, I'm so glad to see you, but I wish it wasn't under such sad circumstances." She pulled Joy into a tight hug, then stood back to look at her. "Young lady, you need to be fattened up. Your Nana would have a fit." She stopped when she realized she had spoken of Joy's grandmother in the past tense. "Well, let's just say she wouldn't like to see what a little bone you've become."

"Nice to see you, too, Izzie. And we both know I am not a bone. I weigh one hundred and six pounds, the same as I have since I was in seventh grade." She said this with a smile. She was petite, just like her grandmother, who also had had reddish-blond hair and deep blue eyes. She resembled Nana more than she did either of her parents. Izzie and her mother had always thought she should weigh an extra twenty pounds.

"You're a twig, young lady," Izzie said. "Now, let's get you something to eat. Most of the guests are out and about right now, so we practically have the place to ourselves."

"That's unusual," Joy said. "Anything going on in town?"

"There's a cookie bake-off at Mary Jane's today. She's supervising; otherwise, she would be here," Izzie explained as she removed large covered bowls from the refrigerator.

"That sounds like fun," Joy said. "Izz, would you mind if I took a shower first? I've got five hours of airplane crud on me and who knows what kind of germs."

"Of course, baby. I'm putting you in the Scrooge Room. It's all that's available."

Joy couldn't help but laugh. "The Scrooge Room? That's a good one."

"Your grandmother's idea."

"It sounds like her," Joy said, her voice full of unshed tears. She dabbed at her eyes with her shirt. "What exactly happened? She never indicated to me that she was sick or felt bad."

Izzie had her back to her as she heated something on the stove that smelled divine. "Like you, I didn't have a clue. She hadn't seen the doctor, that I know of; she didn't complain of anything. She was just her usual self—busy as a bee, and then some. I wish your daddy was here. He would've known if she had a problem with her heart."

Her father had been a cardiac surgeon, her mother a nurse practitioner. "It didn't do him any good, so I doubt if he would've known if Nana had heart troubles. Of course, if he'd examined her, maybe. He used to say the healthiest person could drop dead of a heart attack without a second's notice. That's exactly what happened to him." They'd all been shocked when an autopsy showed he'd suffered a massive heart attack.

"Very true. When it's our time, it's our time. At least that's what I've always believed." Izzie removed a bowl from the cupboard and spooned a delicious-smelling soup into the bowl. "Eat this, and I don't want to hear one word out of your mouth until you're finished."

"But I want to take a shower first," she reminded her.

"Food first, young lady," Izzie said, trying to force a stern tone. She poured her a glass of milk, buttered a thick slice of crusty bread, and put it on a plate, placing it beside the soup. Joy didn't realize how hungry she had been as she delved into the hearty vegetable soup. She ate the bread, then chased it down with milk. "That was delicious, thank you. I guess I didn't realize just how hungry I was; I missed breakfast and lunch." She hadn't eaten anything since lunch yesterday, and that had been half a tuna sandwich and a handful of grapes. She couldn't eat when she was stressed.

"That's why you're so skinny. You want a bit more?" Izzie nodded toward her empty soup bowl.

"Thanks, but I really am stuffed. I just want to shower and prepare myself for . . . Mom," Joy explained.

Izzie nodded. "Where's your luggage? I'll have Lou take your bags up to your room."

Joy fished through her purse for the keys to the rental car. "Here. It's parked next to your Caddy. I can't believe he's still able to"—she paused, not wanting to hurt anyone's feelings—"able to work." She whispered the last words in case anyone was within hearing distance.

"Okay, I get it. You think he's too old." Izzie gave her a mischievous grin. "Your room is on the third floor. The old Jingle Bell Room, now known as the Scrooge Room," Izzie said. "It's the only room available unless you want to stay at your mom's place. Just so you know, she's put it on the market. I wasn't sure if you'd want to stay there with strangers poking around."

Joy tucked her purse beneath her arm. "No, you're right. I'd much rather stay here. Mom should've put the house on the market a year ago. It's too big for one person. She mentioned it the last time we talked."

Her parents had built their dream home while she still was in nursery school. She'd been around three or four when they'd moved in. It was a beautiful house, overlooking the Trent and Neuse Rivers, but it was huge. Her parents had lived in one of the now-renovated guest cottages at Heart and Soul when they were first married. In her youth, she'd always spent as much time at the B&B as her parents would allow. It'd been exciting, especially during the holidays—working, doing anything that required an extra set of hands. All of the guests coming and going, the food, the effort it took to run the place was ginormous, and she'd been captivated by all of the hustle and bustle. Of course, that trip to Colorado all those years ago had totally changed her perspective on her hometown. Maturity and time had mellowed her, she'd realized as she'd driven from the airport earlier. Spruce City was charming, but she'd keep that thought to herself.

"Now go on and get your shower while Lou brings your luggage to your room. It might take him a while. Him being so old," Izzie said.

"I didn't mean . . ." She stopped. "Exactly how old is Lou?"

"Old Lou"—Izzie made air quotes—"is fifty-eight. Six years older than me, young lady."

Joy absorbed that bit of information. "Oh." He'd been

with Heart and Soul her entire life. For some reason, she'd thought him much older, even though he really didn't look all that old, other than his white hair.

"Go on. Us old folks will take care of your luggage," Izzie teased.

Joy nodded and decided it was best to drop the subject. "Thank you."

Knowing why the Scrooge Room was available, or knowing what Izzie and her Nana believed about this particular room, made her laugh out loud as she climbed the stairs. For years, they'd thought the room was haunted. Apparently, word traveled because the local ghost tour guides touted Heart and Soul as one of the most haunted B&Bs in Spruce City. She'd never experienced anything even remotely "ghostly" herself. Her Nana allowed this bit of info to be shared in travel pamphlets and had thought it a great selling point when it came to the B&B. Joy was sure her business acumen was inherited from Nana.

Upstairs in the so-called haunted room, she grinned at the décor theme. The bed, an antique four-poster, was draped with cream-colored sheer panels, giving the giant bed a hazy, supernatural appearance. Joy almost expected to see old Ebenezer himself tucked beneath the covers, but even for Nana, that would've been too much. Though she did notice a copy of Charles Dickens's *A Christmas Carol* on the night table. Apparently, this Scrooge Room was decorated in a similar fashion to the one depicted in the old movie, which starred Reginald Owen, a movie she was quite fond of. Growing up, she'd watched it during the holidays, and when she thought of Scrooge, that room always came to mind. Apparently, Nana's thinking had been the same.

The room was sparsely furnished. A couple of rickety-looking chairs flanked the giant fireplace several feet from the foot of the bed. To the right of the fireplace, the room had a window that overlooked the Neuse River, a grand view. It was wasted with the drapes closed, Joy thought, then pulled the drapes aside. On the left side of the fireplace was a desk, nothing more than a wide plank of wood, with two holes, where one might've placed ink-wells. Joy was surprised Nana hadn't added an inkwell or two, but maybe she hadn't had a chance to complete the décor. Basically, the room was barren, with few extras. However, this was Heart and Soul, and in the far corner of the room a giant Christmas tree filled the room with a fresh pine scent. She touched the tree and discovered it was real. She leaned in to inspect the ornaments—a small wooden chair, a miniature crutch, a turkey, bright golden coins, and little people who on closer examination appeared to be the characters from the story: Jacob Marley, Bob Cratchit, Tiny Tim, Mrs. Cratchit, and the other Cratchit children. She laughed again.

The en suite bathroom had been spared no expense when it'd been remodeled last year. There were marble counters and copper sinks. In the center was a giant soaker tub, and there was a separate, glassed-in shower and a toilet hidden away in a small, closet-like room. For-est-green bath towels and washcloths were placed on a towel warmer, one by the tub, another within hand's reach of the shower. Heart and Soul had its own brand of sham-poo, conditioner, and bath soaps, all scented according to the seasons. Taking a small bar of hand soap from a copper soap dish, she smelled a light scent. Cranberry. *Nice*, she thought. She looked into the mirror above the deep copper sink. "I look like a ghost," she said out loud. Though she wanted nothing more than to fill the tub with hot water and soak until her skin wrinkled, she knew that would have to wait for another time. As in all the guest rooms, there were thick, heavy robes with "Heart and Soul" embroidered in the same forest green as the towels the guests used, and they'd always been available for purchase, too. She owned two, and they were her favorite. Hurrying now, she took a quick shower and washed her hair. Wrapping herself in the plush robe, she located a hair dryer in the cabinet beneath the sink and dried her hair. She saw her luggage inside the room, courtesy of Lou, and quickly slipped into a pair of dark Paige jeans and a cream-colored cashmere sweater. She used a Tom Ford lipstick in soft peach, added a swipe of mascara, then touched her cheeks with the lipstick for a bit of color. She didn't want to look like one of Nana's ghosts. She'd touch up again before she saw Mom tonight. Her heart lurched.

After losing her dad, Mom was devastated, as one would expect. They'd grieved deeply and together, even though she was in Denver; she video-chatted with Mom daily, spoke on the phone, and e-mailed. Gradually, her mother had returned to life, and that was when she discovered how much she enjoyed cruising. Her first cruise had been for widows and widowers, and she'd made new friends; some, Joy knew, would be her mom's friends for life. Grateful her mother had made new friends who were in the same situation, she secretly hoped she would meet someone and fall in love again. As she'd thought many times, her mother was much too young to be alone. Wool-gathering, her Nana would call this. "Stop," she said out loud. Izzie was waiting downstairs.

Before Joy left her room, she quickly unpacked her luggage, thankful there was a large walk-in closet in the room—something, she was sure, that Ebenezer Scrooge didn't have in his fictional life. Dickens, either.

Chapter 3

Joy entered the kitchen and found it empty. "Izzie," she called, loud enough for her to hear if she were close by, but not so loud as to disturb the guests if they were relaxing in the formal area or having a snack in the dining room.

A snack. Yes. Izzie was probably hosting the afternoon snack—an adult snack, wine and cheese, with a variety of desserts from Delirious Delights Bakery. At least, that's how it used to be. Unsure, Joy headed for the dining room.

When she reached the formal dining room, she stopped and stood stock-still. "What are you doing here?"

"Joy Elizabeth Preston, you ought to be ashamed of yourself!" admonished Izzie.

"But . . ."

"Be quiet and come over here and give your mother a

hug," her mom said. Joy did as instructed. Relief flooded her as she realized her mother already knew, and that she wouldn't have to be the one to tell her. She held her mother tight, tears filling her eyes.

"Mom, I'm so sorry about Nana. I . . . how were you able to come home early?"

"Izzie called the cruise line. I was able to take a speed-boat to shore; they have those in case of an emergency. I caught a late flight to Charlotte last night. There weren't any flights to Spruce City until this morning. I didn't feel like driving, so here I am."

Even at fifty, her mother was a stunning-looking woman. Her light brown hair reached her shoulders, and her blue eyes were an identical match to Nana's and her own. She had full lips and a slim figure, was much taller than Joy's five feet, and appeared much younger than fifty. They were often mistaken for sisters. Elizabeth had been a young mother, and though it was true, Joy agreed, that they looked a lot like sisters, Joy loved her like a mother and knew that her mother felt the same way about her daughter.

"Are you okay?" Joy asked in a low tone.

"I will be, sweetie. How about yourself? I know what a shock this must be for you," her mother said.

"I'm sad, Mom. I will be all right, but it will take time. It's like it was with Dad, though I don't think I will ever stop missing him. Now Nana." Tears filled her eyes, and she let them flow. Her mother wrapped her arms around her.

"We will get through this, too."

Joy nodded. "Where is the wine and cheese?"

Izzie looked at Joy's mother.

"Elizabeth, I believe our girl forgets she's on eastern

time now. We had wine and cheese an hour before you arrived. But I do believe your Nana has a fine collection of wines downstairs in the supply room. Come on; you'll both be surprised."

Joy looked at her mom, who shook her head, indicating that she, too, was clueless.

They followed Izzie downstairs to the giant pantry where they stored the supplies for the B&B. There were shelves on each wall, stacked with condiments, canned goods, and all the items they needed that were bought in bulk and could be stored for long periods of time.

"This," Izzie said, holding her hands out as wide as she could, "was Anna's Christmas gift to herself this year."

Joy stood beside her mother, and her jaw dropped in amazement. "A wine cellar, room, whatever they're called," Joy stated.

"Yes, this was something she'd always wanted but made a million and one excuses as to why she shouldn't, but she bit the bullet this past summer and had this mini wine room built. It was supposed to be a surprise," Izzie explained.

Elizabeth shook her head. "Well, if that's what Mom wanted to do, then I'd say she's done a darn good job. I wouldn't have thought of this, but it makes sense. When she went to Paris last year, she came home with a new appreciation for wines. I guess I didn't realize just how much."

"I think it's amazing," Joy observed. "She always hosted wine and cheese time. It makes sense that she would need proper storage. Especially for this," Joy added, removing a bottle of wine from the shelf. "Ghost Pines Zinfandel."

Joy looked at her mom, then Izzie. They all busted out laughing.

"No doubt about it, Mom had a sense of humor. I think we should open a bottle of champagne and make a toast. What say you?" Elizabeth asked, looking at Izzie, then Joy.

"I think it's the best idea I've heard in days," Joy said. And it was. Since Izzie's early-morning phone call three days ago, she'd been devastated but had been doing her best to keep her emotions in check. That was her way, and she knew it was her mother's, too.

"Izz, you do the honors since Nana shared this surprise with you first," Joy offered. "If you want."

Izzie made fast work of removing three glasses from a newly installed hutch. "Of course I want. I'm honored to be the first one to," Izzie's golden eyes puddled with tears, "toast Anna and share this gift with you girls." Izzie twisted open the little wire cage that held the cork in place and carefully began to open the bottle. A soft, hissing sound, then a pop.

"Mom was more of a wine connoisseur than I thought," Elizabeth said as she perused the shelves. "2012 Le Cigare Volant Reserve. 2009 Cos Contrada. These are excellent wines."

"Mom, earlier you said you knew what a shock this was for *me*. Am I wrong to read more into your words?" Joy asked while Izzie poured their wine.

Elizabeth drew in a deep breath. "You're quite perceptive, and yes, Mother had issues that she didn't want anyone knowing about. Given my profession, it was hard *not* to catch all the signs. For the past year, Mom had been short of breath and didn't have her usual energy, that extra zest she was noted for. I asked her about it for months, and she refused to acknowledge she had a problem. Finally, before I left on this last cruise, I told her she had to see Frank Dutton or else.

"He's the best there is. Your father was, too, but . . . no matter. I told Mother she had to go for a checkup, or I would personally drag her to the doctor myself. And I would have. I think she knew it was time. Even though she wasn't that old by today's standards, she couldn't remember the last time she'd had a complete physical, so she reluctantly agreed to go."

Izzie added, "And believe me, it was not an easy task for Elizabeth. Your Nana was as ornery as ever. I had to promise her I would devote every waking moment to the guests before she would go. I just thought she was going for a basic checkup. Nothing serious."

"Sounds like Nana," Joy said. "Stubborn."

"Frank checked her over and sent her straight to the hospital. They did a stress test, then she had a calcium heart scan, which showed some blockages. Frank was concerned enough that he called me and said Mom needed surgery."

"Why didn't she have the surgery?" Joy asked. "It's not like she didn't have health insurance in addition to Medicare."

Elizabeth shook her head. "I know. She wanted to wait until after Christmas, said she wanted to get through one more season, then she would do whatever was necessary. Needless to say, she shouldn't have waited. I should've stayed here and kept an eye out for her."

No one spoke.

Izzie swallowed the rest of her champagne, then refilled their glasses. "I'm here all the time. It was me who should've kept an eye out for her, though I didn't know she was in such dire shape. If I had known, she wouldn't have been working fourteen-hour days. I blame myself for that."

"Look, if there is anyone to blame, it's me. I knew her condition, knew that she was scheduled for a future surgery, yet I chose to go on that cruise. I'm her daughter. I should have been here."

"I'm not going to let myself off the hook, either. She asked me all the time to come and spend November and December with her, and I was, I am always too busy. I could've made the time. Hayley would've covered for me."

"Listen up," Izzie said, with renewed vigor. "Anna would have a hissy fit if she knew we were sitting around blaming ourselves for her passing. And she'd be madder than a hatter if we drank and didn't make a toast. So, I am proposing a toast." Izzie held her glass out. Joy clinked her glass, then her mom followed. "To Anna."

"To Mom. To Nana," the daughter and granddaughter added.

"Since we're here, alone, I'll tell you that Mom took care of her final . . . arrangements," Elizabeth said. "I have, too, just in case. The details are with Will Drake."

"Mom!" Joy bellowed. "I don't want to hear this now, okay? I've had enough grief. And who is this Will Drake? His name sounds like something out of those old *Perry Mason* shows you used to watch in reruns! I bet you still do."

Her mother blushed. "I'll admit I do. With Netflix, I can watch those and a lot of other old programs anytime I choose."

"Is this about TV or your mom and grandmother? 'Cause if it's the former, I've got a ton of programs I can recommend," Izzie said, her voice raised a notch.

"You still haven't told me about Will Drake," Joy persisted.

"He's the family attorney, Joy. He has been for a while."

"What?" Joy asked, her word a bit slurred. The champagne on an empty stomach was starting to have an effect on her verbal filtering process.

"She's too skinny," Izzie observed. "I told her she needs to put a few pounds on, but do you think she'll listen to me?"

Izzie and Elizabeth cackled with laughter again.

"Mom! Izz, what's going on? You're acting like twelve-year-olds. The least you could do is let me in on the joke."

"I think we've all had one too many glasses," her mother said.

"Oh," Joy said, "I think I need to lie down. My stomach isn't working right."

More laughter, then her mother took her hand. "Come on, sweetie, I'll take you up to your room. I think we're all a wee bit tipsy. Izzie, don't finish that bottle by yourself. I'll be right back."

Chapter 4

"**W**hat do you mean? I have a business to run. I live in Colorado now. I can't believe she would do this to me!" Joy practically shouted.

"Look, Ms. Preston, I am not the enemy here. Nor was your grandmother. These were her wishes. As her attorney, I am legally bound to follow her instructions. I am very sorry that you don't agree with them," Will Drake explained.

Will Drake was as handsome as her mother was beautiful. He had to be at least six-foot-three, with shoulders that seemed almost as broad as the desk behind which he was sitting. Those dark eyes glared at her as though she'd just committed the crime of the century. She could actually see the muscles bulging beneath his navy blazer. He did not look like an attorney. He looked like a mountain man. Outdoorsy handsome, with thick black hair that was much too long, with just the right amount of gray at the temples. His shadow of beard couldn't hide the sharp angle of his chin, the jutting cheekbones. Lips that were full and sensual. *Kissing lips*, she thought. Lips like that were meant to be kissed. Maybe a future polish name?

Kissing Lips?

"What you do about the situation is up to you," Will continued. "It is completely your decision whether you choose to follow through and honor her wishes."

Nana's ideas for her arrangements had been simple. She'd wanted a private memorial, with just the family and a few of her closest friends. They'd honored her wishes, and the memorial was held at a church in town. Pastor Antonio negotiated with the bell ringer, a longtime resident of Spruce City, to sound the bell seventy-one times, one for each year of Nana's life. She hadn't wanted a big to-do. No flowers; friends could make a donation in her name to the American Heart Association. Now, with the simple service concluded, Joy and her mother were gathered in Will Drake's office discussing Nana's will.

Joy could not believe the total no-win situation she'd been left by her Nana. If her beloved grandmother were not already dead, she'd personally choke the life out of her. No, no. She would never do such a terrible thing. But her mind was spinning, and her thoughts were all over the place.

"Mother, did you know about this?" she snapped.

Her mother was wearing black slacks, a red silk blouse, and red flats. Her hair had been twisted into some kind of trendy bun. Ruby earrings dangled from her ears.

"Joy Elizabeth Preston, pay attention!" her mother said, her voice raised, a slight edge to it. Joy remembered that tone of voice from her years as a teenager. It wasn't a good sign.

She took a breath, hoping to settle down. *I've got this. I have got this! Really. I. Have. Got. This!*

"Yes?"

"Does this mean you accept your grandmother's conditions?" Will Drake asked.

"What? Of course not! How dare you try and put words in my mouth," Joy said, her voice laced with repugnance.

"I can see that Ms. Preston has a few . . . issues," the attorney said. "Maybe we can schedule another meeting when she isn't so distressed."

Joy practically jumped out of her chair. "Issues? Distressed? Is that what you said? You think I'm distressed? Look, Mr. Perry Freaking Mason, you haven't seen *distressed!* How dare you label me! Mother, I'm leaving. If you want a ride back to the B&B, come on; if not, Mr. Mason can take you home." She grabbed the cross-body purse she'd hung on the back of the chair and reached inside for her keys.

"I'll call you later, Will. I apologize for my daughter's behavior. This has all been a terrible shock to her. She's grieving."

"Of course she is," he said, then stood. "Call Kristabelle; she'll arrange for another appointment. At Ms. Preston's convenience, of course."

Then he actually led her mother to the door. With his hand on her lower back!

Maybe her mother and Mr. Perry Mason, aka Will Drake, had some sort of . . . thing going on between them!

Joy stepped out of the office into a hallway that led to the reception area, waiting for her mom. Two minutes, and she was out of there. Decorated in dark wood furniture, with touches of burgundy and gray, the office screamed traditional male. Paintings of bird dogs hunting, ships at sea, and the classical portrait of a man wearing a captain's cap hung on the wall behind the reception desk. *Is this Kristabelle's desk?* she wondered She didn't remember seeing anyone sitting at the desk when she arrived. She'd followed her mother directly to Will Drake's office. One more reason to deduce her mother's relationship with the attorney was more than friendly. Not that it mattered. She wanted her mother to find love and happiness, but not with *him*.

"Let's go," her mother said from behind her. "You and I need to have a talk."

Joy was only too happy to leave. Her entire life had just been turned into sheer pandemonium.

Inside her rental car, Joy spoke as soon as her mother was inside. "I'm sorry. I didn't mean to embarrass you. I can't believe Nana would do this to me." She eased out of the parking space and drove toward the B&B, an entire six blocks away. "Did you know about this?"

"Would it make any difference?" her mother asked.

Joy thought about that for a moment before giving her answer. "I suppose it wouldn't."

"Okay, then, to answer your question, I didn't know Mom's last wishes. I never asked. I guess I didn't want to know because of what they implied."

Joy pulled the car into her parking space next to Izzie's Caddy. She shut the engine down but remained inside. "Why would she do this? She knew I have a business to run. She of all people, a businesswoman herself, would realize what this would mean." She inhaled deeply and hung her head. Her life was a mess right now, and sadly, she had no one to blame except for Nana. What in the world had she been thinking when she'd added those ridiculous terms to her will?

In order for Heart and Soul to remain in the family, Joy Elizabeth Preston must live at the B&B as owner and operator for six months. If she chooses not to abide by the terms of this, my last will and testament, the property located at 325 Main Street will become the legal property of the state of North Carolina.

"I know this wasn't in your plans, but we can't let her down. She knows, *knew* how much you love the Christmas festivities here. Clearly, she wasn't aware of the hardship this would cause, but, Joy, for a minute, imagine yourself here. Imagine Simply Joy here, in Spruce City. Imagine your business, anywhere in the world. Please, just try. For me."

Joy closed her eyes. Most of her work was done through the Internet. Orders were placed online. Her lab was in New York City. FedEx operated all over the world. Generally, people didn't care where the central offices were located. She opened her eyes.

"Okay, I tried," she said.

"And?"

"And what?" She did not like the direction her thoughts were headed.

"Tell me what you're thinking," her mother said. "And be honest. Not that you wouldn't be."

As much as she didn't want to admit it, her mother's probing forced her to realize she could work from anyplace in the world. She wasn't in a corporate setting, her offices were small, and she rented the space as it was. Her employees, all four of them, were single, and though a few of them had family in Colorado, in reality, she *could* work from Spruce City. If they wanted to relocate, they could decide that for themselves. Hayley and Jessica could come out here. They were her best friends and had a stake in this, too.

"I suppose I could give it a shot. Not that I want to, but I could. For Nana. And you. I just don't understand her reasoning behind this. She knows how much I love Colorado. She accepted my choice to move there when I left for college. Or so I thought." She had to admit, if only to herself, that spending the holidays at the B&B, with all the holiday extravaganza, was very, *very* appealing.

Could she actually pull this off? Maybe. Her mind was churning. If Nana thought she could do this, then maybe she knew Joy better than Joy knew herself.

Chapter 5

"You don't have to decide right now," her mother reminded her.

"I know, but if I'm going to do this, there's no point in putting it off. I can't, anyway. According to the will, once it's read to me, I have seventy-two hours to make a decision, at which point the terms of the will go into effect immediately, one way or the other."

"True," her mother said. "I think I can persuade Will to wait a few days. Take your time. Really think this over." She paused. "Don't worry about me or what I think. Either way, I'll support your decision."

Joy nodded. "Thanks. I've got a feeling I'm going to need all the support I can get," she said, already resigned to the fact that she was about to upend her life as she currently knew it. Hayley had the Valentine's Day dilemma taken care of; the spring color collection was 99 percent handled. A few phone calls and e-mails, and she'd be good to go.

For once, she was grateful she didn't have any pets to relocate. She'd planned on getting a cat a few weeks ago, but with her new plans, maybe she'd get a cat *and* a dog. Or two. She smiled as she imagined her animals roaming about the B&B. Actually, it was a fantastic idea. The B&B would be perfect for an animal or two. She wasn't there yet but added this to her mental "get them done" list.

Animals. Check.

"Woolgathering?" her mother asked.

"Yes, I was. Sorry. I was thinking about getting an animal. Or two."

Her mother nodded. "You should. I've been considering it myself. Going on all my cruises, I couldn't have an animal, but I think I'll be staying home for a while. A German shepherd, I'm thinking. Or a golden retriever. A larger dog. Someone to cuddle up with on a cold night. We could go to the shelter later this week. They're at full capacity during the holidays."

"It's a date. Speaking of dates, tell me if it's not any of my business—I know it's not—but is there something more than friendship between you and Mr. Drake?"

Her mother looked as though she'd been slapped.

"Joy! Have you lost your marbles? Of course there's not! He was your grandmother's attorney. I met him just after he took over his father's practice. He's close to your own age!" She shook her head. "I can't believe we're even discussing this. I'm a little chilled. I'm going inside."

Joy sighed. "I'm right behind you. I'm sorry. I shouldn't have asked such a silly question."

"No need to apologize, but for the record, I'm not involved with anyone at this point. I'm trying to learn how to live as a single, *older* woman."

Joy followed her mother inside. She should be helping Izzie and the rest of the staff. She knew most of them, but Nana always hired a few extra hands to help out during the Christmas season, and she needed to familiarize herself with their duties and the inner workings of Heart and Soul if she was going to operate the place. Had she bitten off more than she could chew?

No, she could do this. A change would work because she was going to make it work. She went to the prep kitchen, where she found Izzie and her mother, heads together, whispering.

She cleared her throat. Loudly.

In a light, teasing tone, she asked, "Are you two talking about me?"

Her mother turned around. "Yes, and it's something you need to hear. Right, Izzie?"

"I'm sure it is," Joy said. She sat beside her mother at the small table Nana had used for herself and her employees when they were taking a break or having a meal. "Go on, tell me what it is I need to hear."

"We're filled to the max right now. Anna always served a formal Thanksgiving dinner to her guests, and the employees and their families. She'd just started planning the menu when . . . this happened. Your mom and I want to continue with her plans, but we want your input since, basically, you're now my boss." Izzie's eyes twinkled.

"Nana ran this place successfully for longer than I've been alive. If she planned a feast for the guests and the employees, then I say we'd best hurry. Thanksgiving is less than two weeks away. What do we need to do?" Joy directed her attention to Izzie and her mother.

"Mom always ordered fresh turkeys from Pickney's and, of course, her hams from Kinston. As for the rest of the meal, the trimmings, I think between Izzie, me, Robert, and Marie, we should be able to pull it off. We'll need your help, too, Joy. Mary Jane says she can help. She'll make sure we have breads, desserts, the usual Turkey Day goodies. Which brings up the day after Thanksgiving, the official start of Christmas season here and in town. The annual gingerbread house competition starts in less than a week, too."

"Why is it so early?" asked Joy. "Shouldn't it be closer to actual Christmas?"

"They do the judging early so everyone can keep the houses on display all through the season," Izzie explained.

"So we'll have Mary Jane make ours," Joy said.

"No, we can't. She's a professional baker, so she isn't allowed to compete," Izzie replied.

"I won't tell if you won't tell," Joy teased. "I helped Nana bake a few times, but I'll have to watch a few YouTube videos. I've never constructed a gingerbread house before."

Her mom and Izzie looked at one another.

"What? I feel like I'm missing something here."

"You really don't know how to make a gingerbread house?" her mother asked. "We're not talking about plain, ordinary gingerbread houses here. In order to enter, you have to make an exact replica of your home, whatever that may be."

Joy took a few seconds to let the words soak in. "I'm in the nail polish business, not construction, plus this place is huge! Three stories. Can you even make a three-story gingerbread house without it falling apart? I don't know, you tell me. Just so you know, my baking skills are limited to canned biscuits and slice-and-bake cookies."

"Of course, you don't have to worry about this. We'll take care of it," her mother explained. "You may want to watch, learn the basics, just in case."

"Why in the world would you say that? Just in case what? Either of you decide to kick the bucket? Please, don't even go there. Nana would not like you thinking this way. She was always positive, no matter the circumstances. At least the Nana I knew was."

"I'm sorry; you're right. Mom was a great woman, and I don't think losing her has really hit me yet. I want to honor her memory, and I know you both do as well. The next time I turn into Negative Nancy, one of you give me a swift kick in the pants."

Izzie rolled her eyes. "We're not going to kick the bucket or kick anyone in the pants. What we are going to do is get busy. You'd be surprised at the work involved. We have one family in the Santa Suite, a husband and wife. We've got four college kids from Duke in the Kringle Cottage. Keith and Kim Moore are back this year. I put them in the Jack Frost Cottage, farthest away, since they've had a baby since they were here last year—Olivia, she's three months old and colicky, cries all the time, poor thing. Kim told me big brother Bryan can't keep his eyes off her. They're here until the end of the month. That's ten more mouths to feed, not to mention the other guests. Mr. Wallace is here until the New Year, and so is Miss Betty. They come every year."

"Aren't they the ones who swear their dearly departed better halves visit them when they're here?" Joy asked, remembering Nana talking about them. They'd been guests for many years.

"The one and only," Izzie said.

"It might be a good idea to stop promoting this ghostly stuff. I know Mother was all for it, but I'm not so sure it's a good idea. Of course, it's up to you now, being the new CEO. You are planning to stay, I hope?" her mother stated.

Joy chewed the edge of her lip, something she did when she was in deep thought. "Yes, I am. For six months. After that, I'm . . . probably heading west again. I can operate Simply Joy here for the duration. Hayley and Jessica should be able to hold the fort, and I'm sure that the rest of the staff will be willing to put in a few more hours. I'll make this work for now. But"—she held her hand palm up—"I have the right to change my mind, too."

"You'd actually consider living in Spruce City full-time?" Izzie asked. "Because that's what Anna really wanted. She'd be so thrilled. A shame . . . well, you know what I mean."

"Let's not put the cart before the horse," Elizabeth said. "I'm sure Joy will decide what's best for her *after* we get through the holidays. For now, let's finish up planning for Thanksgiving."

For the next hour, they planned the Thanksgiving menu. They went online and ordered four turkeys, four hams, and four prime rib roasts. "Do you think this is enough?" Joy asked. "Do we offer doggy bags to the guests? I know I always like a turkey and stuffing sandwich at three in the morning."

Her mom and Izzie spoke at the same time. "That's a great idea."

"So, how do you plan to make this work?" Izzie asked.

"Give them a Ziploc bag and a napkin?" Joy teased. "Actually, I'm not sure. Any suggestions?"

Izzie twisted her long braid through her fingers. "All the rooms have mini refrigerators but no way to warm anything. I suppose we could put a couple of microwaves in the toast-and-coffee area."

Joy raised her brow.

"Weekends, we always set up an area for the early risers. Coffee, tea, toast. Mary Jane's grandson delivers fresh-baked goods Saturday and Sunday. We don't have breakfast until seven on the weekends," Izzie explained.

"So, let's get a microwave or two. We'll put out paper plates and plasticware if anyone does decide to take a doggy bag. I've never met anyone who doesn't like leftovers. We can let the guests know via an e-mail or text message," Joy explained. "That's the way we communicate with our guests, right?"

Smiling, her mother said, "No, we still use the paper method. Sliding it under the doors. If there's a scheduling change after a paper change, Mother always wrote it on the whiteboard."

"Mom, are you telling me Nana still did that? It's so out-of-date. Why not send the guest an e-mail or a text message when there's a change to the schedule?"

"Because some of our guests don't have cell phones or computers. Your grandmother decided to stick to what she knew best. It's worked for a long time, so I wouldn't change it, if I were you."

"I see. Maybe it's something to work on in the future. I'll put it on the back burner for now. Hard to believe people don't have cell phones," Joy stated.

"So, what was Nana's plan for winning the ginger-bread house contest? I know she was very competitive. And when do we have to finish? And who are the judges?"

"We have one week. Judges are random citizens who volunteer to put their names in for consideration. The judges aren't chosen until a couple of days beforehand. They draw the names out of a box. Old-fashioned, but it prevents any bribing or kissing up to the judges.

"The four other B&Bs are just as determined to win as your grandmother was. They've had this unspoken competitiveness going on between them for years. Waterside, The Green Way, The Golden Bear, and Swanson House. All owned and operated by widows. It's almost like an Olympic event around here; as a matter of fact, we refer to this as the Christmas Olympics. The locals love it, and so did Anna. It's worse than one of those cake bake-offs on the Food Channel. She was extremely secretive about her ingredients and decorations. We can't purchase anything local, as Barbara Green owns the local grocery. Her mother, Clemmie Green, is one of the sneakiest women in town, and she's friends with Helen Lockwood. Nosy, too. So we'll have to get our supplies out of town. Raleigh is where we usually go. There's a special bakery shop there," Izzie explained. "I'm surprised Clemmie hasn't discovered the place herself."

"Do you know that she hasn't?" Joy asked.

Izzie rubbed her hands together. "Actually, I don't."

"Then we can't go there this year. Too much risk. We'll order everything we need online," Joy said.

"That won't work," her mother offered. "Jack and Lola Waldie run the post office. They're almost as nosy as Clemmie. They're loyal to her, too. So I don't think that's an option," her mother said. "They'll check the return address on whatever comes through."

"This is why I like Denver. No one pokes into your business; it's to each his own," Joy explained. "Does anyone know I'm going to be here for six months?"

"No, because we didn't know it ourselves until a few minutes ago," Izzie told her. "Why?"

"Does FedEx deliver directly?"

"I think so," her mother said.

"Then we'll use them. Now, we need to make a list of everything we need. We can probably get most of our supplies on Amazon. And, of course, we have to make sure we have FedEx deliver the stuff overnight."

"Won't that look suspicious if we start getting deliveries every day?" Izzie asked. "Because they'll all be watching us and each other."

"Who's to say the deliveries aren't for me? Nail polish. Samples, work-related packages." Joy shook her head. This might be crazy, but it sounded like a challenge she was up for. And when Joy was given a challenge, she played to win. "You ever thought of having Mary Jane order for you? She owns the local bakery? Couldn't we have her order whatever we need?"

"Tried that a couple of years ago. They caught on," Izzie said. "The idea is to have a gingerbread house that's like your B&B. It's the decorations that we need to be unique, extra special."

"Hang on a sec," Joy said, taking her cell phone out. She hit a few keys, then said, "Voilà!"

"What?" Izzie asked.

"There is a place in Illinois, Global Candy Art. Look." She handed Izzie the cell phone. "Does this have what we'll need?"

"Elizabeth, take a peep at this." Izzie passed the iPhone to her.

"They have everything and then some," her mother said.

"Let's place an order. The website says they do overnight deliveries," Joy said.

For the next half hour, they pointed and clicked, then placed a huge order that was promised for delivery tomorrow afternoon.

"Perfect," Izzie said. "We've got all the silicone molds, and tomorrow I'll start baking the gingerbread. Then it's game on!"

Chapter 6

Will Drake couldn't get the image of Joy Preston out of his mind. Petite but mighty, he thought. Beautiful, too. She'd ripped him to shreds two days ago, and he admired her even more for that. Not many people stood up to him the way she had. Since her office visit, he'd done a bit of research, discovering that she was a rising powerhouse in the business world, too. No wonder she'd been so upset when he'd read her the terms of her grandmother's will. Life in a small town versus the big city would be quite the concession. He wouldn't accept the terms if he were in her position, but giving up a family business as successful as Heart and Soul wouldn't be a wise move, either. Since he hadn't heard from Ms. Preston, he assumed that she had already returned to Denver and they were putting off telling him for obvious reasons.

When his father had decided to retire at the beginning

of the year, Will was only too happy to take over for him. He'd been a one-man operation and said he had no regrets. Will himself had been a criminal defense attorney in Charlotte for ten years. He'd seen more than his share of all walks of life—some good, some not so good. It was the not so good that made him jump at his father's offer to take over his practice. Plus, he wanted to fish, one of his favorite pastimes. There was plenty of fishing around Spruce City. His father was retiring to Florida, so he could catch the bigger fish, he'd said, and Will didn't blame him one bit. He'd make sure to visit as much as he could. From the looks of things, it was very likely he'd get to spend plenty of time with his dad on the new fishing boat he'd just purchased.

His father had practiced civil law for thirty-plus years and said it didn't compare to the excitement of catching a two-hundred-pound marlin. Not that he'd ever caught one, but he said that if he did, he just knew it would far surpass the excitement of anything that had happened in his legal career.

Will had inherited a secretary named Kristabelle. She loved her work at the firm and did an excellent job. She was a widow who had never gotten over the loss of her husband.

Much to his surprise, Will was learning that Spruce City was full of widows. Joy's mother, who seemed much too young to have suffered such a loss, had been widowed three years ago. All of the bed-and-breakfasts in town were owned by widows. He knew this because they had all been clients of his father's and now were his. Wills, legal documents, nothing mind-boggling. Another widow worked at the local bookstore. She was somewhere in her early forties and had flirted with him every time he had stopped by to purchase a novel. There wasn't much nightlife in Spruce City, certainly nothing like what existed in Charlotte. Cherry Suds was the only watering hole in the city, and it was truly a hole. In the men's room, the floor had a hole the size of a small crater. In order to get to the urinals, you had to jump over it. It was located on the outskirts of town, and Will found himself going there for a beer in the evening a couple times a week; on weekends, if there was a sporting event being televised, he'd pop in for a few beers. He'd met several of the locals, many of them friends of his father, and some were just curious about the new guy in town. Competition was fierce in Spruce City over single males, according to Artie, the owner and bartender. Said there were five women for every man. He'd laughed but thought there might be some truth to it.

"Mr. Drake, you need to take this call," Kristabelle said from the doorway to his office. Forget interoffice phones here; he found he liked this personal aspect of the firm. It was old-school, though they did have a website and used e-mail to communicate with clients as needed.

"Sure, I'll take it," he said. Must be important. He nodded to Kristabelle and picked up the phone.

"This is Will," he said casually. He disliked formality, and his father had, too, so his easygoing ways wouldn't seem unusual to his clients, though he'd been anything but casual when meeting Joy Preston.

"Mr. Drake, this is Joy Preston. I've decided to accept Nana's terms. I'll do the six months, and not a day more, okay?"

So much for hello.

"Of course," he said politely. He knew he'd come off as stern at their first meeting. His deep voice could be intimidating, and now he wanted her to have a better impression of him. Yes, she'd ripped him a new one, but he liked that about her. Not afraid to speak her mind. "I'll need you to come in and sign a few papers."

"When?" she asked.

"How about now?" He looked at the gold Rolex on his wrist, a gift from his father when he'd graduated from the Duke University School of Law. Almost noon. Maybe she'd have lunch with him? Maybe he was acting a little bit juvenile?

"Okay, I suppose I can," she replied.

He heard the hesitancy in her voice. "If it's not a good time, we can schedule another day."

"No, no. Today's fine. I need to get this over with. I'll be there in fifteen minutes."

Will's mood went from a low six to a high ten. "That's perfect. I'll be waiting." He broke the connection, not allowing her the opportunity to change her mind.

Her file was on the desk. He picked it up, scanned through the terms one more time, then stacked the papers in a neat pile. "Kristabelle, Miss Preston is on her way to the office now. Don't worry about hanging around for her. I'll listen for the door."

"As you wish," came her reply.

He couldn't help but laugh. "Enjoy," he called out to her, knowing exactly where she'd go for lunch and what she would eat. She'd walk down to the waterfront, sit on the bench behind the local supermarket, and eat her tuna sandwich. He'd walked with her a few times, and each time was the same.

Five minutes later—he knew this because he was watching the time as though his life depended on it—he heard the door open, then close.

"In here," he called out.

Joy appeared in the doorway seconds later. "No secretary again?"

"Kristabelle is on her lunch break. Noon every day, she is out of here," he said, hoping he sounded a bit more friendly to her than he had the other day.

Nodding, she said, "Now, about those papers. I've got to hurry back. Mom and Izzie are about to decorate the gingerbread house, and I don't want to miss it."

"Ahh, the annual contest," he said as he motioned for her to sit down.

"You know about that?"

"Sure. I'm one of the judges," he said, a huge grin on his face. "Most of the local businesses tossed their name in a bucket, literally, and Bob Harper, the mayor, drew the names."

"You're serious," she said, taking the seat in front of his desk.

"I am."

"Well, you don't seem like the kind of guy that—"

"Judges gingerbread houses?"

She had the good grace to blush. Who would've thought this spunky woman blushed?

"What's so funny?" she asked, out of the blue.

Caught red-handed, he said, "If I lie, you'll know it, so I'll tell you the truth. You're blushing, and I find that rather . . . surprising."

She stared at him for a couple of seconds. "I'm not sure if I should be insulted or take that as a compliment." She adjusted herself in the large chair. He'd bet the bank her feet didn't touch the floor.

"It's a compliment. I hope you're not offended."

"I'm not easily offended, so no worries," she said, "but

I really am in a bit of a hurry, so if we could just get the papers taken care of, I'll be on my way."

"Of course." He took the stack of papers in front of him, flipped through them, then turned them so that they faced her. "If you'll just sign, here, and here." He pointed to the spaces for her signature.

She signed the papers, then stood. "So, Heart and Soul is legally mine for the next six months?"

"That was your grandmother's wish, so yes. It's all yours. You've got plenty of help, according to your grandmother."

"We do, and they're probably waiting for me right now, so I'll be on my way unless there's something else you need?" She stared at him as though she were checking him out.

He needed to invite her to dinner, but his fear of rejection kept him from asking her, which was very odd for him. "No, nothing. These papers are signed and sealed. I'll file them with the clerk of the court to make it official, but that's it."

"Well, then, I'll see you around town. I guess," she said as she walked to the door.

He followed her down the hallway to the entrance. He needed, *wanted* to get to know this woman better. Why not chance it, he thought, as she stepped outside. "Joy, I know this is going to sound bold, being that we barely know each other, but I thought maybe you and I could . . . have dinner. Sometime. Together." He watched her, waiting for her answer, a reaction, but she just stood there, a huge grin on her face.

"You should come to the B&B tonight. Izzie made a killer lasagna this morning. You can have dinner with us if you'd like?" She was blushing again. "See how we operate."

While it wasn't his first choice, he wasn't about to turn her down. "That sounds like an excellent idea. What time do you want me . . . uh, there?" He hesitated. "I'm pretty much finished up for the day."

"How does seven o'clock sound?" she asked.

"Perfect. I'll see you then," he said.

"Okay," she said, then hurried down the steps to her car, which was parked in front of his office.

He gave her a wave, then returned to his office.

Chapter 7

Joy pulled out of the parking space in a little bit of shock; she could not believe what had just happened! Never in a million years had she expected Will Drake to invite her to dinner. Just a few days ago, she hadn't liked him one little bit. He came off as arrogant and sounded like a total smart aleck. Now she was inviting him home for dinner! She could not believe what she'd done. Her mother would love it, and so would Izzie. They were always after her to get out and "meet someone nice." Did Will Drake qualify as nice? Unsure, she pulled into her parking spot, next to the silver Caddy in its usual space. Wait until she told them what had just taken place.

"Mom, Izzie! You're not going to believe what just happened," she called out as she came in through the back door.

Her mother and Izzie were seated at the table in the

kitchen, the gingerbread house dominating the center of the table.

"You told Mr. Drake a thing or two, I'm sure," her mom stated.

"That poor guy, I bet his ears are still burning," Izzie added. "He's actually a pretty nice guy, you know."

Taking a deep breath, Joy sat down in the spare chair. "He's coming for dinner. I told him you made a lasagna this morning."

"What?" Izzie said. "When in the world do I have time to make a lasagna? It's all I can do to get breakfast on the table, and I have help. Why in the world did you tell him that?"

Joy raked her hand through her hair. "He invited me out for dinner. I . . . it just came out of my mouth. I don't know. I'm stressed. I have an enormous amount of responsibilities with this place and Simply Joy. I probably think he's hot, too." She could not believe she'd said that. She'd thought this the first time she saw him, but he'd ticked her off, and she'd focused on that. Not his looks, or the broad shoulders, or the sexy, too-long hair or the deep voice that gave her shivers the minute he'd spoken her name. No, not any of that.

"I'll get a frozen one from the supermarket. We can put it in a dish, make out like you made it yourself," Joy said.

"*We?* There is no *we* here, kiddo. If you want to invite someone over for dinner, be my guest, but don't get me or your mom involved. Right, Elizabeth? Besides, I don't think I've ever made a lasagna in my life."

Joy looked at her mom and Izzie. They weren't going along with her plan. "Okay, so I stretched things a bit."

"Stretched? You mean you told a flat-out lie? Correct," Izzie called her out, but she had a huge smile on her face.

"Okay, I lied. So what am I supposed to do now?"

"If it were me, I would've taken him up on his offer to go out to dinner. You could use a break, as I think you really are stressed, sweetie. But, if you've invited Mr. Drake for dinner, we'll see if we can help out." Her mother was so kind, it almost brought tears to her eyes.

"Thanks, Mom. You're the best."

"And what about me?" Izzie asked.

Joy laughed. "You are second-best. But only because you can't make a lasagna, which I don't believe for one minute. You're practically a world-class chef. I don't know any chef that couldn't whip up a lasagna.

"I told him to be here at seven. That gives me six and a half hours, enough time to get myself out of this hole I've jumped into. I'm going to look up a recipe for lasagna. I'll make one myself. It's about time I learned to cook anyway."

"I'll make that blue cheese salad that you like," her mother offered.

"I suppose I can make garlic bread and dessert," Izzie volunteered. "Being that you're making the main course and all. I can't wait to see how this turns out."

Joy clicked away on her cell phone. "Here, this looks simple. I can do this. I'll just run to the store. Oh, and by the way, Will is one of the judges in the gingerbread-house contest. Just so you know."

"Is that why you invited him for dinner?" her mother asked.

Joy smiled. "No, but you have to admit, it's a good idea having him here. Tomorrow is the official judging for the contest."

"No, we can't do this. It will look bad. The others, they'll accuse us of bribery or some such harebrained scheme. You need to call him right now and uninvite him. Seriously, Joy. He can't have dinner with us. If he's judging tomorrow, it will look . . . underhanded, sneaky," her mother said.

"I can't do that, and I won't," Joy said firmly. "I'm almost thirty years old, and you can't tell me who I can and can't have over for dinner. Besides, I'm in charge of all this . . . this stuff now."

"Hold on, young lady," Izzie said. "You need to listen to your mother. Unfortunately, she's right about this. You've been away too long. You don't know what these women are like. They're die-hard cutthroats to the bitter end. If they get even a whiff of suspicion, they'll . . . well, let me tell you a little bit about them. Then you'll understand.

"Edna Blakely owns Waterside, the giant white place that faces the Neuse. She's been widowed for more than thirty years. The woman lives her life to gossip and loves to make others as miserable as she is. She and your grandmother were known adversaries. They were both widowed young, both in the same business, so they became quite competitive. Anna tried being friendly with her throughout the years, but Edna refused her overtures. I don't know why, other than she's just an old sourpuss. Frowns all the time. I saw her in the supermarket a few weeks ago. I said hello, and I swear to you, that woman gave me the nastiest look I've ever seen. I smiled at her, and that made her even madder. If she found out that Will Drake was here the night before judging, trust me, it wouldn't be pretty.

"Then there is Juanita Howard; she owns The Green

Way. She changed the name a dozen or so years ago. Used to be called Howard House. She's all uppity and new-age-like, hence the name change. She advertises a lot and always emphasizes how she's saving the earth. Now, don't get me wrong, there's nothing wrong with that; I'm all for recycling, doing what we can to save the planet for our future, but Juanita takes it to the next level. I don't think there's been a soda can in her house since her husband passed away. She has this compost area in her front yard, and it smells so bad, most people are turned off by it unless they're greenies like her. She has no air-conditioning or heat other than the fireplaces in the house. Nothing that isn't recycled paper, no computers, doesn't allow guests to use their cell phones on the premises. However, she is absolutely brutal when it comes to the contests we have here in town. Spares no expense to have the finest, most organic foods, and this applies even to the gingerbread house. She gets her organic ginger from some gal in England who owns a bakery, uses organic eggs, even raw cane sugar—you get the picture. She wants to be number one and will let you know it. Last year, her gingerbread house was trimmed in real pearls and rubies, even though the rules state the houses must be entirely edible. She's never won any of the contests, which makes her even more determined each year.

"Now Amanda Swanson, over at Swanson House is a . . . well I won't call her the name that comes to mind, but she is hardcore and ruthless. Her place is beautiful. There's no denying that, but the woman is the opposite of Juanita. She's so cheap, she uses her daughter's washer and dryer for all the linens from Swanson House, and the breakfasts she serves are really nasty. Now this is according to a few of her guests, ones who have left the place and had to relocate here. She doesn't provide soaps or any toiletries at all. No cheese and wine, nothing to snack on. One guest who came here to stay said the bread she used for toast was actually moldy. Now, if that isn't cheap, I don't know what is. She resoles her shoes, and they look like something from the Depression era. The entire town knows she's loaded, but rest assured, when there is a sale at the supermarket, she's waiting at the door so she can stock up. She spends her days figuring out new ways to save money, and again, there's nothing wrong with that. She's never been competition in any of the contests, but she enters them because all of the B&Bs in town do. Last year, she used candy wrappers from Olive Garden for grass. Who has grass with a gingerbread house?

"Our biggest competition, actually, is Helen Lockwood over at The Golden Bear. She's the biggest priss you'll ever meet. We think she has OCD. She's constantly washing her hands and rearranging her furniture so that everything is all symmetrical. Even the guest rooms. She makes her guests remove their shoes before they step in the house. I could go on and on, but this woman is such a perfectionist, we have to watch her. She's nosy, too. Most of the widows in town are gossips. They have nothing better to do. Helen's husband, Larry Lockwood, died in his sleep eight years ago. She was devastated, and I can't blame her, either. Larry was a great guy, friendly as can be. Something changed when he died, and she's turned into this obsessive-compulsive. So, these are a few reasons why you can't have Will Drake over for dinner."

"All of this nonsense is about to change," said Joy. "I don't care what any of those women think. We're all in this for fun, and I'm going to make the best of it, for Nana. It's Christmastime, my favorite time of the year, and I am not going to allow a bunch of gossipy widows to run my life or determine what goes on here. I can't believe you both would get sucked into such silliness. Now"—Joy stood up—"I'm going to the supermarket to pick up the ingredients for dinner." And before they had a chance to stop her, she was out the back door in a flash.

Izzie stared at Elizabeth. "That girl is gonna cause a boatload of trouble, mark my words."

Elizabeth nodded. "She has no idea what she's about to stir up."

"As she said, it's her place now, let her handle it. She's a big girl," Izzie said.

After Joy did her part in preparing for dinner, she had about ten minutes to make herself presentable. In the Scrooge Room, she took a quick shower and washed her hair. She smelled like garlic and hoped Will Drake wouldn't smell it on her when he arrived. As she let the warm water soothe her stiff muscles, she wondered if she'd seemed too eager when she'd invited him to dinner. Mom and Izzie were probably right. She should have gone to dinner with him; she could've saved herself a lot of trouble. Maybe this contest thing was all in their heads. She just couldn't imagine grown women, *older women* being so aggressive over a gingerbread house.

She dried her hair and dressed in a pair of black jeans with a dark green sweater. It was chilly in Spruce City, but nothing like it was during the winter in Colorado. She could get used to mild winters and loads of sunshine, no doubt about it, but she didn't want to think about that now. A touch of blush, lipstick, and mascara, and she was good to go. She didn't want to fuss too much with her appearance. Didn't want Mr. Will Drake to think she was trying to impress him. Though she was, sort of, but she'd keep that thought to herself.

Downstairs, her mother and Izzie had the formal dining room set up. She hoped none of the guests would be traipsing through the room, but if they did, she'd manage. This was a B&B, filled to capacity, and she couldn't expect total privacy. She would have to get used to that as well. She'd been alone for so long, being around people all the time was going to be a bit of an adjustment.

"This looks perfect! Thank you both for doing this. I know you think it's going to stir up trouble, and if so, I will deal with the ladies. I think it's time for the widows of Spruce City to make friends," Joy said as she admired her Nana's blue-willow china. That might've been a bit too much, but it was too late to say anything. She looked at the clock. It was five minutes to seven. He would be here any minute now if he was punctual.

Since this was a B&B, they didn't officially lock the doors until eleven, and the guests had a key card if they were out late, Joy didn't expect Will to knock on the door.

"I'm glad you approve," her mother stated. "Though I disagree with your thoughts on the ladies. They're as vicious as Izzie said, maybe even more so."

"Trust me, Mom, I'll take care of them."

She heard voices coming from the front entryway. Will was here. She smoothed a hand over her hair and brushed imaginary lint from her sweater. He was punctual. Seven o'clock on the dot. She'd give him points for that.

When she saw him, for a split second, it took her breath away. He was beyond good-looking. He wore jeans and a black turtleneck sweater, with a black blazer. His hair was wet, and he looked as sexy as ever. She could get in trouble with this guy, she thought as she walked from the dining room to the main entry.

Unsure what to say, with Izzie standing there giving her the evil eye, she went with her gut and said, "I hope you're hungry. We've got a huge lasagna. Let's eat it before it gets cold."

"I can't wait. I've forgotten the last time I had a good homemade meal. I'm not much of a cook myself, though I'm big on frozen dinners," he said; his dark eyes were bright and filled with what she thought was interest as he gave her the once-over. Of course he was interested. He wouldn't have accepted her invitation if he wasn't.

"Mr. Drake, I'm Izzie, Isobel Carter. It's nice to meet you," she said, introducing herself.

"I'm sorry, I should've introduced you. Izzie runs this place. Don't let her tell you otherwise," Joy said, as the three of them made their way to the dining room. "It would fall apart if not for her."

"Thank you, Joy. You're a sweet girl," Izzie said, then added, "Sometimes."

"I heard that," Joy responded.

They entered the dining room. Will looked surprised when he saw how formal the setup was.

"Mom and Izzie thought it was a good idea to eat in the formal dining room. Our gingerbread house is on the kitchen table, and it's probably not a good idea for you to see it before the contest judging tomorrow."

"Probably not," he agreed.

Feeling odd just standing there, Joy said, "Let's eat. I am starving."

Her mother entered the room. She'd changed into a pair of navy slacks with a light blue silk blouse. Her hair was in a topknot, and as always, she looked stunning.

"Good evening, Will," her mother said, holding out her hand. Will shook her mother's hand, then proceeded to pull out a chair for her.

"Is this all right?" he asked.

"It is; we have no assigned seats around here. I can't even remember the last time I actually had a meal at this table. Mother always uses, *used* this room for the guests' breakfast, even though we have our social room with tables and chairs for those who prefer a more casual setting."

"Then I'm honored to sit at your table," he announced, taking a seat.

"I say let's eat," Izzie broke in.

For the next half hour, they ate and offered up small talk. Joy learned that Will's mother had died when he was a baby and that his father had never remarried. Though he'd dated off and on, he said he could never find a woman who would even compare with Jenny, his wife, and was content with just himself and Will. Will had left Spruce City when he was thirteen. He went to a boarding school, he told them, and that's when he became interested in studying law. He graduated, came home for two weeks, then moved to Durham, where he went to Duke University for four years, then went on to study law there as well.

"So how do you feel about living in a small town? After Denver, I would think it's quite a change," Will said to Joy.

"I grew up here, so I know the ins and outs of the place. I don't know that I could ever live here permanently again. I've spent my entire adult life in Colorado, so coming back is . . . different, but I am here for the six months Nana asked for. When that's over, I'm going home. I've got a business to run," Joy said.

Her mother looked as if Joy's admission upset her. "I thought you said you could operate your business from here. Didn't you tell me that, or am I imagining that you did?"

"I can run Simply Joy from here easily enough. I'm not sure my employees would be willing to relocate. I've only told Hayley and Jessica about Nana's will, and I made them swear to keep this to themselves until I make a final decision."

"So does that mean that you're considering moving here?" Will asked.

Joy took a deep breath. She wasn't sure of anything right now except for the fact that she found Will Drake way too appealing. "I can't make that decision yet. There is a lot to consider. For now, I will abide by the terms of the will. I said I would, and I will. So, what about you, do you miss Charlotte? The nightlife? Because there's nothing here in Spruce City, though I suppose you know that by now. And I do mean nothing."

They all laughed.

"There's Cherry Suds. That's good enough for me. I was never one for bar hopping or partying. I guess I'm a bit boring. I'm happy to stay home most nights and dig into a novel. I've always been an avid reader," Will explained. "Plus, I'm too old to be out late at night." He smiled when he said that.

"Exactly what do you call old?" Izzie asked.

"Thirty-five," he answered.

"Then I'm on my way to old. I'm almost thirty. Does life end at thirty-five?" Joy asked Will.

"No, but that's when we get really smart," he said in a teasing tone.

"Really?" Joy said, grinning.

Out of nowhere came a loud, terrifying scream.

"What, who is that?" Joy said, as they all jumped up from the table and headed for the stairs.

"Help! Help!" a shrill female voice screamed.

The noise was coming from Miss Betty's room.

Upstairs, Izzie knocked on the door, then gently pushed it aside. "Miss Betty," she called out. "Are you all right?"

The little woman was huddled beneath the covers on the giant bed, her white hair poking out, but the rest of her remained under the covers.

"It was Herman," she whispered. "But . . . But . . . he wasn't alone this time." Miss Betty's green eyes peered out at them. "I'm . . . I'm scared."

Joy, her mother, and Will remained in the doorway. She couldn't believe this was happening. Tonight of all nights. She whispered to her mother, "Is she one of the regulars who's here to visit . . . her dead husband?" She felt silly asking the question, but if she was going to run the place, she needed to know as much as humanly possible.

"Yes, she's been swearing for years that he visits her during the Christmas season. Of course, no one has witnessed him doing so. At least no one that I know of." Her mother didn't sound as though she believed her own words.

Izzie was trying to calm Miss Betty down. "You all come in and meet Miss Betty." Her tone left no doubt they'd better not refuse her.

"Uh, sure," Joy said, looking at Will, who seemed to be enjoying this insight into what went on at the B&B.

"I'd be delighted to meet her, too," he said.

They all entered the Patchwork Suite, an adorable hodgepodge of items, culled from all the special events in their families' lives going way back. Quilts made from a special article of clothing, such as a wedding dress, a christening gown, a first-day-of-school outfit—all of these items were used to make the drapes and the chair coverings, hence the name. This part of the décor never changed, but they more than compensated with additional items at Christmas.

There were three small Christmas trees, each decorated in a different theme. One had a wedding theme—the decorations were all white, soft creams, and antique whites; another featured a baby theme; it was decked out in pink and blue ornaments, all with a Christmas flair. The third tree was simply an old-fashioned spruce with what Joy knew to be a collection of holiday spangles her Nana had picked up on her many travels. How Miss Betty could see a ghost in here was beyond Joy's wildest imagination. The rest of the room was bright and colorful, everything Christmas should be. Greens, reds, and golds. Nana really did go to extreme lengths decking out the place for her holiday guests.

"Miss Betty, this is Elizabeth, Anna's daughter. Do you remember her?" Izzie asked. By this time, the small woman was sitting up in bed, the covers held tightly against her chest. She nodded.

"And this"—she motioned for Joy to come and stand at her bedside—"is Joy, Anna's granddaughter, Elizabeth's daughter."

Joy sat on the edge of the bed. "I've heard a lot about you, Miss Betty. I'm so sorry you're scared right now."

Old Miss Betty glared at Will, who was now standing at the foot of the bed. "That's not my Herman! Who is he?" She raised her voice and pointed an arthritic finger in his direction.

"This is Mr. Drake. He was Anna's attorney. He is having dinner with us tonight. There is no reason for you to be afraid of him. He's a good guy," Izzie explained to her. "We were about to have dessert. Why don't you come downstairs and join us? I've made tiramisu. It has a bit of Kahlúa and espresso; I think you might enjoy a piece."

Miss Betty lowered the covers. She wore a hot pink track suit that on anyone else would have been considered loud and ridiculous-looking, but on her, it was perfect. "You said Kahlúa, right?"

"Lots of it, too," Izzie gushed. "More than the recipe calls for."

Miss Betty pushed the covers aside and hefted her tiny, C-shaped figure onto the floor. "Well, what are we waiting for? Let's go. The heck with Herman tonight. He's made me mad and scared the bejesus out of me. I don't think I want to see him anymore, at least not tonight. Mean old troublemaker."

"Come along then. Elizabeth and I will do our very best to help you forget old Herman for tonight." Izzie placed her arm around Betty's little waist and led her out of the room and downstairs.

"Now, you sit right here, and I'm going to get dessert. Joy, you and Will get the coffee cups while your mother and I get the tiramisu and coffee, okay?"

"Yep, that's all fine by me," Miss Betty said. All traces of her former frightened self were gone.

Joy opened the antique hutch and removed the blue-willow cups and saucers. She gave Will a stack of saucers and two cups. She held the remaining three looped between her fingers, then closed the glass door. This china was very delicate. Hopefully, Miss Betty wouldn't drop any, as her poor little hands were twisted with arthritis, like an old, gnarled tree limb. On her back was a small hump, and she faced more toward the floor than ahead. Joy felt so bad for the little woman. "So tell me about yourself, Miss Betty. Nana said you visit every year?"

"Yep. Since Herman passed. You know, he does visit me every year. He told me he would, and for the past eleven years, he's kept his word. Until tonight."

Joy was hoping to distract her while they waited for dessert, but she'd done just the opposite. "You're very committed to Herman. That's to be admired, don't you agree, Will?"

"One hundred percent. Herman was, *is* a lucky guy," he said, as though he had conversations like this all the time.

Miss Betty nodded. "He was the best husband I ever had. The first two kicked off so fast, I never had the chance to have children. By the time Herman and I got together, we were too old to even consider the possibility of a family, so we took trips. Lots of them. We traveled around the world once, were gone an entire year. Best trip of my life," she reminisced.

Finally, Izzie and her mother entered, each carrying a tray.

The smell of freshly brewed coffee was a lifesaver. Joy was addicted to the stuff.

"Here, let me help." She took the tray from her mother

and placed it in the center of the table. She removed the carafe of coffee, with the sugar bowl and a creamer that looked like a mini pitcher.

"Will, would you mind grabbing another cup from the hutch?" Izzie asked.

"Sure," he said, and quickly found another blue-willow cup and saucer.

"Are we missing something?" Joy quizzed. "Five people. Five cups."

At that moment, Lou entered the dining room. Out of his work clothes, Joy hardly recognized him. Had it not been for the white hair, she wouldn't have known him. Incredibly handsome, he wore jeans and a bright red sweater, which provided a perfect background for his caramel-colored skin and white hair. He smiled, and Joy felt a rush of happiness invade her body. Izzie and Lou were an item. *How perfect is that?* she thought, as Izzie introduced him to Will.

"So, is he your boyfriend?" Miss Betty asked as soon as Lou took a seat next to Izzie.

Lou laughed. "I think you could say that. Right, Izzie?"

Izzie turned to look at him. "I'm not so sure about that just yet." Then she leaned over and kissed his cheek. "You're gonna have to convince me. Later."

Joy shot a glance at Will. He was staring at her, and she quickly turned away. This evening was becoming more embarrassing by the minute. What had she been thinking when she'd invited him over? Didn't matter now. This was mild compared to what it could've been had the guests been in and out, upset, or who knew what? Lucky for her, most of them were still out for the evening—where, she hadn't a clue, but nobody had showed up with a complaint or a compliment, and for that she was grateful.

"I will do that, Izz. I promise," Lou said and returned the kiss.

Joy rolled her eyes. "Come on, you two. Can't this wait until after dessert?"

"Miss Joy, this *is* the dessert," Lou said, his green eyes warm and full of love for Izzie. It was written all over their faces.

"I'll bet she is," Elizabeth said. "Now who wants dessert? It's a bit . . . potent, with however many extra shots of Kahlua that our dear baker insisted on adding. We'll be lucky if we're able to walk after this." She shot Izzie an ornery look.

"So tell me about the gingerbread houses," Will said. "I understand this is quite a big deal around here."

"It's more like a mudslinging contest, if you must know the truth. The other four B&Bs, plus Heart and Soul, are the only contestants. Anyone can enter, but they don't because they like to hear the gossip that goes on during the three days building up to what's referred to as Judgment Day around here. I suspect there will be a lot more mudslinging this year, given that we've had a few changes since Mom's . . . passing," Elizabeth said before taking a sip of coffee.

"Why is that?" Miss Betty asked. "They don't have a life or what? No men or women, kids in their lives?"

Everyone laughed.

"I wish that was the case, but it's really a bunch of silliness," Elizabeth said, then gave a brief summary of each woman and her history.

Will stood up. "Then I'd best get out of here. If they discover I'd had dinner and dessert with such a lovely group, their competition, then I'm toast."

"Burnt toast," Joy added. "Let me show you out the back way."

"Thank you for the lasagna, Izzie. It's some of the best I've had, and Elizabeth, I'm happy to see you're doing well, given your recent loss. Lou, anytime you're up for a day of fishing, call me. It's not often I meet another person who is quite as enthusiastic as I am about the sport. Miss Betty, you take care of Herman. I'm sure I'll be seeing you around."

Each said their good-byes, then Joy led Will out through the back door in the prep kitchen, avoiding the table where their gingerbread house sat waiting for its final decorations. "That was fun," she said. "I hope it didn't scare you off." Oh crap! She couldn't believe she'd said that. He'd think she was desperate for sure now.

"Not at all. It takes more than a few ghost stories to scare me off," Will said. "Old houses, old towns—it's not unheard of."

She walked with him. "I'm assuming you're parked out front?"

"I am."

"Then why are we walking in the opposite direction?"

Will stopped, took her hand in his. "Because I wanted to spend time alone with you." He pulled her close, then gave her a gentle kiss. "And do this."

His kiss was surprisingly sweet, yet full of promise. She touched her lips, surprised that such a light kiss could send shivers of delight down her spine. She took a deep, shaky breath to still the waves of longing that wafted through her. It had been a very long time since she'd been in any kind of relationship, yet she couldn't recall any first kiss being so . . . *sexy!*

"Have I assumed too much?" he asked.

Unsure how long she'd been standing there, she shook her head. "I was, uh . . . thinking about the . . . contest. It's really like a full-time job." She really was turning into a habitual liar. Especially where he was concerned.

"I'm sure it is, and if that's what's on your mind, it looks like I haven't done my job," he said, reaching for her again. This time, when his lips met hers, she actually felt weak in the knees. He tightened his hold on her and pressed his lips to hers, only this time, the kiss was intense, deep, yet tender. His mouth caressed hers; his lips were warm and tasted of the dessert they'd just consumed. Sweet and satisfying—the thought skittered through her mind.

He gently released her, yet his arms remained loosely around her waist, almost as though they'd done this a thousand times before. If anyone saw them, they would assume they were a couple and quite at ease with one another.

Unsure of a response, Joy smiled up at him. "You're doing just fine." And he was, but she couldn't allow herself to get involved. She was only in town for the required six months, then she was going back to Denver and Simply Joy. With that in mind, she stepped out of his embrace. "I'd better go before anyone sees us together."

He chuckled, and his dark eyes glinted from the streetlight above him. "Ashamed to be caught in public, huh?" he teased.

"Not at all. It's those ladies. Can you even imagine?

It's a gingerbread house!" She giggled like a teenager, and it felt really good. *She* felt really good.

"I'll look forward to a good laugh tomorrow."

She thought he was going to kiss her again, but instead, he brushed his fingers across her cheek.

"I'll see you tomorrow, Joy." He turned and headed toward the B&B, waving.

She lifted her hand, returning the wave, and couldn't remember being this excited, this elated in . . . forever.

Chapter 8

Joy read the list of requirements for the gingerbread house competition.

The annual contest was unlike any other she'd known, though she'd only known of a couple, so she didn't have all that much to compare it to. Nonetheless, these rules were ridiculous. Each entrant had to construct an exact replica of her bed-and-breakfast. Each gingerbread house had to be one hundred percent edible, so no rubies and pearls—for this year. A Christmas-tree-shaped piece of gingerbread had to be available for the judges to taste-test. The overall aroma and taste accounted for 10 percent of the total score, with general appearance worth an additional 40 percent. Technical difficulty accounted for another 20 percent, with uniqueness, piping work, and the decorations used each worth 10 percent.

According to her mom, last year's judges had over-looked the use of rubies and pearls, but it hadn't mattered because Heart and Soul had won, as it had every year since the contest's inception. With Izzie, her mother, and Robert, Izzie's full-time assistant, involved in creating the gingerbread house, the odds of their losing were very low.

As always, they used Anna's great-grandmother's recipe for the gingerbread, as taste was one of the many areas to be judged. "I can't believe you all take this so seriously," Joy said, as Izzie and her mom took pictures of the edible house from every angle possible.

"Well, it's fun, if anything," Elizabeth said. "Your Nana delighted in this contest every year." She laughed. "To be absolutely honest, I think what she enjoyed more than anything were the gossiping and the hoopla. These women believe—I heard this through the local gossip line—that because Mother is no longer here, Heart and Soul won't be much competition this year. She was the best, and they knew it, but they forgot about me. I'm not just a nurse. When I was old enough to talk, Mom started teaching me how to bake. By the time I was eleven, I could put a gingerbread house together like a pro."

"Why didn't I know this?" Joy asked, incredulous. How could she not know this about her mother?

Elizabeth stepped away from the table in the kitchen to take another shot. The sound of the camera's clicking was the only noise in the room. "I guess you didn't need to. I never involved myself with this place once you were born. Then I went back to work with your father, so the opportunity for you to learn about my baking skills never came up."

"I learn something new about you every day," Joy said. "Amazing. So these other ladies have no clue about your skills? I love it!"

Her mother laughed, the first genuine laugh Joy had heard from her since Nana's passing. "Nope, they have no clue. Between Izzie and me, we're gonna tear those old gals to shreds—or crumbs, in this case. Wait until the Parade of Homes gets under way. Spruce City lights up like the Fourth of July, and I'm not just talking about the Christmas lights, either. Tempers are like a tightrope around here. One wrong move, and boom, you're out cold!"

"Exactly when is that? I haven't seen you prepping anything special," Joy said, waiting for another surprise from her mom.

"Mother and her decorators took care of that. The rest of the outdoor decorations go up Thanksgiving night. The official Christmas festivities start December first, but as you've seen with the guest rooms, the preparation for the following year's Parade of Homes starts practically right after the annual winner is chosen on Christmas Eve. It's a constant cycle here, and part of Spruce City's charm—at least, I like to think so. We're pretty famous around here and throughout the state and beyond during the month of December."

"I remember. I loved working here during the holidays, helping Nana, seeing all the visitors coming and going. Each time someone new came through, it was like viewing all of our hard work over and over again, just by keeping an eye on the looks on their faces," Joy said, reliving those times again as she spoke of them. "Though I don't recall this gingerbread stuff."

"That only started eleven years ago. Next to the Parade of Homes, this is now the biggest deal for the locals," her mother said, glancing at the time. "We need to get a move on. We've got exactly one hour before the judges make their appearance. I'm going upstairs to clean the buttercream icing off myself. Then let the games begin."

"I'll be up in a few," Joy called out.

Izzie and Marie were in the dining room attending to the few guests who'd lingered over breakfast, making sure there was plenty of hot coffee to go around all day. Joy was just beginning to realize how many people it took to keep the B&B up and running.

Izzie, who was basically in charge of everything and everyone since Nana had died—not to mention the gourmet breakfasts she managed to create daily—carried the bulk of the responsibilities. She had Robert, a chef from Raleigh who'd worked here for the past six years, then Marie, a local young woman who'd just gotten married and needed the extra income. Chandra, a college student, took care of the dishes and anything extra Izzie needed her to do. She couldn't forget Lou, who was the jack-of-all-trades handyman. He'd been at Heart and Soul for as long as Joy could remember, and now that Joy knew he and Izzie were a thing, she thought their storybook romance sweet.

Brett and Sal worked in the elaborate gardens, creating a rainbow of cheer year-round. Joy couldn't believe only two men were able to accomplish this. Jeanette Holcomb, a classmate from her high school days, was in charge of the cleaning staff. Laticia, Angie, and Cheryl were angels when it came to keeping the B&B white-glove clean. Add in the decorators and occasional part-timers, and this place was a little industry all its own. In some ways, it reminded Joy—on a much smaller scale, of course—of the Biltmore Estate in Asheville, with its winery, restaurants, horses, cows; the estate grew most of their vegetables, not to mention the dairy, the elaborate gardens, and the tremendous Christmas trees in the many rooms. And those were just a few of the things she recalled offhand. There had to be hundreds, if not thousands, of employees to keep the place up and running.

She was excited about the upcoming contest, and if she was honest, she was most excited because she knew that Will Drake would be passing through with the five other judges as they made their way across town to each B&B in order to view each gingerbread house. With that in mind, she hurried upstairs to her room—a room she was now sharing with her mother, as the real estate agent had so many prospective buyers coming in and out of Elizabeth's own house, her mother said she no longer felt at home in the place. Joy didn't mind; it gave them a bit of private time together.

"How does this look?" her mother asked. "I just grabbed a few outfits at the house for now. I can go back when the place is empty."

Her mother wore an Oscar de la Renta scarlet-colored dress with three-quarter-length sleeves, a wide belt that showed off her small waist, and a flared hem that swirled in a perfect circle when she turned around for Joy to view.

"Mom, that's beautiful! You look fabulous, as always. I'm almost jealous," Joy said, smiling.

"You don't think it's too much? You're more of a city girl than I am; you know all about this designer stuff."

She grinned. "I know that dress you're wearing is a designer dress, and it set you back a few thousand dollars." Joy raised her brows up and down, earning a roar of laughter from her mother. "To be honest, I don't get to experience all that much of Denver. I'm so busy that, by the end of the day, I'm too wiped out to even think about going out on the town, though I have made a few ski trips to Vail with Hayley and Jessica." The three of them adored skiing and made it a priority to hit the slopes at least once a month.

"Oh, sweetie, you should make the time to get to know the city you live in. If that's going to remain your home forever, don't neglect what it has to offer."

"Mother, I know what you're asking, and I'll tell you just like I told Izzie and Mr. Drake. When the required six months is over, I'm returning to Colorado. As you said, it's the city I live in. My business is there; you know I can't just . . . *leave*."

"Of course, you say you can't, but think about it. I know, I know, you're a successful businesswoman, and I am very proud of all you've accomplished, plus I adore all the free nail polish you send, but it's not impossible, is it?" Her mother's voice was serious. Joy recognized the tone well.

"Are you wearing Ravishing Reindeer Red on your nails?" Joy asked, hoping to change the subject, but she knew that her mother could be relentless when she was fired up.

"I know you're trying to change the subject, and I understand, and yes, this is Ravishing Reindeer Red. I know the designer," she admitted, a smile softening her face.

"We'll talk later. I promise, okay?"

"I'll hold you to that. Now, what are you wearing? You know that Will really likes you, don't you? He couldn't keep his eyes off of you last night."

Joy turned away from her mother so she couldn't see her face. If she did, she'd see the hot flush her comment had caused. Did he like her that much already? Wasn't it too soon to be thinking . . . there was a chance of a . . . *relationship? A long-distance relationship? No way, no how.*

"He's a nice guy, Mom, but that's it. We're just friends." Here she goes again. Lying. What had gotten into her? They were friends at this point, but that kiss last night was not the kiss of a mere friend. She was not a liar but felt compelled to prevaricate whenever the subject was Will Drake.

"Maybe we can date while I'm here." There, that took away some of the guilt she felt for lying to her mother.

It suddenly dawned on her; not only was she lying about Will to her mother, and to him, she was lying about him to herself! She had to admit that she already had some feelings for this man, despite having known him for only a few days. This wasn't like her. Something in her had changed. Later, she would delve into her psyche.

"I like him, too. He seems very relaxed and fits in with our little town. Moreover, all the locals seem to like him, so he's scored points there," her mother said. "He's local, just been away most of his adult life. All right, enough of my blabbering, I need to get downstairs and get ready for the big competition."

"I'll be down in a few minutes. I need to change into something appropriate." What she really thought, of course, was that she needed to change into an outfit that would impress Will Drake. One that would knock his socks off!

Chapter 9

Joy wished that she had brought a few more dressy outfits when she'd packed to return to Spruce City, but at
the time, she had only been thinking of Nana and the loss
she was feeling. She'd never expected this trip to rock the
world she'd created for herself, at least not in the way it
was now. Finally settling on a navy wrap dress, she slid
into a pair of nude Christian Louboutin heels, the only
pair of designer heels she owned. She applied a soft, fawn-
colored eye shadow, lined the top of her lids, added two
coats of mascara, and her favorite Tom Ford lipstick,
which she used for her blush. She looked in the mirror,
fluffed her hair, and decided this was as good as it gets.
She'd taken more time with her dress and makeup, yet it
wouldn't appear as if she was trying to impress people,
and certainly not Will Drake, because everyone in atten-

dance would be wearing their Sunday best. At least, that was what her mom had told her.

Heading downstairs, Joy felt a shiver of excitement knowing she would see Will Drake, if only for a few minutes.

Will, along with the five other judges, was standing around the table in the kitchen inspecting the replica of Heart and Soul. Barbara Green, owner of the local supermarket, had been selected as an alternate judge and was there since Ray McGuire, a seventh-grade teacher, had come down with the flu. Carolyn Anderson, who ran Create Salon, the only place for a decent cut in town and the only person her mother would allow to touch her hair after a disastrous cut from Norma Yost at Teases and Tangles years ago, was also judging the contest this year. Harold Higgins, the president of First Savings and Loan, would undoubtedly judge the five edible houses as if he were considering giving their owners a mortgage. And, last but not least, was Rose Baker-Gentry, the owner of Pure Bliss, a day spa in Spruce City, which carried Simply Joy polishes exclusively. But Joy was interested only in the attorney.

Her mother and Izzie stood in the corner of the kitchen while the judges inspected their work. She tiptoed around the judges and joined them. She was about to speak, but her mother silenced her with a finger to her lips. Joy nodded and gazed at Will as he followed the others around the table. They all carried a sheet of paper and a pencil. She assumed this was for keeping score. Stretching as high as her five-foot-nothing allowed, she tried to sneak a look at Rose Baker-Gentry's paper. Nope, too short.

Her mother touched her arm and shook her head from side to side, mouthing, "No."

She gave her a big, toothy smile and a thumbs-up sign.

For the next ten minutes, the staff of Heart and Soul watched as the judges admired the gingerbread house, tasted the piece provided for that purpose, and marked their score sheets. When they were finished, Will said, "Good luck," and the others mumbled something, but Joy hadn't paid attention as she'd only had eyes for Mr. Will Drake.

Dang, but this man was causing her heart to beat at an unhealthy staccato. As soon as they left, she let out a sigh. "Whew, I'm glad that's over with. How can you stand this?" she asked her mom and Izzie. "It's like they're judging the final vote in a fraudulent political election!"

They laughed at her description. "I wouldn't say that, but they do take this seriously, as they know all the hard work that has gone into constructing the houses," her mom said.

The Heart and Soul gingerbread house was three feet high, and they had used around five hundred pieces of gingerbread. Almost sixty pounds of icing trimmed the windows, doors, and chimneys. It was the glue that held all the parts together. Izzie swore they'd ordered a hundred pounds of the unique candy parts, courtesy of Global Candy Art. Peppermint sticks and multicolored gumdrops were used in so many different ways that Joy would never look at them again and think they were silly or boring. Marshmallows shaped like mini Christmas trees were on the lawn, along with gingerbread that was shaped to resemble large pine trees, courtesy of Izzie's artistic ability. A sleigh sitting on the roof by the chimney and Santa doing his best to slide down the chimney were both made of icing, and very delicate. It was one of the reasons they'd decided to keep the gingerbread display in the kitchen. It was very fragile, and the foot traffic in this room was minimal. After the judges finished observing it, they would move the house to the formal living room, where it would be on display during the Parade of Homes.

"It was important that you not say anything while the judges were doing their job. They all know that if they show any sign of likes or dislikes, the judge who does so will be disqualified, another judge brought in as a replacement, and they'll have to start all over again. They've already used Barbara Green as an alternate, and if I'm correct, they only pick three, so there are just two left."

Joy shook her head in amazement. "This is so . . . silly, but I get it," she said, placing her hands in front of her. "So, we wait."

"No, we get out of these clothes and get to work. We're not going to hear who won until Christmas Eve, so we put it out of our minds until then," Izzie said.

Joy felt let down a little bit, but she'd get over it. She'd gone to the trouble of wearing makeup and a dress. Had Will sneaked a look at her? She wasn't sure but hoped her efforts had been worth it. She was used to wearing jeans and a sweater, with comfortable Uggs. It was not full-on glam, and certainly not a dress, but it worked in her chosen profession.

She had a few e-mails to answer and a very important phone call to make. "I've got some Simply Joy business I need to take care of. Give me an hour, and I'll be down to help out."

Once she was out of her dressy clothes, she put on her Paige jeans, and because she felt fantastically cheerful, she wore her red Rag and Bone sweatshirt that was anything but a sweatshirt. Jessica had introduced her to Neiman Marcus, and she'd discovered an entirely new way to shop. Not that she shopped very often, but when she did, she didn't look at price tags anymore. She had made that promise to herself when she started Simply Joy. As soon as she became financially successful, she was not going to look at prices in clothing stores. She now had enough money to last her a very long lifetime, and with her smart investments, she wouldn't have to worry about retirement, either. So now she wore a two-hundred-dollar sweatshirt that didn't look or feel like a sweatshirt. The Paige-brand jeans that she'd become so fond of because of their comfort weren't cheap either.

Sometimes she felt guilty, but she also made sure to donate to several charities, plus she gave an extremely large donation to the ASPCA every single month. She'd set that up three years ago simply because it was the right thing to do. She loved animals, and now that it was in her power to help those who needed it, she had no regrets whatsoever. "And I'm getting a dog or a cat as soon as possible." So there. She'd said it out loud. Her personal rule was that if you say that you are going to do something out loud, that means you have to do it. It was silly, she knew, but it worked for her, kind of like her "get them done" list.

She opened her laptop, logged onto her business account, and answered her e-mail. Complaints were few, but when she had them, she liked to take care of them herself with either a personal e-mail or a phone call. Today she faced a couple of complaints, but, thankfully, nothing serious enough to require a phone call. As soon as she finished the e-mails, she checked on the Valentine's Day labels on Simply Joy's website and liked what she saw. Hayley had had a rough start, but in the end, she'd created something that she'd set out to do—a label that stood apart from her competitors'. She'd buy the next round of lift tickets for her and Jessica, who'd managed to get the labels up on the website in record time.

With her online work finished, she had that phone call to make; then she could go and help Izzie and her mom. She had the number stored in her cell phone and hit the name. Her call was taken immediately. She spoke for twenty minutes, then ended the call. Happy now that that was off her chest, she headed downstairs. Her leg muscles were getting a workout in the short time she'd been here. A good thing for sure.

In the kitchen, Chandra was cleaning pans, and Marie was at the island, chopping vegetables for tomorrow's omelet lovers. "Where's the boss?" Joy asked.

Both women laughed. "I didn't know we had one," Marie said, "but if you're talking about Izz, she and your mom are working on the whiteboard. Said they had to make a few menu changes."

"Thanks," she said and went to the main entrance, where the guests checked in. A giant whiteboard behind the counter gave the guests the breakfast menu for the next day. In addition, any new Heart and Soul activities, as well as all local events that were Christmas-related, were added daily.

"I like the red and green," Joy said, looking at the two women. Her mother had beautiful handwriting, and Izzie could draw just about anything. Between the two of them, they made the board look like a work of art instead of looking tacky and out of place. Though Nana had been as talented as her mother and had done this task before she passed away, now that her mother was involved in the day-to-day operations, she realized that running the B&B came as natural to her mother as it had Nana. Why hadn't she left the B&B to her only daughter? She lived here and loved it. Why she'd made her will so difficult for Joy, she would never know. But she'd accepted the terms, and here she was.

"Did you get your business taken care of?" her mother asked her, finishing up what she was writing on the whiteboard.

"I did. This board is fantastic. You two make quite a team, you know," Joy stated as she observed Izzie drawing a red basket with mistletoe weaving in and out of the handle. "What's in the basket?"

Izzie laughed. "You are a big pain in my neck, girl. There is nothing in that basket, it's just for looks. I'm guessing if it were real, it would be full of pine cones. How's that?"

"Pine cones work," Joy responded, as if they were discussing an important subject.

"I'm glad you approve," Izzie said. She made a few touches with the red and green markers, then stood back to admire their handiwork. "Not too bad for two old gals, huh?" She looked at Elizabeth.

"Not bad at all. We're good at this," Elizabeth said. "Old age and all."

"So, seriously, what's on the agenda for today?" Joy asked.

"Thanksgiving preparations. We've got five days. FedEx delivered our turkeys and hams last night—can you believe that? The prime rib roasts are supposed to arrive sometime later today. We've got sixteen guests who've confirmed they're staying for dinner. We'll have to arrange seating. With so many, we're going to have to use all the tables we have. I'm thinking we should set this up smorgasbord style. Do either of you have any suggestions?"

"I've never planned a Thanksgiving meal, so I'll do whatever you all need me to do," Joy said, knowing she was totally out of her comfort zone and wondering again why in the world Nana had put her in such a predicament.

"Let's go to the kitchen," Izzie said. "My menu is in there."

Joy and her mother returned to the kitchen, the hub of the B&B, where Izzie made it all come together.

"Here it is." She picked up a small notebook from the counter and sat down at their usual table, which, though it still held the massive gingerbread house, had enough room for the three of them to squeeze in close enough to have a conversation, plus a few inches of space for Izzie to set down her notebook. "Obviously, we're having turkey, and Elizabeth, could you make your corn-bread dressing? No one makes it like you do."

"Consider it done. I'd planned on making that red-velvet cream-cheese cake, the one that was on the cover of last year's *Home Sense* magazine, too. And we'll make Mom's red devil's food cake. She always served that on Thanksgiving when I was growing up. I always liked that way more than pumpkin pie."

"Perfect. Make double of all the desserts, and I'm guessing at least five pumpkin pies. We'll need fruit pies, too. A lot of our guests—heck, I think most of our guests—are from up North. I know they're noted for their traditional Thanksgiving desserts, but add in a sweet potato pie and a pecan, too. Do you think you can handle that?" Izzie asked, a huge grin showing her gleaming white teeth.

"Yep, I do. Joy can help. I'll teach you how to make the flakiest piecrust in the South. Are you up for all of this, Joy?" Her mom turned to her. "It's fine if you're not," she added.

"Isn't this the operations part of running this place? I'm certainly willing to give it my best," Joy said.

"I know you will," her mom said. "What we can do is start making our piecrusts. Then we can freeze them; that'll make things a lot easier given that we're baking for a small army. What else can I do, Izzie?" Elizabeth asked.

"You want to do more?" Izzie shook her head, her long braid hitting the back of her chair and making a thumping sound.

"I'm trying to make up for lost time," Elizabeth joked. "Really, I want to do as much as I can. I have Joy, and you've got Robert and Marie. We can handle this. Mother did it long before we were able to lend a hand."

"True," Izzie said. "Okay then, Elizabeth, you're the official dessert lady. Joy's your assistant and owner in training. We need to thaw those hefty birds out a couple days beforehand. I'll need to keep the sinks empty and get out a few of those old lard containers we've hung on to. They'll hold the hams as well as the prime rib roasts. I'll have Lou bring them down from the attic."

"I know you two know how this all works, but if we've got the kitchen commandeered, where are we going to get all the breakfast stuff prepped?" Joy asked.

"I'll set up a couple of tables in here, so we should be okay. We only make that one meal, so it's not like we're in here cooking around the clock. We'll work it out. Now,

I suggest we start off by making a list of what we don't have. Joy, you can go to the supermarket and pick up everything, if you would."

"Sure, I can do that. What else?"

"That's it for now. Elizabeth, am I forgetting anything?"

"I don't think so. Joy, is there anything you think we might've missed?" her mom asked.

Joy chewed on her bottom lip. "Do we have horseradish for the prime rib?"

"I didn't even think of that. Add that to my list," Izzie said, handing over her pencil. "Elizabeth, we'll have this girl running the place in no time. Then you and I can go on one of those cruises you're always trying to get me to go on."

"Works for me," Elizabeth replied. "Just tell me when, and we're out of here."

"Okay, cruisers, I'm going to the supermarket. If you think of anything else while I'm gone, call my cell," Joy said, then took the list and stuffed it in her pocket.

Chapter 10

Outside, the November air was cool and refreshing. After being cooped up in the house all afternoon, Joy relished the fresh air. She pulled into the parking lot at Green's Supermarket, surprised to find the place packed. Inside, the small grocery hummed with the sound of shoppers picking up the makings of Thanksgiving dinner and the wheels on carts squealing. Joy found a shopping cart and took out her list. Up and down the aisles she went, locating everything on the list except for pecans. "Okay," she muttered. "Pecans have to be with the peanuts. A pecan is a nut."

"Excuse me?" came that familiar and *sexy* voice.

Surprise siphoned the blood right from her face. "Oh, hey, what are you doing here?" she asked, then realized how stupid that must sound. Buying food, most likely. It's what you did at the supermarket, isn't it? Unable to stop herself, she gave a quick glance at his attire. He wore black dress slacks and a crisp white shirt with French cuffs and gold cuff links, though she couldn't tell the design. *Men still wore cuff links?*

"Stocking up on frozen food," he answered. "What are you doing here? Don't you guys get your food from one of those restaurant-supply companies?"

"No, at least I don't believe we do. We did order the turkeys online, but—" She stopped. Taking a breath, she started over. "There's a special farm where we order fresh turkeys. Hams are Smithfield, of course, and the prime rib comes from . . ." Where had they ordered those from? "I haven't a clue."

He laughed, catching the attention of several shoppers. "You'll learn," he said. "For the B&B's future orders, I'm sure," he assured her, smiling the entire time.

"Excuse me, you two are blocking the aisle," shouted a woman with yellow hair, blue eye shadow caked on her eyes, and white jeans, in an atrociously nasal voice. "*Excuse me!*" The woman tried forcing her cart between their two carts, which was impossible.

Will pushed his cart a few feet down the aisle, then said, "Ma'am, now you can get through."

She gave both of them a dirty look, then slammed her cart past them. The woman muttered something, but Joy couldn't make out the words.

"She's here every Saturday. Double-coupon day."

Joy could only nod as her mind went completely blank.

"Would you like to meet for coffee later?" he asked. "Joy, are you okay?"

Snapping back to reality, she spoke up, "Sorry, I think I went to high school with her." She nodded toward the yellow-haired woman, who'd stopped at the end of the aisle, reading the label on a jar of marshmallow fluff. Joy suspected she was listening to their conversation.

"Looks like life hasn't treated her too kindly."

Glass shattered, and they both turned their heads. The yellow-haired lady had dropped the jar of marshmallow fluff.

A young boy came around the corner with a broom and mop. He was there so quickly, Joy thought he might've been waiting for a mess on aisle three. She smiled.

"Are you finished with your shopping?" Will asked.

"I . . . pecans, I was looking for pecans."

He turned around, searching the top shelves. "How many bags do you want?"

She looked up to see bags of pecans on the top shelf. She glanced at her list. It didn't specify how many, so she said. "Six." Surely that was enough for a pie or two?

He took six bags off the shelf and put them in her shopping cart. "Looks like a ton of food."

"Thanksgiving is this Thursday, and we're making dinner for all the guests and the employees." She peeped at the contents of his cart, hoping to spot a small turkey, a ham, something indicating he had plans. When all she saw were frozen dinners, three of them turkey and mashed potatoes, she said, "Why don't you come for dinner? There's going to be enough food to feed half of Spruce City."

"Are you asking me because you feel sorry for me with all this frozen turkey stuff in my shopping cart?" He grinned. "Or are you asking because you'd like my company?"

Caught, she thought about how to answer. "Both."

"I'll come on one condition."

"And that would be?" she said, playing along.

"That you have coffee with me after we take our groceries home and put them away. I could meet you at Uncommon Grounds in, say"—he glanced at his watch—"half an hour?"

"I'm not sure that's such a good idea. The gingerbread thing—"

"We've already turned in our votes," he told her.

"That was quick," she said. She'd assumed they would discuss how they'd voted among themselves, then take a day or so to make a final decision.

"It was. It's just a simple vote; there's no real debate," he explained.

"I know, it's just that the way they've been acting at the B&B, one would think this was a presidential election."

"So, you'll meet me in half an hour? I'd better go to the checkout before this stuff thaws out."

Knowing she shouldn't but wanting to, she nodded. "I'll be there in thirty minutes," she agreed, then pushed her cart to the front of the store.

Fifteen minutes later, she was at the B&B. Lou helped her unload the groceries; then her mother and Izzie put them away.

"I'm gonna meet Will for coffee," she announced, out of the blue.

"Ah-ha! I had a hunch you two would hit it off," Izzie said. "The way you were making eyes at each other while he was trying to judge our gingerbread house. Shame on you both, though he is a handsome man, and smart, too. You two make the perfect couple."

"Izzie! You're talking about me like I'm sixteen. We're nothing more than friends."

"Let it be, Izz. She's not committing to a relationship because she'll be gone in six months, and that wouldn't be fair to Will," her mother called out from the giant walk-in freezer.

Joy rolled her eyes.

"Joy Elizabeth Preston, now *that's* acting like you're sixteen," Izzie said.

"It is, you're right. I'm just going to meet Will for a cup of coffee at Uncommon Grounds. Nothing more. At least not tonight," she added, knowing that her mother was listening to every word she and Izzie had to say.

Chapter 11

Uncommon Grounds was like most coffee shops across the country. The rich smell of coffee, yeasty pastries, and shout-outs for one vanilla chai latte, two espressos with milk, extra hot, a decaf—the usual barista lingo.

Joy would never be able to remember this stuff if she were a barista. She did love coffee, though. It was one of her weaknesses. She'd had several cups already, but the stuff at the B&B wasn't very strong. She stepped up to the counter, ordered a large coffee, asking for their strongest roast, with milk. As she reached into her purse to get her wallet, she felt a presence come up behind her. "My treat," he said, and gave the cashier a twenty-dollar bill.

She smiled. He was *that* kind of guy. Joy liked old-fashioned men. It wasn't so cool these days, but it's what she preferred. Her father had been that kind of man. A true gentleman.

"Thank you," she said.

"A man invites a lady for coffee, he pays for it. Pure and simple," he stated as he carried their paper cups of coffee over to an empty table. "You're good with this?"

Joy felt as though he'd read her mind. "Absolutely."

The place was almost empty, and she was glad. After all the people coming and going at the B&B, then the noisy supermarket, she was in need of some quiet time. They sat across from one another; the table was very small, so when they reached for their cups, their hands touched. He took her hand in his. "We can do this, right? Here in public? No angry high school sweetheart's going to fly through that door and challenge me?"

Joy shook her head, laughing. "Are you kidding? I didn't even have a boyfriend in high school. I was a total geek."

"No boy geeks in school?" he asked.

She thought back to her high school days. "I'm sure there had to be a few, but none I remember. I worked at the B&B all through high school and during summers. I didn't have a lot of friends back then." She hadn't felt like she'd missed out. She'd had her family and Nana, and the B&B kept her occupied. It wasn't until that vacation they took the winter of her senior year that she'd had any thought of leaving Spruce City, let alone moving out west, when she was barely eighteen. She'd fallen in love—with a city—and hadn't ever looked back. Until now. Nana's death had changed things. The thought that you could always go back home, that the life you knew as a child, a teenager, would always be the same, was simply untrue. People died, places changed. Minds changed, too, she thought as she took a sip of her coffee. "Oh, this is the best cup of coffee I've had since I left Denver."

"One of the chain coffee shops?" he asked.

Joy took another sip. "No, not my taste, but there is a blend at Coco's Coffee Cafe in Denver that's worth standing in line for. It comes from Hawaii, and it's expensive. I can't seem to get that extra zing with any other coffee. Silly, huh?"

"No, not at all. If you like a particular brand of . . . anything, or anyone, and they, *it*, makes you happy, why not?" He took a sip of coffee. "This stuff is pretty decent."

Joy understood his insinuation. Should she take the bait? Why not? "I agree—whatever makes you happy. I'm all about being happy." She sounded like a teenager, but at that exact moment, that's exactly how she felt. If this is what her classmates had been all giddy about in high school, then she really *had* missed out.

"You only get one life," he said, his tone somber.

"Is there more?" she asked, knowing, somehow, that he would know exactly what she meant.

"I guess I'm trying to say life is what you make of it. If you see something you want, grab it, because we only have this one life, one chance, to find our true happiness." He took another drink of coffee. "That sounds completely corny."

"Yes, it does, but remember, I'm a geek, and I like corny. Speaking of food—you know, corn, corny—you never told me if you were coming over for Thanksgiving." It wasn't like one more person would matter, but this one person had the power to make her day. Unsure if she liked giving up control of choosing her own happiness . . . Stop, she told herself, you are *choosing* this, *him*, to share your time with.

"I'll accept your invitation on one condition: you let me take you out to dinner. Someplace nice," Will said, squeezing her hand. "Maybe we could drive to Raleigh or Charlotte. They have a few fancy restaurants we could try."

"What makes you think I like fancy?"

"I don't know, maybe the fact that you're a very successful businesswoman, you work hard, you appreciate the rewards your work brings? I'm guessing here, so speak up anytime," he quipped, his voice light and playful.

"Okay. Fancy. It depends. I appreciate hard work, and the changes you can make not just in your own life, but in the lives of others, too. I do my best to give back when I can. Most of my time is spent working in the office, so it's not always easy to actually get out there physically and lend a hand, but I can help financially, so I choose that way for now."

Their cups were empty, he hadn't let go of her hand, and Joy was completely comfortable with it. Normally, this wasn't her way, but her thinking process where Will Drake was concerned was anything but normal. "You haven't accepted my invitation yet."

He finally let go of her hand. "I'll be right back." He took their cups and tossed them into a garbage can. Two minutes later, he was back with two fresh cups of coffee. "Okay, now. What time would you like me to arrive? I'd ask if there was anything I could bring, but you saw what was in my shopping cart. We both know if I brought something edible, it would be frozen. Dad never cooked when I was a kid, so I never really learned how. Is that a good excuse?"

"Yes, it is. On the other hand, I grew up with a mother and grandmother who could make a slice of bologna taste like prime rib, but I can barely boil water. When I'm at the B&B, I try to pick up a few tips, but as soon as I get home, it seems that I forget all about them. We order a lot of takeout."

He jerked his head up so fast it startled her.

"Are you all right?" she asked, alarmed at his sudden change.

"You said 'we.' Is there someone at home?"

She relaxed, letting out the breath she hadn't been aware she was holding. "Just so we're clear, 'we' usually consists of Hayley and Jessica. They both work at Simply Joy. They've been with me since the beginning. So when you hear 'we,' it's usually the girls. If there was someone, I wouldn't be having coffee with you right now. I'm a bit old-fashioned that way. I know it's not cool, hip, or whatever they say these days, but I can't change who I am or what I believe in."

The beginning of a smile tipped the corners of his mouth. "I'm not cool or hip or any of those things, either. I like old-fashioned, Joy Preston. A lot." He traced the red fabric around her wrist. "Before you ask, there is no one, hasn't been in a long time."

She knew that he had told her this just to make clear they were on the same page, not just morally but emotionally. He wasn't in a relationship. That was a good thing. She didn't have time to get involved . . .

Wait! Isn't this exactly what I'm doing? Leading Will to believe there could be more than this? That they could, if they chose to, get involved?

"Is it something I said?" he asked. "I admit, I'm a little rusty, but if I said anything offensive, I apologize."

"No, no, it's not you. You're perfect," she said, then gave a half laugh. "I take that back."

"Now I'm offended," he said jokingly.

"I can't let 'perfect' go to your head, now can I? I was thinking about Thanksgiving, wondering if you uh . . . prefer mashed potatoes, sweet potatoes, or both? Or baked. Or cooked both ways. Because we always run out of regular mashed potatoes. They're everyone's favorite. I want to make sure we don't run out, that's all." The childhood phrase "Liar, liar, pants on fire*"* clanged like a cymbal in her head.

"I like both. I may be imagining this, but I don't think potatoes is what you're really thinking about."

"It is now," she retorted, and grinned. Why was she always overthinking every situation, she wondered? Especially now. Will had read the terms of Nana's will to her himself. He knew how long she planned on staying in Spruce City. If hanging out together for a few months instantly meant they were in a relationship, then her definition of a relationship needed to be reexamined. This was a *friendship*. "The thought did cross my mind. I'm insane when it comes to mashed potatoes. Any potato actually. I microwave them a lot. At home. When I'm alone."

"I'll keep that in mind when I invite you to my place

for dinner." He looked at his watch. "I guess I should let you go. I know you've got your hands full at the B&B right now. All that baking."

She hadn't told him their baking plans. Or had she? It didn't matter. "Actually, I do need to go. I'm sure between Mom and Izzie, they've made a list of all the things I could be helping with. If I'm going to run the place, I should know everything that goes on behind the pretty linens and gourmet breakfasts." As she stood up, he took her empty cup again and tossed it in the garbage.

"Yes, I agree. Let me walk you to your car," he said when they stepped outside. She'd parked in the alleyway and didn't need an escort, but he'd said he was old-fashioned, too, so she walked with him to the back of the building.

"One o'clock," she said as she rummaged through her purse for the key fob. "Thursday."

He leaned down, kissing her on the cheek. "I can't wait."

"Me either," she said. "And fancy is good. Sometimes."

He opened her door and gently closed it, motioned for her to hit the LOCK button, then watched as she backed out of the alleyway. As she pulled away, she looked in her rearview mirror. If anyone else watched her like this, she would immediately think they were creepy, too controlling, stalker-like. But she trusted Will. Nana and her mother were wise women, and she knew she had their seal of approval. Even though Nana wasn't there to voice it, Joy just knew. And maybe she was just beginning to get some inkling of why Nana's will read the way it did. Or maybe she was just overthinking again, which she seemed to be doing a lot lately.

Chapter 12

The Day Before Thanksgiving, 2018

Brett and Sal had spent the past three days turning the outside of Heart and Soul into a visual autumnal feast. Planters with white camellias and yellow and purple chrysanthemums flanked the main entrance. Garlands of magnolia leaves were draped around the wooden doors. Giant orange and yellow pots filled with more brightly colored mums were placed all around the porch. Gourds in all shapes and sizes were arranged in baskets and positioned just so on small tables and in once-empty corners. Pumpkins of different sizes, shapes, and colors lined the walkway. Decorative pillows patterned with autumn leaves were tucked around on comfortable chairs and in nooks where one might hide away with a good book on a breezy afternoon. Burgundy, gold, and orange leaves were scattered all over the porch, almost as though they had accidentally landed there to add to the brilliance of the autumn colors. A faint breeze fluttered, causing the swing at the end of the porch to sway back and forth, giving off a slight creaking noise.

Knowing this lazy fall scene would have to come down in the wee hours of the morning in order for the team of designers to begin decking out the house for Christmas made Joy a little sad, but the Christmas décor would be worth the sacrifice. The day after Thanksgiving in Spruce City was the official start of the holiday season. The annual Parade of Homes began the first of December. The gingerbread competition was downright dirty; the parade wasn't even comparable, according to her mom.

She had heard someone at the supermarket say that this was the beginning of what some of the locals called the Christmas Olympics. If you played, you played to win. If your house didn't inspire jaw-dropping *oohs* and *ahhhs*, as strangers, friends, and members of your family pranced through your mind-boggling display of whatever theme had been chosen, then one might as well call it a day and hide one's head in shame.

"I hate to see all this taken down so soon, but we don't have a choice," Joy said to her mother. They were taking a short break from the activity in the kitchen. "It seems strange without Nana here now. She lived for this day. All the bells and whistles, the buildup. I remember the last time I was here during the pre-Christmas season. You would've thought we were the Biltmore Estate. There had to be at least thirty people working to make this place look magical, and all of it done in just one day. It is kind of magical, don't you think?"

"I do, in spite of our loss. It was a nightmare when we lost your dad. I had your grandmother to lean on then. I should've stayed with her instead of cruising the world," her mother said, as tears eased down her face.

"Mom, stop, please. I know you feel guilty. I do, too, but Nana would have our butts if she thought we felt this way. This sounds crazy, but I sometimes think I can feel her presence when I walk by Miss Betty's room. Am I letting this ghostly gossip get to me? I've never felt anything like it. I've kept it to myself, but it makes you wonder," Joy admitted, wrapping her arms around herself. "It's a bit scary."

"I'm not discounting any of the stories I've heard. I'm sorry for just . . . falling apart, sweetie. Sometimes it just hits me, and I try to keep it to myself. Like daughter, like mother."

They both laughed.

"Let's get back to the kitchen before someone realizes we're gone," her mom said, trying to regain her composure.

Once they were back in the kitchen, Joy quickly found herself up to her ears in flour. "I can't believe we're doing this again." Two days earlier, they'd made so many piecrusts that she'd lost count. She didn't understand why they couldn't just let Mary Jane make the pies since she owned the bakery. She said as much to her mother.

"She's baking pies for half the town already; plus, I want the guests to smell us baking in the kitchen. Smell stimulates memories, and we want our guests walking away with good memories. Like the smell of baking pies. They remember where they were, and that, of course, means Heart and Soul. And once that memory is set, they'll come back the next year and the year after that. They become like family after a while," her mother added, wrapping another disc of dough in plastic wrap and placing it on a large baking sheet.

The first batch of piecrusts was a disaster. After they'd finished rolling out the dough and putting the crusts in pie tins for freezing, her mother couldn't stop talking about them, saying something was not right. She removed one from the freezer, added a mixture of pumpkin and a few spices, and baked a "trial pie." When they'd tasted the pie, it was confirmed. When asked to get the butter from the freezer, Joy had done just that. No one specified what kind of butter. Apparently, she'd grabbed the salted butter, and according to their family recipe, you never used salted butter when making piecrusts. It had tasted terrible, hence the second round of baking.

"I get it. The entire house smells like cinnamon, cloves, and buttery pastries. It smells divine. I can't wait to dig in to that red devil's food cake. And the pecan pie."

That particular pie reminded her of Will. No smell needed. She hadn't seen him since their coffee date, if you called that a date. She would see him tomorrow, and that made her happy. Humming a Christmas tune, she brushed the flour aside into a little pile. "I'm ready for the next batch."

This time around, her mother made sure that she got all the ingredients herself and had Joy *watch* her make the crust. They decided she would roll out the piecrust.

Another round of patting and rolling, then she returned the discs to her mother. She'd put them in the freezer, and in the morning, they would start baking. Joy was excited. It was the same sort of excitement she used to feel as a child on Christmas Eve—anxious and excited in a happy sort of way.

Maybe she knew why she was so happy but wasn't ready to reveal it just yet. She was not even sure that she'd truly revealed it to her adult self. It was much too soon and much too easy to go along with all the match-makers. Right now, she was happy and not thinking clearly, but her responsibilities were overwhelming; she loved them, too, but it was just nice to be here now. She hadn't thought much about Colorado other than work. She didn't find herself craving a five-mile run down a black diamond. Hometown life was much less intent than life in Denver. She hadn't remembered Spruce City being quite so relaxing. She had always thought life back home was a bit slow, but right now, at this very minute, life here was sweet and joyous. To be sure, she might change her mind in another hour. Who knew?

She sneezed. "Okay, if you all don't mind, I think I deserve a five-minute break to go outside and shake the flour from my clothes."

"Elizabeth, that girl is the boss; she can do whatever she wants!" Izzie said, trying to sound serious.

"You two need to take a time-out for acting like three-year-olds," Joy said, trying hard not to burst out laughing. Let them think she was testing the waters.

"I don't think she's serious, Izzie. She hasn't mastered my version of the time-out voice yet, so she just wants us to think she is," Elizabeth said to Izzie.

Joy burst out laughing. "I think you two ornery old gals need to spend some time in detention. Sit in your rooms."

Her mother and Izzie started untying their aprons. "We want to go to our rooms," Izzie pleaded. "Please."

Joy rolled her eyes again. "You can follow me out if you like. I'm just cleaning the flour off myself. Really."

Joy stepped out into the back parking lot, where her rental and Izzie's Caddy were parked side by side. She went to the end of the lawn, walking toward the edge of the property that led to the river. She leaned into the bag she'd brought along and brushed the flour from her shirt into it. Same with her apron, though she brushed her jeans off with her hand. She didn't want to give anyone a chance to say she wasn't hypervigilant when it came to caring for the environment. She heard her mom and Izzie as they walked across the lawn, the crisp autumn leaves crunching beneath their feet.

"I know you think I'm meeting Will out here, but you two can go back inside. I really wanted to clean off this flour and get a minute or two of quiet time. I've lived alone for so long," she explained. Though she was happy to be at the B&B, which was filled with happy people, every once in a while she needed a quiet break. "I needed a moment."

"I understand. It does get noisy in there, but that's exactly what appeals to most of the guests at Heart and Soul. They know when they check in that it isn't a spa resort. Though I'd like to think the rooms offer much more than a spa would," her mother said.

"Except for Scrooge's old room, each guest room looks like a mini soundstage. All the work that has been put into them is phenomenal, and those bathtubs are like something out of a dream." Joy brushed her pants off one last time, and, teasing her mom and Izzie, said, "We can go back in now."

Inside the kitchen, Joy returned to the pie-rolling station she'd set up. Now it needed to be cleaned for the next round, whatever that might be. They'd been baking since before breakfast had been served to the guests, and Joy wondered when they'd have enough pies. "Mom, are we baking more pies?"

"Let me think. There are six pumpkin pies, three pecan pies, three apple pies, three sweet potato pies, your devil's food cake, the red-velvet cream-cheese cake, and I'm making a banana pudding in the morning. It's expected in the South, no matter what holiday. That's all I can account for. Izzie, did I forget anything?"

"The corn bread for the stuffing?"

"Yep, I'm just about to get started on that. Joy, clear me a little space, and I'll show you the beginnings of a family tradition."

In response to her mother's directions, Joy pushed two canisters of flour aside, wiped the countertop, then dried it before putting another disposable plastic sheet on top. "I'm ready," Joy said, stepping to the side so her mom could have the space she needed.

"I think I've got everything I need here," Elizabeth said, placing a tray on top of the counter.

Izzie called out, "If it's not all there, don't you dare send Joy after it."

Joy laughed. "Hey, I heard that."

"I meant for you to," Izzie said. "You think you can learn to operate this place in six months?"

Joy shook her head. "No, not if I tried. There is more than just checking the guests in and out, keeping their rooms clean, having breakfast ready. I know all the basics, but you know full well I couldn't do this without all of you." She saw Marie and Chandra happily chopping away at the island in the center of the large prep kitchen. "And you, too," she said to them.

"Thanks, Miss Preston," Marie said.

"Please call me Joy. Miss Preston sounds like an old spinster aunt." They all laughed at this.

For the next fifteen minutes, Joy learned the Southern way to make corn bread. When they were ready, she carried the two pans and placed them in the already-steaming-hot oven. "Set the timer, Izzie. Mom says to tell you this even though you're right here."

"Oh, I thought she was helping Lou rearrange the tables in the formal living room," her mom said.

"I'm back. Lou just wanted to kiss me. That's all. He's had those tables in place since midnight. We take this stuff seriously."

"The kissing or the work?" Joy taunted.

"Both," Izzie said, and there was more laughing.

"Good to know," Joy said. "For the future."

Her mother raised her eyebrows at Joy, inquiringly. "For future employees, Mom. Some businesses don't allow employees to date. I'm glad Heart and Soul isn't one of them."

"I am, for sure, and Lou, too," Izzie added, though in a teasing way, as she started peeling potatoes at one of the smaller of the four prep sinks.

"Good. Now we all know where we stand. So, if we see employees sneaking a smooch here and there, it's okay as long as their work is finished?" Joy questioned.

"It depends on the work, so each situation would be different. Let's say, for instance, if Izzie's peeling away, and her significant other, her boyfriend, comes inside for a drink of water or an iced tea, and just happens to give Izzie a quick kiss in passing, then that would be just fine," her mother explained.

Joy grinned at her mother. After the sadness that had overtaken them earlier, they'd both managed to find and focus on that bright light called happiness. Heart and Soul liked their employees to be happy. Its new proprietor ran Simply Joy the same way. Given that she had been at Heart and Soul for such a short time, it was virtually impossible to believe all the changes that had taken place in her life. Staying in Spruce City for six months, learning all she could to keep the bed-and-breakfast going, competing in contests, and having dinners and coffee dates with *one of the judges!*

What if she decided to move to Spruce City permanently? Would her being just a regular citizen of a small town appeal to Mr. Will Drake? Or is he more attracted to the professional woman who runs a company located in Denver, Colorado? Would whatever was happening between the two of them lead to something more serious? Or was she just overthinking again?

The latter, she thought to herself. Will Drake liked her, and she liked him; it wasn't time to think about wedding dresses and names for the babies they'd have. No, she did not want to go that route. Not yet. She'd worked hard in order to achieve her small bit of success. Having spent so much time focusing on Simply Joy's day-to-day operations didn't allow for a lot of free time to plan where you wanted to be in the next five or ten years. She would think about that on a more personal level. Even though she'd already financed her retirement, one couldn't be too careful with one's investments. Just as with one's romantic life, they came with a risk.

Just as that thought passed through what remained of her mind, the oven timer went off, jarring her back to the moment. "The corn bread—I'll get it. Where are the oven mitts?" She searched the area for the mitts, finding that they'd fallen into one of the sinks next to the giant industrial oven. She put them on—luckily, they were still dry. She did not want to be blamed for burning the corn bread. Opening the oven door, she pulled out one perfect yellow-gold pan of corn bread, followed by a second. She took a deep breath. This would be perfect with butter. Right now, she thought. She found a small knife, cut into the steaming-hot corn bread, and carried two slices over to the small refrigerator they used in the prep kitchen. Locating a dish of butter, she sliced off a square, then put it between the two pieces of corn bread. Taking a bite, she closed her eyes, and marveled, "Oh my gosh . . . I don't know when I've had anything so . . . perfect. You know, something I cooked, and all? Though I didn't make this, did I? Never mind. Mom, this is the best ever. I don't know what your trick for this is, besides using unsalted butter, but this stuff is too good for the dressing. I know butter isn't in this recipe."

Everyone in the kitchen laughed.

"Thank you. It is good. A trick is to not overmix your cornmeal. Mother taught me that."

Joy finished eating the two slices of buttered corn bread and indicated, "And a good thing you listened. I haven't had this in forever. Right out of the oven, too."

For the rest of the evening, they prepared what they could in advance. Tomorrow was the big day.

Joy just hoped Will showed. Especially after telling everyone that she'd invited him. She should have kept quiet until he walked into the house. Too late now, she thought. If he didn't show, maybe he'd have a good excuse. He had to bail someone out of jail, was pulled away by a big client, on and on. In his profession, he could have a million excuses.

She would find out tomorrow at one in the afternoon.

Chapter 13

Thanksgiving Day, 2018

The dining room and the main living room could hold up to fifty people. They could actually squeeze as many as twenty-five people around the main dining table, but Izzie said only around twenty would show up. The guests, especially those staying inside the house, knew how busy they'd been and didn't seem to request a lot during their Thanksgiving preparations, which was very kind of them.

The only downside, at least for Joy, would be for Will not to show. She'd thought of nothing else since she woke up this morning. She'd utilized the soaker tub, relaxing for more than half an hour in cranberry-scented bubbles. The entire time, she daydreamed about Will Drake. Sick, she thought. Especially at her age. She'd be thirty in February. Grown women don't act like this, do they?

"Joy, could you supervise the guys picking up the fall décor? They're pulling up now," Elizabeth Preston said, interrupting Joy's noodling about what grown-up women did and did not do.

"Sure thing," she said, and rushed outside. She'd put on jeans this morning but planned to change into something a little less casual before dinner.

A box truck slowly backed into the empty parking area reserved for that kind of thing. The truck's backup alarm beeped repeatedly, then stopped when the edge of the back wheels touched the concrete edge. A man in his midfifties, tall and lean, with a shiny bald head, jumped down from the cab and said, "I'm here from the shelter to pick up the pumpkins." He said it as if it was something they discussed daily.

"Over here," Joy said, pointing to the dozens of beautiful pumpkins and gourds.

Lou rounded the corner, hand waving in the air. "I got this, Joy. You can go on in."

She waited for Lou; then, as he started tossing the pumpkins to the man, who was now standing in the truck, Joy started helping out. When they were finished, the man hopped down and came around to where she stood. "I can't thank you enough. This will be enough for at least fifty pies. It'll keep Lana busy for a few days. Thank you, miss." He nodded, hopped back into the truck, and drove away with the pumpkins that would keep Lana occupied.

Lou stood beside her. "That's such a good idea. Getting rid of the pumpkins. I'll see you at dinner, Miss Joy."

"Sure," she called out, but Lou had already left.

Inside, she found her mother up to her elbows in more dough.

"First, please tell me you're not baking more pies. We have enough pies to feed the entire town. And who gets those pumpkins? The man thanked me like I'd given him the winning lottery numbers."

"That's James Albert. He runs a shelter for battered women and their children. He and his wife, Lana, run the place on donations and money left to him when his father died about fifteen years ago, though he didn't start the shelter until six or seven years ago. They're really invested in helping abused women and their kids. Lana uses the pumpkins to make pies. He'll use our donation for his Christmastime pumpkin pies."

"Now, that is a very good man, if I say so myself. What a fantastic way to use your inheritance. Helping battered women." She thought for a moment. "Mom, would it be . . . I don't know, weird or silly if I were to send a bunch of nail polishes and nail-care kits to them? We have them for small children, too. Something Hayley talked me into."

"You are my daughter, no doubt. That's a fantastic idea. You remember, it's what started your business. All women like pretty fingernails. I think those gals at the shelter would be thrilled to have something fun and frilly in their life. I can put in a call to James and Lana, if you'd like?"

Joy looked down at the two-hundred-dollar jeans she wore and the shoes that cost more than some people earn in a week. She needed to give back in smaller ways, locally, and not just by signing those checks, however large, to be donated to her chosen charities. She needed to see if her donation of nail polish would make one of the shelter women happy. Even if it was just for a few minutes. An idea had blossomed, and she needed to act on it now.

"That would be terrific—thanks. Let me run upstairs to make a call. I'll be right back to help," she assured her mother. Back in her room, she took her cell phone from the charger and dialed Hayley's cell.

Hayley answered on the first ring, which, given the two-hour time difference, said a lot, as Hayley was definitely *not* a morning person.

"Happy Turkey Day," Joy said cheerfully, knowing this, too, would irritate her as she wasn't a big fan of perkiness. In fact, she hated it, at least early in the morning.

"Yeah, whatever, Happy Turkey Day right back at ya," she said, her hoarse voice indicating that she'd just woken up.

"I've got a job for you. Today—and before you tell me, I know it's a holiday—but you'll like this idea."

Joy explained what she needed for the shelter.

"That's the best idea I've heard all day," Hayley said, her voice now filled with excitement.

"It's the only idea you've heard all day," Joy shot back. "Seriously, I think this is something we could do all the time. Not just on holidays. I'm not one hundred percent sure the shelter approves just yet, though I discussed this with my mother. She thinks it's a terrific idea, and she's calling the couple who run the local shelter now, just to make sure we're not stepping on toes or anything."

"I hear that. Do you want me to go ahead and get started with the packing? And should I send this to the B&B or to the shelter?"

Joy thought for a moment. "Just send it to me at Heart and Soul. I'll personally deliver the boxes to the shelter. I'd like to see if something as simple as a bottle of nail polish can bring a ray of sunshine into the lives of the women there. It's apparent they're not there for a holiday. I feel terrible about their situation, and I've never even set eyes on any of the women. We need to make this something permanent. Not just at this shelter, but at as many shelters around the country as we can. See if Jessica can start the ball rolling, get the addresses, clear it with the powers that be," Joy said. Excited that she might be able to add this to her "get them done" list, she was sure that with Hayley and Jessica's help, it would most definitely happen.

"I'm on it, and, Joy, what we discussed yesterday is okay by me. Just so you know."

Surprised, Joy said, "Really?"

"Really."

"Then that puts an even brighter light on what we talked about, but you cannot breathe one word of this to anyone yet."

"Does Jessica know?" Hayley asked.

"No, but I plan to call her tomorrow. I know she's spending today with her family, so I'll wait until she's home."

"Thanks a lot. You know how hard it's going to be to keep my mouth shut?" Hayley asked.

Joy burst out laughing. "Okay, okay. I get it, and you're the best secret keeper ever, so don't cut yourself short. I'll call her as soon as I hang up, just so you won't have to worry about making a slip of the tongue and all. Hayley, I don't know what I'd do without you. And Jessica. I just want you to know, I could not run Simply Joy without you two."

"We know," Hayley said.

"You're a prize. I'm hanging up and calling Jessica right now. Talk to you later."

Joy ended the call before their sparring could continue, as past experience showed that it could go on for hours on end.

Though she hated to interrupt Jessica's time with her family, Joy dialed Jessica's cell.

"Happy Thanksgiving, girl!" Jessica was the polar opposite of Hayley. "Perky" was her middle name, no matter the time of day.

"Thanks, Jess. You too. Listen." Joy could hear voices in the background. "Can you talk for a few minutes, or do you want me to call later?"

"I can talk. I'm at home, not at the White House. So what's up? It's got to be super, super important for you to call this early on a holiday."

"I keep forgetting about the time difference. Sorry. I've had a bit of a brainstorm of an idea here. I just spoke with Hayley, and she, too, thinks this is a good way to give back."

Joy explained the plan, then went on to discuss the possible future of Simply Joy.

"Fantastic, Joy, seriously. I'm thrilled to help, and no worries on the other stuff. I'll keep it to myself," Jess said.

"I really appreciate this. I'll treat you and Hayley to a ski trip after the holidays," Joy said.

"I'll hold you to it," Jessica said. "Now, go on and get back to what you were doing. We've got this end handled."

Downstairs, Joy filled her mother in on the details of her conversations about making donations to shelters.

"I called and spoke with James, told him what you proposed, and he told me to tell you to 'go for it. Anything to make the ladies happy.'"

"Good, because Hayley's going to overnight everything I asked for later today. It should arrive tomorrow," Joy explained. "I want to give back, and these women and the shelters are going to be hearing a lot more from Simply Joy." She stole a glance at the clock. It was ten o'clock—only three hours to go.

Feeling as though she'd accomplished something she had control over, Joy looked around the kitchen, enjoying the atmosphere. Everyone seemed to be really cheery, doing their assigned tasks and being pleased to do them. At least that was how it appeared to her.

"That's truly what this day is about," her mother said. "Being thankful, helping others, being a part of whatever makes you happy. I didn't realize just how much I've missed all this," she said. "I canceled the Christmas cruise I booked last year. I want to be around family and friends, now more than ever."

Joy hadn't really thought too much about the Thanksgiving holiday other than her nail polish colors for the season. Then there was what they had learned in first grade. She remembered making Pilgrim hats and wearing hers until the construction paper was completely destroyed. *Do they still do this*, she wondered?

"Are you sure? You know how much you've been enjoying those cruises. We can handle things here if you really want to go," Joy told Elizabeth.

Her mother walked over to the sink, took the giant pot filled with potatoes, and put it on the stove. "We'll need these last. Sorry, I was thinking out loud. To answer your question, I am one hundred percent sure. I'm not saying I won't take another cruise, but for now, I'm a bit of a burnout. I think I've been on what, at least, twenty cruises? More than most people go on in a lifetime. I'm here to stay." She put the lid on the pot.

"Good, not that you can't come and go as you please. While I totally dislike the reason I'm here, being here feels good right now." She emphasized the last two words. Joy didn't want to say anything to encourage her mother to question her further, especially regarding a move back to Spruce City, which was why she had said nothing at all about the second part of her conversation with Jessica today and Hayley the other day.

"That's true. Mother always had a way of making strangers feel right at home, that's why she is . . . *was* . . . so successful. People were drawn to her, and I'm sure she's looking down on us now and thinking, 'They're getting behind,' which we are." She paused for a second. "I need to make sure Chandra set out extra plates. Lou added two microwaves to the coffee station, so if anyone takes leftovers, they'll have a place to warm them up. This is a great idea. We've got Ziploc bags, plasticware, paper plates, the whole shebang for those who want a midnight snack."

"I'll be having a turkey sandwich for sure. I like the leftovers more than the meal. Is there something I can do now? If not, I'm going upstairs to get changed."

"I can't think of anything now. We've got things covered for a while. Go on and take your time. Soak in the tub."

"Been there, done that, but I think I will again. Thanks, Mom. I'm really grateful you and I are here together. It's different without Nana, but together, we'll make this work."

"You know we will," Elizabeth Preston encouraged. "Now go on and get ready before the guests start coming down for Thanksgiving dinner."

"Okay, I'm out of here. For now." Joy winked at her mom, then headed upstairs.

Chapter 14

Joy stole one last glance in the mirror before heading downstairs. She wore her usual Tom Ford lipstick, eyeliner, and two coats of mascara. This is as good as it gets, she thought, though she'd taken more time than usual with her makeup.

She'd originally planned to dress up, then decided against it and wore her black Paige jeans with a gray silk blouse and black ballet flats. With the exception of the navy dress, which she had already worn, the outfit was the dressiest she had brought with her from Denver. The jeans were appropriate because not only would she be having dinner herself, but she was also "working the meal," as Izzie had informed her earlier. That was fine by her, as anything she could do to avoid thinking about Will was a welcome distraction. Though she had been looking forward to seeing him for days, now that the time had arrived, half of her dreaded seeing him again. But her other half couldn't wait. That half of her felt like a little girl getting up early on Christmas morning to see what presents Santa had come down the chimney with.

With nothing left to keep her upstairs, Joy headed for the kitchen, where all the action was taking place. The prime rib roasts, hams, and turkeys rested on giant platters, covering fully half of the available counter space. Casserole dishes holding green beans, cranberry salad, a corn soufflé, candied yams, sweet potatoes, both whole and mashed, and, of course, the corn-bread dressing covered the other half. Joy had never seen so many mashed potatoes in her entire life. In addition, there was a broccoli, tomato, and Bermuda onion salad as well as a plain tossed salad. There was so much food, they'd have leftovers until Christmas. The yeast rolls were just out of the oven, and the house smelled delicious. Just as her mother had said it would.

"You look pretty," Elizabeth said. "Your eyes match the sky today."

Joy looked at her mom. She was wearing a plain black shift dress that clung in all the right places. Of course, her mother would never look in a mirror and say this. She, too, wore flat shoes. *She doesn't look a day over forty*, Joy thought.

"Thanks, Mom. You are stunning," Joy said. "As usual."

She peeked at the clock. Twenty minutes before one.

"What can I do to help?" she asked.

"I think we've got it all handled," her mother said, gesturing toward the platters of food. "The girls will take all of the scrumptious food to the dining room; then I believe we're all set. Izzie had Chandra put candles on the small tables. The floral arrangements for the main dining table arrived while you were upstairs, plus those three big boxes from your office arrived. I had Lou put them in the wine room." She paused, then went on, "I've checked and rechecked the dishes. We're using last year's bone china, so if anyone drops their plate, we have extras. These aren't the expensive set, but still," her mother said. "If it was just family, I'd bring out the good stuff, but these dishes will work just fine."

"Mind if I take a look?" Joy asked. Her mother was getting skittish, and that meant she was nervous. She talked way too much when she was nervous.

"I'll go with you."

The formal dining room was massive and could hold as many as thirty-five people. The antique Victorian table dominated the center of the room. It could seat as many as twenty-five in a pinch, but that made for elbowing one another; today it was set comfortably for twelve. Lou placed the four smaller tables strategically, giving everyone a view of the massive buffet tables. There were candles and autumnal flowers on all of the tables, but the largest centerpiece was laid out on the Victorian table. The floral arrangement was long and low—deep orange-red roses along with tiny baby yellow roses, all adding to the room's autumn décor. Everything was simple but elegant.

"We can seat everyone comfortably this way," her mother said. "What do you think?"

"Nana would love this. It's just what I'd envisioned."

"Yes, she would no doubt be pleased as punch."

"And tonight, after the Thanksgiving dinner is over, this entire room will be totally decked out for Christmas? That's amazing," Joy stated. It had been a while since she had had a behind-the-scenes view of what took place to make Heart and Soul one of the top B&Bs in the state. She couldn't wait to see how the day turned out.

"It's always amazed me. Even though Mom didn't do all the decorating, she always hired the best and the fastest. Of course, this all came with a heavy price tag, but it was well worth it. Mom had this year's theme prepared months ago with her team, so this year we can sit back and watch, but next year, this will be up to either us or the state."

"And which it is hinges on my decision?" Joy turned, heading for the kitchen, her mother right on her heels. Suddenly, she felt as if her world, the world she'd created for herself, was about to come crashing down in one giant swoop.

"I don't understand it either, Joy. It makes me wonder if Mother was in her right mind when she had her will revised. I wish I knew why she did this, but all I know at this point is that it is legal and binding. Follows the letter of the law. I could ask Will if he'd mind going over it one more time. Maybe he missed something. His father drew up the original will, and it's possible he misinterpreted her words. I don't know. I guess anything is possible."

"I'll remind you to ask him," Joy offered. "Though not today. Let's save this for another time, if that's all right with you."

Her mother shot her an amazing smile. "Yes, that's fine. Another day. Now, we best get our rear ends busy because it's almost time to serve dinner."

Joy could hear voices out in the main room. She tried to listen for that deep, *sexy* voice, but didn't hear it. Maybe he'd decided to stay home with his frozen dinners. She wasn't sure of anything where Will Drake was concerned, but today was all about being thankful, and Joy would do her best to make sure she was thankful for all the blessings she'd had in her life.

The next half hour was total commotion. People finding seats, saying grace, then standing in line to fill their plates with all the incredible food they'd worked so hard to prepare. Eighteen guests joined them for dinner, and this did not include themselves or the employees.

Nor did it include Mr. Will Drake.

Every two minutes, she'd made an excuse to return to the kitchen in order to pass by the front entrance, hoping she'd catch a glance of him, but nothing.

Nada. Just as she'd imagined.

Her head began pounding, and her vision was slightly blurred. She should eat, but she was too busy mentally kicking herself for telling anyone she'd invited him as her personal guest. The pitying looks she received from the staff were enough to send her straight to the airport to catch the earliest flight back to Colorado.

"Hey, young lady," Miss Betty called out. "Aren't you eating with us? You're skinny as a beanpole."

Mortified that the attention of the entire room was focused on her, she waved and smiled. "Just busy, but I'm starving, so I'll be there soon."

"I'm counting on it. I've got a secret to tell you folks," Miss Betty told her.

Taking a very deep breath, Joy dug deep inside herself for a shred of patience. Miss Betty was old. Very old. She was most likely senile and imagining things, such as the ghost of her dead husband coming to "visit" her every Christmas. *Poor little woman*, Joy thought. *She just wants attention.*

"Then you'll tell me as soon as I grab a plate of food," she called out to Miss Betty in the most cheerful voice she could muster.

"I'm saving this seat just for you," Miss Betty said with a mouthful.

Everyone seated at the Victorian table laughed, and Miss Betty turned her attention to them.

In the kitchen, Joy took a bottle of water, gulped it down, then reached for another.

What is wrong with me? She felt as if she were on a precipice, ready to fall into nothingness. Her head felt as though it were filled with cotton.

Was all this because Mr. Will Drake failed to show up for Thanksgiving dinner? Did he not have a phone? Of course he did. Did he not have a vehicle? Of course he did. Did he not have any manners? Of course he did not. Joy wasn't sure if she should laugh or cry at the irony. She'd worried herself into a frenzy, more so out of embarrassment than anything, or that's what she kept telling herself. It wasn't as though she were madly in love. That was absurd. She was an adult woman, not a teenager. This was the part of small-town life she disliked. By tomorrow morning, the entire town would know that Will Drake ditched her for . . . who knows what? Or whom? Doing her best to pull herself together, she took another bottle of water from the fridge, and headed back to the main room.

Every single eye in the room was focused on her. Even Keith and Kim Moore's newborn daughter stopped crying when she entered the room.

Am I the new cure for a colicky baby?

Holding her head as high as she could, without it appearing as though this was what she was attempting to do, she walked around to the side of the table and took the empty seat beside Miss Betty.

"So, how's the turkey?" she asked, realizing how stupid she sounded the second the words were out of her mouth and seeing that Miss Betty's plate had not a shred of turkey on it.

"I don't like turkey. Went for the prime rib myself," Miss Betty explained. "I never could figure out what people saw, or tasted, in an old turkey. They're just birds. Give me a big slice of beef any day of the week. You're still too skinny; you young kids think that if you eat a bite, you'll gain a pound." Miss Betty took her spoon to tap on her glass of iced tea. "Listen up. All of you! If any of you sees Herman, I want you to come to my room. Bring that ham with you because Herman always liked ham." After making her announcement, Miss Betty sat back down. "Herman had a great big—"

Again, Joy didn't know whether to laugh or cry. This little woman wasn't herself, anyone could tell; nonetheless, she'd opened the door and invited Herman to visit her and the guests.

"Who's Herman?" asked one of the male Duke University students. Joy sent up a silent prayer of thanks for the interruption.

A few other people whispered among themselves about the whereabouts of Miss Betty's other half, but no one questioned her directly.

"Herman was, *is* her husband," Joy answered as politely as she could, even though she felt as if her head were about to explode.

"Oh," came the reply.

As if this weren't bad enough, a loud commotion from the entryway caught the guests' attention again.

Suddenly, Joy burst out, "Mother, could I see you and Izzie. In the kitchen?"

She didn't wait for either of them to answer, and she seemed ready to blow up. "Why are you two . . . why aren't you helping me out there? I'm totally humiliated as it is, and all this . . . bull crap happens, and you say nothing to help me out! Is this supposed to be some kind of joke? Are you all testing me to see if I have what it takes to operate this . . . this . . . *place*? Tell me, because if this is a test, I've failed miserably." Her heart slammed against her rib cage.

"Sweet girl," Izzie said, wrapping her arms around her, "there is no way I or your mother would purposely do or say anything to cause you pain. Of any kind."

Elizabeth grabbed a paper towel and handed it to Joy. "Honey, please, it's going to be okay. I know you've had more than your share of disappointments lately, so if you want to cry and scream, just do it. I don't care if the entire world is listening. This is your home, and you can do whatever you darned well please! So curse if that helps! Kick something or someone," her mother said, and it was so unlike her that Joy and Izzie stopped to stare at one another, then at her mother. Who never raised her voice. Or cursed.

Joy pushed away from Izzie in order to get a clear view of her mother. "Are you giving me permission to curse? I'm almost thirty years old, and you're really giving me permission to curse? Well, okay. I can curse with the best of them. Sailors. Truckers. Shit. See? I can curse. Dammit to hell and back! Does that make you feel better? Because it sure as hell made me feel better! I'm going to start cursing the guests. I'm sure they'd like their damn rooms cleaned twice a day. No, let's do it three times a day!" Before she could utter a curse word, what was left of her composure disappeared completely.

"What's that damn noise? Mother? Isobel? You both work for me now. Go and see what the hell is going on out there!" Joy shouted, full of fury.

Am I having a nervous breakdown? Is this how one loses control of oneself? Of reality? Why is everything so out of focus? Or was this another bout of what she'd recently been told by her doctor?

"Izzie, see what's going on, please."

"Sure thing, Elizabeth." But Izzie waited, staying in the kitchen for a few minutes.

The sound of Izzie saying her mother's name in such a serious tone forced Joy to focus. "What am I doing? What . . . tell me what's going on, I swear—"

"No! Stop, don't say another swear word, please," Izzie begged, as Joy's eyes widened in fear.

Joy began to cry, and she never cried. She didn't act like this, she rarely said a cussword, and now here she was screaming obscenities on Thanksgiving Day of all days, and hopefully the guests hadn't heard her. "The truth, please, Izzie."

A low growl forced her attention away from Izzie. "What in the hell?" She couldn't help herself anymore. If she was going to curse, today was the perfect day to start slinging the words around as though they were nothing more than "if," "and," or "but."

Izzie followed her gaze. "What in the world?"

Standing in the doorway was an extremely large and smelly dog.

A dog.

Attached to the dog's collar was a long leash. At the end of the very long leash was Will Drake himself. In person. The real deal. With a giant dog. He was with . . . a *dog?*

More confused, and more frightened than ever, Joy closed her eyes. This was a dream. A bad dream that had turned into a nightmare. She would open her eyes and find herself back in Denver in her office. She opened her eyes. No, she hadn't imagined this at all.

"Joy, uh, Mr. Drake has arrived," her mother said.

"Duh," Joy replied. Her eyes doubled in size. The real and very truthful thoughts she had were escaping from her gray matter without going through her verbal filtration system. Again. She was doing this again. What was wrong with her?

"I don't think now is a good time. I'll just head home," Will stated, looking at her mother, then Izzie, and lastly at her.

"So why bother in the first place? You're late. You don't have the common courtesy to call, you've brought this mangy-ass," she turned to her mother as she said *ass*, then returned her attention to Will Drake, "dog into my kitchen without my permission, and you've turned my damned life upside down, and you have the nerve to even . . . I don't know! Just leave. Go home." Joy shouted, and at this point she couldn't care less if the guests or Herman or any other living creature heard her.

"Will, would you please excuse us?" her mother said as she placed both arms around Joy's shoulders. "Izz, the guests."

"Why don't you follow me, Mr. Drake. And this one, too," Izzie said in a sweet voice, patting the oversized dog on its head.

"Thank you, Izzie," Elizabeth said, then turned her full attention to her daughter. "Joy, let's go upstairs."

She guided her daughter out of the prep kitchen to the Scrooge Room. Joy nodded.

At least she could still understand direction, Elizabeth thought. She had never seen Joy react so strongly. Ever. Not even when Joy's father, Joseph Preston, had died three years ago. Leading her to the bed, she helped her lie back against the fluffy pillows. She removed her ballet flats, then went to the minifridge for a bottle of cold water and a piece of fruit.

She sat on the edge of the bed. Joy did not look good. Her pupils were dilated. As a nurse, Elizabeth noticed these things. The veins in her slender neck showed that her heart was beating much too fast. She gently took her wrist, careful not to bring on another . . . fit. It was the only word she could come up with that appropriately described what had just taken place downstairs. Her pulse was as fast as it had physically appeared from the veins pulsing in her neck.

"Joy, can you understand what I'm saying?" Though Joy was much too young, Elizabeth wanted to make sure she had no symptoms of a stroke. She did a quick assessment, and though Joy had lost control of her emotions, Elizabeth saw nothing that would indicate she'd suffered a stroke. "Sweetie, can you hear me?"

"I can, Mom. I'm okay now," she said in barely a whisper.

"Here." Elizabeth held the bottle of water to Joy's lips. "Drink this, and take a bite of this apple."

Joy sat up and drank from the bottle of water, took a bite from the apple, then fell back into the plush pillows. "I don't know what came over me . . . It happened so fast."

"When was the last time you ate a full meal and drank something besides all that coffee?"

"I had that corn bread."

"That was yesterday, Joy."

"Yeah, I guess I should eat something."

"I think you're dehydrated," her mother said. "Mind a little pinch?"

Joy shook her head.

Elizabeth took her hand and gathered a bit of skin between her thumb and index finger. When she let go, Joy's skin was slow to return to normal. "You're definitely dehydrated, and I think that's why you've been acting so out of character. Add the lack of food, your grief about your grandmother, and all this stress you're under, it's a miracle you didn't snap sooner."

"*Snap?* What do you mean? In relation to me?" Joy asked, sitting up in bed.

"Downstairs. You just lost control of yourself."

Sighing, Joy said, "I guess I did."

"Yes, and if you don't remember, I think you need to see Frank. This could be serious."

Joy appeared to be confused. "So you think there's something physically wrong with me? Besides being dehydrated?"

"I don't know that for sure, but you should have Frank check you over. I can call him now."

"No, don't do that. I'll be fine. As you said, I'm dehydrated."

"I can't force you, but you should have a doctor check you over. Dad didn't think he had anything wrong, either. He . . . well, he was young, you know that. And your grandmother, she wasn't old, either. If this is a genetic thing, don't you want to know?"

Joy swallowed another sip of water. "Mom, I know I acted like a fool downstairs, okay? I'm just too ashamed to admit it. Yes, I feel light-headed and a little dizzy, but I'm not about to keel over from a heart attack. I've got low blood sugar. This has happened before. I need to eat, and when I am stressed, food is the last thing on my mind. I have an unusual reaction when my sugar is low. You're welcome to check this out with my doctor, at *home*."

"Why haven't you told me? I'm a nurse, Joy. I need to know these things about you, regardless of your age." Elizabeth was relieved but wished Joy had trusted her with the details of her health. It wasn't as though she tried to interfere. As a mother, she simply needed to know if her daughter was ill.

"I know that, I'm just not used to . . . all of this attention. I probably should eat something, so I can go downstairs and apologize."

"I'm going to bring you a plate of food. Do not get up."

Without another word, her mother left the room. Joy finished off the bottle of water, ate the rest of the apple, and felt somewhat better. But she realized that she needed to eat more often. She would let the time get away, and if she waited too long to eat, it could spell disaster. Her doctor at home had told her this, as she'd experienced a couple of low-sugar meltdowns already.

Not more than five minutes passed, and her mother was back with a tray full of food. "You don't have to eat all of this, but some carbs will raise your sugar. Go for the mashed potatoes first," her mother instructed.

Joy did as she was told. She ate the potatoes, the green beans, a slice of turkey, a small slice of prime rib, two buttered yeast rolls, and a glass of sweet tea. The more she ate, the better she felt. "I feel like a total idiot. I can't even begin to imagine what the folks downstairs are thinking. I'm so embarrassed." It embarrassed her to even *think* how she'd ranted and raved at her mother and Izzie.

"You don't have to worry about that. No one heard you except Izzie and Mr. Drake. Luckily, the guests were too busy being entertained by Miss Betty," her mother assured her. "I checked with Izzie."

Joy took a deep breath and released it slowly. "That's a relief." She needed to apologize to Will Drake. Whatever chance she'd had with him, she was certain she'd sent him running. And that . . . *dog!*

"Mom, did Will have a giant dog with him?" Again, she was afraid of the answer but needed to know she wasn't losing her grip on reality, sugar or not.

"Yes, that's why he was late, according to Izzie. He's still here if you want to see him."

"He's still here? After all the horrible things I said?" She felt the heat rush to her face. She'd have a hard time explaining herself to him, but she'd have to sooner or later.

"No, but you weren't in your right frame of mind."

"I'll go downstairs and try to explain." Joy set the tray on the side table, then swung her legs to the floor. She waited a couple of seconds to make sure she wasn't going to have another bout of lightheadedness, then stood up.

"Walk around the room a bit, get your circulation going. Stairs aren't a good idea right now," her mother informed her in what Joy thought of as her "nurse voice."

"I need to speak to Izzie. And Will," Joy stated flatly. "If you'd ask them to come upstairs, I'll try to explain."

"If you're sure? Why don't you sit down? I won't feel comfortable leaving until you do."

Joy returned to her spot on the bed. "Okay. I'm sitting. I promise not to get up."

In order to keep herself from getting up, she admired her nail polish, Berries in the Snow, a darker shade of red with silver undertones. Hayley had come up with the name, she recalled. That was the fun part of being in the nail polish business. She never tired of coming up with unique, and sometimes silly, names for her polishes. There was a tap on the door. "Joy," her mother asked, "is it okay if we come in?"

Why was she asking? "Of course, the door is open." Dreading this, but knowing that if she put it off, she'd never be able to show her face to Izzie or Will, she sat up straight, brushed crumbs from her jeans, and fluffed her hair.

Izzie was followed by Will, minus the dog, and her mother. Suddenly, the room seemed much too small for the four of them. Another deep breath, in and out. In and out.

Before she lost her nerve, she spoke. "I am so very sorry for the horrible things I said. To both of you. I know you have no clue, not that this excuses anything, but I have a bit of a low-sugar issue. When it gets out of hand, it seems I get out of hand. I was irresponsible, allowing myself even to get in such a state. I know this is a crazy excuse, but it is what it is. Again, I'm sorry for those awful words I said." Tears welled up in her eyes. She didn't bother to try and still them. She needed a good cry—a *cleansing* cry, as Nana used to say.

"Hey, there, now don't you worry about old Izz here.

I've heard much worse. You really didn't say anything all that horrible, right, Elizabeth?"

"Right."

"And I second that," Will said. "I wasn't offended in the least. I think Rex might've been a bit frightened, but he'll be okay."

He looked amused, and Joy found herself smiling at him. "I want to ask who Rex is, but I'm assuming it's the dog."

"Yes, the mangy one, which I need to explain." Will pointed to the foot of the bed. "Mind if I sit down?"

"Please. Mom," she said, "Izzie, sit down," she added. Not wanting to come off as bossy, she added, "Pretty please?"

Everyone laughed, easing the slight bit of tension she felt. "Tell me about Rex."

"I found Rex sitting on my doorstep last night. I kept hearing a noise, thought it sounded out of place. Not the normal night noises I'm used to. I went outside to see where the noise was coming from, and there he was. Freezing, curled up in a ball, trying to keep warm under my welcome mat. I brought him inside, poor guy. He was freezing, and starving.

"I fed him three frozen dinners, dried him off, then looked to see if he had any tags. Nothing. I called the local animal shelter this morning to see if anyone had reported their dog missing, and, of course, no one had, so here I am."

"Do you think I am the most heartless, hateful person in the world?" Joy said. "I won't blame you one bit if you do. All I can say is, I was totally wrong. About a lot of things. But how do you know his name is Rex?" She laughed. "I mean, you said you didn't know who the dog belongs to, but you know his name."

"Yeah, I gave it to him. He just looks like a 'Rex.'"

"More like a *Tyrannosaurus rex*," Izzie said.

"What are your plans?" her mother asked. "If you don't mind telling us."

"I'll try to locate his owner, contact the vet's office, see if he has a chip, put up flyers. If no one claims him, I'll keep him. He seems friendly enough, looks like a labrador and shepherd mix. I got involved bathing him, then had to chase him around in order to dry him off, but he wanted to play. We played, then I saw the clock, and you know the rest."

"Boy, this is one Thanksgiving we're all going to remember. Where is Rex now?" Joy felt like the biggest idiot in the world. A man who takes in stray dogs! He comes for dinner, and she cusses him out! Hayley and Jessica would have a field day with this info. But she didn't have to tell them, so she was safe in that regard. She wished she could hit a real-life rewind button, get a do-over, anything to forget yelling at him and the dog, and at her mother and Izzie. More tears filled her eyes. Taking a tissue out of the box on the bedside table, she wiped her eyes.

"Lou is looking after him. He is just fine. That dog probably just had the best meal of his life. Prime rib, turkey, and ham. And green beans, too," Izzie said. "He's good."

"Okay, I'm going downstairs to apologize to Rex." She held up a hand. "Don't any of you try to stop me. This day has been awful for all of you. I'd like to make up for it in some way, and I can start by apologizing to Rex."

"Just take it slowly," her mother advised in her nurse voice. "I don't want you falling down the stairs."

"Sure, Mom."

Downstairs in the kitchen, they found Lou and Rex. It seemed Rex had a new best friend. "I told you not to feed him again! You're gonna make him sick," Izzie said.

Apparently, Lou had decided to give Rex all of what was left of the two prime rib roasts they'd had. Joy saw the dog's belly, and it looked like he'd swallowed an entire cow rather than just part of one. "Good grief, Lou, I have to agree with Izz. This dog is gonna burst."

Rex lay contentedly on his side, his long tail sweeping across the wooden floor. He didn't have a care in the world.

Will stooped. "You're a happy dude, huh?" He fluffed the fur between Rex's ears. As Rex wagged his tail even faster, Joy lowered herself to their level. After she let Rex sniff her hand, he rolled onto his back, where he proceeded to get a belly rub from her. "You do deserve this today. But don't get used to it, because this is probably the last time we'll meet, but I'm sorry you heard me yell. I hope I didn't frighten you any more than you were already."

"Rex doesn't look very frightened to me," her mother pointed out. She grinned. "In fact, Rex looks very content. As if he were already in doggy heaven."

"He does, doesn't he?" Will said. "The walk home will burn off those calories, and the fresh air will be good for both of us."

"You walked over here?" Joy asked, pushing herself up off the hard wooden floor.

"I did, with Rex. I tried getting him in the car, but he went berserk. Whatever happened to him, I'm guessing a car was involved. It's not that far, and once I managed to get the leash on him, he behaved just like a gentleman."

"I'm going to make a fresh pot of coffee," Izzie said. "Lou, why don't you join me? And Elizabeth, you too. Remember you were saying you wanted a fresh cup of coffee?"

Joy watched Izzie's eyes going back and forth between her and Will. She knew exactly what she was up to.

"You know, a cup of coffee is just what I need, too."

In a louder-than-normal voice, her mother said, "No, Joy, you absolutely do not. That's the last thing your body needs. You are dehydrated. Caffeine will only make it worse."

"You're right. I'll just have an ice water."

Always polite, her mother asked, "Will, what will you have?"

"Nothing, thanks. I need to get home. I just bought the latest John Grisham novel. I plan to spend my holiday weekend reading."

"Does this mean you're not going to hang around and watch the designers do their magic? You and Rex. You guys could watch. With me." Joy practically had to pull the words from her brain, slowly, just in case she'd say something she'd regret.

"I'll wait for the end result, but thanks for asking. I know the Parade of Homes is one of the big events in town. Does City Hall still have the annual Christmas tree lighting in the town center? I remember my dad taking me there when I was a kid."

"I'd forgotten all about that," Joy said. "We always went for the tree lighting, too, when Dad was alive. It's a big deal around here. I think everything is a big deal in our neck of the woods right now. The gingerbread houses, the parade, trees being lit up all over town, people trying their best to out-decorate one another. It's the most Christmas-oriented town in the state."

"It is, and I have to admit, I get a little bummed during December. I may take Rex to Florida; we can visit Dad. He'd love that," Will said, a faraway gaze in his eyes. "But I haven't decided on that just yet. I have a few things that need my attention in town."

"You're depressed in December?" Joy blurted out. "No, that isn't what I meant. There is a disorder—SAD, seasonal affective disorder; a lot of people in Colorado go through it during the winter months. You need sunshine."

"All the more reason I need to visit Dad. You could be onto something. I'll give this some serious thought." He took the leash from his back pocket, and Rex jumped up. "He knows we're going outside," he explained, as if he'd had the dog forever.

Joy thought his devotion to the stray dog, Rex, only added to his charm. His good looks, his sexy voice, everything that constituted Will Drake was almost too good to be true. Other than his December disorder, she thought. "Then you two should go. Mom, can we make up a doggy bag—no pun intended, Rex—for these two gentlemen? I'm sure Rex would appreciate a late-night snack."

"If word of all this attention gets out, I'm in trouble. At least with the gingerbread judges."

"Mom, could you make up a couple of large bags for these two? I need a minute," she said in a firm voice, hoping her mother would get the hint.

"Oh, yes. I'll do that right now." And she left the prep kitchen without saying a word.

"So, you wanted to get me alone to take advantage of

me?" Will asked, then burst out laughing. "I'm sorry, I shouldn't have said that."

"No, no, it's fine." She searched for the right words to say, words that didn't make her appear crazy or childlike. "I . . . are you angry with me?" There, it was out. Sure that she'd ticked him off, she hadn't been able to get this thought out of her head since coming downstairs. Will was usually asking her out before the end of the date— at least he had the few times she'd been alone with him. *One date. At the coffee shop! One really, really good kiss . . .*

"Absolutely not. What gave you that idea?" he asked. Rex stood between them as though he were protecting them from one another.

"I certainly wasn't very welcoming when you arrived," she said. "I guess I feel like I need to apologize again. I'm"—she looked away—"ashamed of myself."

Again, her eyes gushed with tears. And again, she allowed them to fall.

Will stepped to the side, away from where Rex stood separating them. "You don't need to keep apologizing. We're adults. Adults get pissed off. I cuss when I'm mad, and trust me, what you think of as horrible language is mild in comparison." He placed his free hand on hers. "Why don't you come for a walk with us? We can walk downtown, see what's going on in the town center? We could watch the tree lighting, too."

So he wasn't mad!

"I could use some fresh air, too. Let me grab a jacket, and I'll take you up on your offer." Before she could change her mind, or he could change his, she raced up the stairs, all traces of her earlier, low-blood-sugar craze gone. In the Scrooge Room, she grabbed her Columbia ski jacket since it was all she had brought with her.

Three minutes later, she was ready. Will and Rex waited at the main entrance.

Saying, "Let me tell Mom I'm going out," she headed in the opposite direction, to the dining room. The guests were gone, and the furniture with it. All that work, erased. Her mom, Izzie, and Lou were directing the first arrival of the B&B's Christmas trees. Probably not the best time to leave, but she didn't plan on being gone too long. "Mom, I'm stepping out with Will. I'll be back in a little while," she called out, then once again headed for the front door. Joy wasn't going to hang around and wait for her mother to answer. She was an adult. Telling her mother she was leaving was simply a courtesy, especially after the earlier episode.

"Okay, let's go," she told Will, slightly out of breath.

As soon as they stepped out the door, Rex went into a barking fit. The designers and decorators were arriving all at once.

"It's okay, boy," Will said. "I don't think he's used to being around so many people."

She laughed. "I'm not either."

"Then let's make a run for it before any more of them arrive," Will said teasingly.

If you had told Joy an hour ago that she'd be going on a walk with Will and his newly acquired canine, she would've told you that you'd lost your mind. *How fast life moves*, she thought. "Let's go," she agreed, and picked up the pace. This must be what it would have felt like to sneak out, had she done so as a teenager. No wonder most girls in her senior class were grounded on the weekends! She smiled at the thought.

The town center was packed with locals and tourists. The shops remained open, and vendors from all over were packed between the local barbershop and the florist. A young woman selling sweet cinnamon sugary pecans had a line as long as the eye could see. Next door, Mega Fitness, which was usually open twenty-four hours, had put their CLOSED sign up. It was Thanksgiving, after all. No one in their right mind would be working out today even if a good workout was what was needed to compensate for the Thanksgiving Day dinner.

"Rex doesn't seem to mind all the crowds now," Joy observed. She reached down to pet the dog, and his ears moved back and forth as she did so. "I think Rex is a ladies' man. He likes this," she said as she rubbed his head.

"Smart boy," Will said, and navigated through the crowds of people, trying to get them as close to the giant Christmas tree as they could. Many of the people in the crowd were tourists. Joy was sure a few of them would be visiting the B&B when they had the doors open for the Parade of Homes. For two nights only, thank goodness. She wasn't too keen on this part of the festivities, but she was sure that she would survive. Given the way she had made a fool of herself today, Heart and Soul would be lucky to have even one visitor during the two-day event.

Shouts from moms and dads, laughter from all directions, the occasional crying of a baby, and the starting of an engine were all background noise as Joy and Will tried to talk. He pulled her close and whispered in her ear. "You want to go to my place? For coffee? We can come back when it's dark. See the tree."

Would she ever, but she was afraid one of the local widows would see her and find out, and that it would jeopardize the chance the B&B had in any of the contests this year. Beyond trite, she knew, but this was a very small, conservative town. And according to her mom and Izzie, those widows thrived on gossip. No way was she going to give them the pleasure of having something to gossip about, so she said to Will, "I'd love to, but not today. After Christmas. When all this hoopla and competition calms down."

He shook his head. "I understand, but that doesn't mean we can't enjoy ourselves now, does it?"

Rex barked, and again, they both laughed.

"This dog is a smart fellow, and yes to your question. We should enjoy ourselves, I think after today it's deserving, even though I'm the culprit."

For the next hour, they roamed through the shops, admiring their Christmas decorations, all the little trinkets that came out of hiding during the holidays. The shop owners remembered her, and this made her happy for some strange reason. One minute she longed for the anonymity of the big city, and the next, she delighted in knowing that this or that person remembered her from fifth grade or high school. An older couple recognized Will, and they stopped to chat for a few minutes. When they were out of the main crowd and heading back to the B&B, Will stopped to let Rex off his leash to do his business.

While they waited, they discussed Rex and wondered if his former family had been in the town center.

"He would've found them, I'm sure," Joy said. "Maybe his owners were tourists, and he got away?"

"Could be, but who'd miss a dog the size of Rex?"

"That's true," Joy agreed.

"Rex! Come on, boy," Will called, then placed his fingers in his mouth and whistled.

They waited for a few minutes for the dog to return. When five minutes passed, and there was still no sign of Rex, Will whistled again. "Maybe Rex found his home."

"Come on, let's walk in the direction he took. We'll find him," Joy said. "He might be chasing a squirrel."

"Good plan," he agreed, and they walked toward the river. The sun was starting to set, the evening air became chill, and the Christmas lights began to twinkle across the water, marking the unofficial beginning of the holiday season as the residents of Spruce City began their own celebrations.

"Rex! Here, boy, c'mon!" Will whistled again. "Probably not a good idea. We'd better forget about finding Rex."

"No, we aren't forgetting about Rex. We're going to keep searching until we find him. If it takes all night."

Joy continued walking, away from the river, heading toward a residential area where two other B&Bs were located. She doubted anyone would be outside as most people were at the tree lighting. "Follow me," she told Will. "Could be Rex has found another doormat."

Will laughed. "I didn't think of that, but I would like to find him. I'm attached already," he said, and while he was a pace behind her, Joy's heart started that insane staccato that would send someone older into tachycardia. "I'm attached already." Did that mean her? Rex? Both? Either way, she couldn't allow herself to read more into his words every time he said something that implied, however remotely, that they were exclusive.

A lone bark in the distance sent her running. "That sounds like Rex," she called over her shoulder. *Good thing I loaded up on all those carbs*, she thought as she ran full force toward the barking. She stopped when she reached the end of the block. Waiting for Rex to bark again, she got her wish.

"That's definitely Rex," Will said when he caught up with her.

"I thought so, but he's stopped barking. We can't just parade through these lawns."

"I can," Will told her, then proceeded to call out to Rex. This time there was an insane amount of barking, but it wasn't the kind of bark they'd heard minutes ago.

Screw rules, she thought. Following Will to the back-yard of a private residence, she searched for the dog, calling his name, but not as loudly as before. "Rex, come on, big guy," she said as she rounded the corner.

Will met her at the corner, saying, "He's not here, but he's close by. Let's try that place." He pointed to the two-story home next door.

Joy saw the small wooden sign that read, in delicate script, THE GOLDEN BEAR. "I'd better not step on their property. This is Heart and Soul's worst enemy, according to Izz and Mom. You go ahead, and I'll wait here." Feeling cowardly, she motioned for him to go on. "Just hurry."

The front lawn was small and neatly kept. Flower boxes overflowing with red and white poinsettias were in all the downstairs windows. Suddenly, the front lawn was lit up with white lights, thousands of them, shining on her, as she stood on the sidewalk in front of her biggest competitor. "Crap," she said out loud. Joy walked away from the B&B, hoping no one had seen her. Will must be in the back gardens. She knew this place, though not so much about the owner; the back lawn was always plush with blooms of color in the spring and summer. She remembered walking past the property in her youth. Why she remembered all the flowers, she hadn't a clue. But since they were deep into a North Carolina winter, the flowers had probably died off.

"Come on, Will," she said to herself. Retracing her steps, she again stood directly in front of the large house. It couldn't have been more than a minute when Will came out from behind the house with Rex. He'd put the leash on. But that isn't what surprised her. She knew they'd find him, but she did not expect to see an older woman marching directly behind Will.

When they reached the front lawn, the woman, who she guessed to be Helen Lockwood, had a plastic bag in her hand. "You let that mutt in my yard again, and I'll make sure to call animal control. We have a leash law in this town!" She hurled the plastic bag in the air, and it landed right in front of Joy's feet.

"What!" She didn't have to pick the bag up to know what was inside. The smell alone told her that Rex had definitely completed his mission. She couldn't help but smile at the irony of where he chose to relieve himself. Carefully, she picked up the bag, planning to dispose of its contents properly.

Will ignored the woman as he and Rex walked toward Joy. She could see he had a grin on his face the size of the moon. "That woman had no clue I was one of the judges in that crazy gingerbread contest. I'm guessing it's too dark for her to see." He laughed, and Joy did, too.

"Let's get out of here before she calls animal control. From what Mom and Izzie say, she's one mean, old, wicked woman."

They jogged down the sidewalk, Rex happily keeping

up with their pace. When they reached Main Street, they stopped to catch their breath. "I need to get rid of this," Joy said, holding the odoriferous bag away from her.

"Here." Will took the bag from her. "Be right back." He jogged over to a community garbage can and dropped the strong-smelling sack inside.

"Sorry about that," he said.

"Why?" she asked, not really knowing what he was apologizing for.

"The bag of dog poo," he reminded her. "Most women would've flipped out."

"Then you've been hanging around with the wrong kind of women," she teased. "I guess this makes us even. My sugar fit, Rex's poo."

"We are most definitely even. You're a couple of points ahead, though," Will shot back, his tone reflecting the humor of the situation.

"I should get back now." Joy could have stood there all night, just listening to Will's sexy voice. "Mom and Izzie are probably going crazy. All those decorators in the house, plus we've had to ask the guests to either remain in their rooms for the night or help deck the halls. Nana started this, and apparently the guests were always thrilled to be included." She stopped, realizing that she was rambling.

"Between you and me, from what I could tell, The Golden Bear doesn't stand a chance for the Parade of Homes. White twinkle lights covered the gardens, but that was it, though it could be they're not finished. But from what little I saw, I wasn't impressed."

"Good to know. Do you want to come with me to pick up the doggy bags?" She leaned down, gave Rex a little hug, and fluffed between his ears. Joy hoped Will would keep the big guy, because anyone who saw him with this lost dog would agree that they looked like they belonged together.

"I'd forgotten all about them. Sure, I think Rex would agree with me, too."

Joy's heart sang with delight. She was blissfully happy to be here with Will even if it was for just a few extra minutes. She couldn't recall ever having such a total and heightened sense of life. Before this she had thought that flying down a black-diamond slope was the ultimate. But it didn't compare to what she was feeling at that moment. Partly frightened by this sudden euphoria, yet thrilled, too, she needed to think through these new emotions. No more rash, sugar-deprived decision making. This was serious, as she had never had anything like this connection in any of her past relationships. She only hoped it was mutual.

"Good. We don't want Rex eating another frozen dinner. Or his owner," she added.

"I will assume you mean you do not want his owner eating another frozen dinner, not that you do not want Rex eating his owner. And, Rex," Will said as if he were having a real conversation with the dog, "we have found that pot of gold at the end of the rainbow."

Heat rushed to her face, and she was glad it was dark outside. Maybe he was referring to the doggy bags they were going to take home? Maybe *she* was Will's pot of gold at the end of the rainbow? Or maybe those were just words to fill the empty space? Again, as seemed to be happening again and again, she was overthinking the situation. She forced herself to look down the street at all the vehicles parked at the B&B. "Criminy, would you look at all those cars?" she said.

"Now, that's a party," Will joked. "Might not be a good idea to bring Rex into the mix, especially if there's a tree around."

Joy chuckled. "I understand. I'll run in and grab those doggy bags and bring them out. We don't want Rex getting into any more trouble."

As they approached the B&B, Joy heard shouting, followed by squeals of laughter. "You're okay staying here for a few minutes?" Joy asked.

"Go ahead, I'll be waiting."

She picked up her pace, hurrying so she didn't keep Will and Rex waiting too long.

Joy entered through the prep kitchen, as she didn't want to disturb the crowd decorating the formal living room. She found several bags of turkey and ham in the fridge, with Will's name written on them. She took the doggy bags and hurried back to where Will and Rex were waiting patiently. "Mom actually had these labeled, just for you."

"I'll thank her the next time I see her," Will said.

"Well, then, I guess . . ."

She didn't have a chance to finish talking, for Will's lips touched hers, and all logical thoughts disintegrated into the cool night air. There wasn't any hesitation in this kiss. As Will pulled her closer, he pressed his lips harder against hers. And she kissed him back with as much passion as he was showing as he kissed her, savoring every moment. Her breath quickened, and a shock wave went through her entire body. The kiss was so powerful, so strong, she felt as if her insides were on fire. Telling herself this wasn't the time and place, she let that thought skitter by so fast, it was hardly a thought. However, Rex had other ideas.

"Woof! Woof!"

Will released her from his arms, slowly. His gaze lingered on hers. She saw passion in his eyes, and something else she couldn't name, but she knew this kiss was just the beginning of something new and wonderful. Joy couldn't disguise the emotions soaring through her, but she stepped back, too, allowing Rex to stand between them. "He smells this," she said, holding up the Ziploc bags.

Joy gave the bags to Will.

He took a shaky breath. "Yeah, we'll both enjoy those tonight, and you"—he pointed to another truck backing into the space reserved for deliveries—"are going to be up decorating Christmas trees all night."

"Probably," she agreed. Though she wanted to invite him in for a cup of hot cocoa, she refrained from asking. A feeling of déjà vu hit her. It hadn't been that long since they'd kissed in this exact spot. "Are you putting up a tree at your place?"

"I don't know. As I said, December is usually an off month for me, though I have to say that November has been off the charts."

"And why is that?" she asked.

"Because I was lucky enough to be able to take over my dad's practice, which introduced me to you. And on and on," he teased, "I hope."

His last word was more of a question than a statement. "I hope so, too." Okay, she'd taken a step without overthinking it, though she had to remember why she was in Spruce City. She didn't want the problems that came with a long-distance relationship. If she kept seeing Will, that's exactly what would happen. She took another step back, hoping to put some physical distance between them. If she leaned forward far enough, even with Rex between them, she could still reach his mouth. No. She wasn't going there again. She took another step back. "If we have any leftover Christmas trees, I'll save one for you." Rex licked her hand. "And a great big chewy for you."

"I'll be seeing you," Will said, and he walked away, Rex at his side.

Chapter 15

Joy poured the last of the coffee into a mug for Lou. "I'll make another pot," she said to Izzie.

The last decorator hadn't left until after four in the morning. Thirty-seven people, plus herself and all the employees, had trimmed three twelve-foot-tall Fraser fir trees for the formal living room. There were four ten-foot-tall Fraser firs in the dining room. Still another—the tallest, at fourteen feet—was placed in the entryway next to the staircase. It was Joy's favorite. Snowmen of all shapes and sizes clung to the branches, and sleighs carrying giant, candy-wrapped ornaments were attached to a sheer white ribbon that wrapped around the entire tree, making it appear as though they were all racing one another on a snowy road. Red and green ornaments the size of small dinner plates were arranged perfectly. It wasn't the most sophisticated of the trees, but to Joy, it was a happy tree.

There were three other trees that were much more elegant. One was completely decked out in red poinsettias, with gold ribbon woven through the branches. Hundreds of tiny white lights encircled the giant evergreen. This tree was centered between the two floor-to-ceiling windows. Two small dining tables flanked it, each adorned with candles, fresh greenery, and poinsettias.

An angel tree, with years' worth of Nana's angel collection, was in the far corner of the room. These ornaments were very delicate, so the tree was placed in a corner to lessen the chance of the tree's falling. It was the only tree on which personal ornaments were used.

Finally, there was a tree hung with a variety of Santas. This one was Joy's second favorite among all the trees. The Santas were of all shapes and sizes. They had long beards and short beards. Some wore glasses, some touted a big belly, others were long and skinny. Old-fashioned red and green lights glistening on the Santa tree reminded Joy of the tree her family had had when she was a little girl. Dad had always used those big bulbs, and she would stare at them for hours, watching them blink on and off.

Heart and Soul had its own ornament, a replica of the outside of the house. Another tree was covered in real gingerbread houses, courtesy of a bakery in Raleigh. "You've got to be kidding me," she'd said when she saw this.

The fireplace mantel was decorated with fresh evergreens, holly berries, and golden ribbons, with a matching wreath above the mantel.

Every room in the house was decked out. The evergreens throughout the house reminded her of Colorado.

There were tall evergreens on her favorite ski run, and she would always take a minute to stop and breathe in the fresh scent whenever she skied.

She'd been so busy working on the inside of the house, she hadn't been outside to see the decorations that had been placed there. Her mother had kept her busy orchestrating the designers.

"Girl, what in the name of Pete is taking you so long to make a single pot of coffee? We've still got breakfast to prepare, we're completely out of those little pods for the coffee makers, and now I want that cup of coffee!" Izzie was overtired.

"It's finished," Joy said, filling Izzie's mug with coffee. "I'll take care of making the coffee. I'm a pro. We still have this," she informed Izzie, holding up the carafe of coffee. "I'll run to the supermarket tomorrow. If there's anything else we need, I can pick it up."

Joy planned to spend the afternoon making up spa gifts for the women's shelter. At almost literally the last minute, Hayley had decided that this should be done, and they'd agreed via a hasty text message that Joy would put the nail polish kits and the hand lotions in the fancy cloth bags that had been included in the package. She was excited, as this was a deed that was bringing out the best in her. She was a giver, always had been. The biblical admonition that "It's better to give than receive" was something she had always believed in and acted upon. Even if, given the constraints on her time, she had, in the past, always had to limit her giving to writing large checks for her favorite charities, the ASPCA being foremost among them.

"I'll make up a list," Izzie said. "We're gonna feed these

people again, then I am taking the afternoon off. Of course, if you approve, you know, you being the boss and all."

Joy rolled her eyes. "You're worse than Mom, sometimes. Do whatever you want, Izz. You're not doing one thing that you didn't do when Nana . . . when she was here." Her eyes teared up, and she wiped them with a dish towel. "I'm not going to run this place, Izz. Just keep doing what you've been doing. When my six months are up, Mom can act as the official owner. You take the afternoon and do whatever you want. Tell Lou he can take the afternoon off, too. With pay."

"Your grandma was very generous, but not *that* generous. I'll take the afternoon off, but it doesn't affect our wages, silly girl. We're all on a salary."

As an accomplished businesswoman, Joy felt like a fool. She hadn't asked and really didn't want to know the financial side of Heart and Soul, but Nana had left this responsibility to her, and she needed to know the money end of things. Since she had grown up with Heart and Soul in the family, she didn't look at the B&B as a place of employment. It had been, to her way of thinking, just a big, old, beautiful house where strangers came and had breakfast. That's what she had thought when she was little, though as a teenager, she knew people had to pay to stay there. Still, she had never given a lot of thought to payroll, taxes, and business expenses. It was just Nana's house. But now, in essence, at least for the next six months, it was essentially her house, her business. And these were things she absolutely needed to think about and take care of.

"Did Nana have an accountant?" she asked Izzie. "I should know this, but I don't." She supposed she should be asking her mother about these things, but Elizabeth was still outside in the wee hours, directing the placement of all the outdoor decorations.

"She did. Mr. Norton of Norton, Inc. He's the only accountant in Spruce City. He's good and honest. Your Nana's words. And he's a good man, too."

"I'll call him and arrange to have a look at the books. I do not like this, Izzie, not one little bit. I'm kind of ticked that Nana did this to me. She knows, *knew* my life in Colorado was my dream. Why would she want to take that away from me? And do this to me? Yes, I loved working here when I lived in Spruce City, but now? I wish I knew what the heck she was thinking when she added this to her will."

Joy wondered if Nana might've been a little senile. She hated thinking like this, but everything that had happened since she had come from Colorado was just so unexpected. Of course, Nana's dying was, too, but add her little "Joy must live here for six months" to the mix, and it did make her wonder.

On the other hand, she was having her share of fun. She'd learned a few baking skills, and now she sure as heck knew that you didn't use salted butter for piecrust, at least in her mother's recipe. Include Mr. Will Drake in the mix . . . *and could that be, maybe, why Nana had added that condition to her will?*

Chapter 16

At ten that morning, Joy was dragging. After being up all night, she'd spent the entire morning making coffee, putting pans of biscuits in the oven, and watching Izzie make Nana's famous sausage gravy. As if that were not enough, her mother had then insisted she needed to learn how to make crêpes, as they were always on the breakfast menu in the summertime. Despite her protestations that, when summertime rolled around, she would be back in Denver, her mother had insisted. So, by the time she'd learned the art of crêpe making, she was so tired, she could barely make it to her room. Thankfully, it was quiet upstairs. Most of the guests were out and about. Today was Snow Day in the town center, and there was a play being performed by the students at the high school. There were snowmen, fake snow, and a snow slide to entertain the youngsters there with their parents, as well as the locals, for hours. This was a new addition to the holiday activities. If she hadn't been so tired, she would've taken a ride down the slide herself, but she needed to get some sleep before going to the shelter.

She slipped on a nightshirt, set the alarm on her phone, and crawled into bed. But, as tired as she was, she could not get to sleep. She got up, drank a bottle of water, and had a couple of bites from a plate of cookies her mother had put in their room. Since her low-sugar episode of the night before, she was making sure to eat something every couple of hours. If she had to go through that humiliating experience again, she would totally croak. She tossed and turned, knew she was overtired, and when she was like this, it was almost impossible for her to get to sleep without a Tylenol PM. She got back up, went to the en suite bathroom, where her toiletry case was, found the much-coveted bottle of pills, and took two. She picked up the copy of *A Christmas Carol* that Nana had put in the room and started reading.

Marley was dead . . .

A strange noise, like a howling sound, roused her from the effects of the sleep aid. She tossed the covers aside, grabbed her Columbia jacket for a robe, carefully opened her door, and peered down the hallway. She didn't see anything that looked out of place. No weird animals were roaming the house, there were no babies in residence, other than the Moore baby, and the Moores were in the guesthouse. In short, there was nothing to be seen or heard.

Maybe it was the whirring sound of a tool, she thought, maybe a drill or something. Lou was probably working, even though she'd told him and Izzie to take the afternoon off. She closed the door, took off her jacket, and once again crawled into bed, hoping she would be able to fall asleep. Not being a daytime sleeper didn't help, either.

Again, she picked up the book and started to read. She felt her eyes getting heavy, and her head felt like a lead weight. She drifted off into a deep sleep and slept heavily for three hours. When her phone alarm buzzed, she jumped up so fast that she banged her head on the bedpost. "Crap!" she shouted. "What a way to wake up."

Joy took a shower and put on a different pair of jeans and a black turtleneck sweater. Black Uggs would keep her feet warm; she did not like having cold feet—a big pet peeve of hers. She wore socks to bed at home but hadn't bothered here simply because it wasn't that cold.

Using a pair of cuticle scissors, she ripped through the packing tape and opened one of the three boxes. In this one, Hayley had sent mini bottles of hand lotion, cuticle cream, nail-polish-remover pads, the Simply Joy brand, and a fragrant hand sanitizer. The second box had the Christmas line of polishes plus their classics. Yule Love was a cherry red with sparkly gold undertones. It was their biggest seller year-round. Another holiday favorite was Merry Me Man!—a deep rose that flattered all skin types, young and old. Joy opened the last box, which was filled with the nail kits for women and children. Each kit contained a nail clipper, a file, and a cuticle tool. The children's kit was aimed more for girls, but boys could use it, too. It contained colored pens for drawing on the nails, press-on nails for fun, and a nail buffer. These would be dispensed accordingly. She didn't want a two-year-old eating the press-on nails. She made a mental note to check the ages of the children, if there were any at all, before she left the kits. This seemed like a good idea, but now she felt that it wasn't enough. It was Black Friday, so maybe she could add a few extras before delivering them to the shelter. There was much to be done, to be sure, but she had made this promise to herself, and she *would* hand-deliver these gifts. She'd made her "get them done" list on her cell phone. She added a note to call Mr. Norton so she could go over the books, but she would wait until Monday to make that call. Though she had e-mails to sort through, that chore could be left until tonight. So she spent the next hour packing the pretty pink cloth bags with goodies, then put them back in the boxes.

One by one, she carried the three boxes to her rental car, and, surprisingly, she didn't run into her mother or any of the guests. Even though Heart and Soul was one of the top B&Bs in the state—nay, the South—especially during the holidays, she didn't see a lot of people hanging around, enjoying all the Christmas decorations. She still hadn't seen the outside of the old house since the decorations had been put up, but she would tonight.

Spruce City was packed with shoppers hoping to get deals on Black Friday. By the time she stopped at the bank and located the shelter on her GPS, it was after four o'clock. She'd called James Albert to let him know she was on her way. The shelter was located ten minutes from the town center. Joy was sure she knew the place and was almost certain that a friend from high school had lived there at one time. She was curious as to how the house came to be a shelter for battered women. James had told her to park in the vacant lot across from the house for security reasons. Joy got this, but thought cars parked in a vacant lot might appear more suspicious than a car in a driveway; however, it wasn't her place to make decisions about security for the shelter.

As instructed, she parked in the lot and crossed an empty street. This was definitely the house of her former classmate. She recalled it from their school-bus rides all those years ago. It was a white two-story with dark green shutters and a neatly kept lawn, and there wasn't a single sign that anyone was home. She walked up the steps, pausing for a few seconds, then rang the doorbell. The door was answered by James himself.

"Miss Joy, please, come inside."

Smiling, she stepped inside to a small entryway. She recognized the lemon-scented furniture polish. It was the same type they used at the B&B.

"Thanks. I've brought three boxes of gift bags—about fifty in all, I'm guessing." She wasn't guessing. She knew exactly how many bags because she'd opened each little pink bag after her trip to the bank and added a crisp one-hundred-dollar bill to each. She wished she could do more this year, and next year she hoped to be able to help several shelters. Using the proceeds from Simply Joy to give back made her feel that all her hard work was worthwhile.

"I'll help bring them in. We have four ladies here now, and three kids. Two girls and an infant boy. They're at the town center this afternoon. My wife, Lana, drove them in the van. There's a Christmas performance by the high school, and she thought it would be good for the two little ones, as well as their moms. She stays with them . . . we have to be very discreet. So many women, so much suffering. It's so sad, but we do what we can in order to give them a second chance."

"This is going to sound crazy, but I have to ask. When I was a kid, I rode the bus to school. There was a girl, I think her name was Pamela, and she used to live here. Do you know what happened to her?" Joy saw the man's face turn as white as Herman's so-called ghost.

"I'm sorry, I . . ." Standing in the entryway, she felt like turning around and heading straight back to the B&B.

James Albert cleared his throat. "Yes, yes, her name was Pamela. She is, *was* my daughter."

Joy took a minute to comprehend his words. "*Was* his daughter." Damn. What could she say?

"I remember her," was all she could come up with. It was the truth. Pamela always carried a red-plaid lunch box. Some of the kids used to make fun of her. They were probably in fifth or sixth grade, when it was no longer cool to bring your lunch to school. Joy wished now that she'd stood up for her, told the bullies on the bus to leave her alone.

"She was a beautiful, kind, and caring girl—our only child."

"You speak of her in the past tense," Joy said.

He nodded. "Pam was a schoolteacher. In Durham. She adored those kids; I'm telling you, that's all she talked about. Her second year of teaching, she got married to a fellow from Texas. He seemed like a decent enough man. Pam was head over heels in love, too." He smiled. "I think that's the happiest she ever was. She doted on him."

This was not going to be a happy story, and Joy didn't really want to know what had happened to the girl on the bus, but James continued telling her about his daughter.

"She stopped calling as often. Then when she did call, she didn't sound like herself. Lana and I questioned her, but she always told us everything was fine. At one point, three weeks had gone by, and we hadn't heard from her. Her mother and I decided that a trip to Durham was needed. When we arrived, Pamela didn't look like the same young woman that we knew. She'd lost so much weight . . ." He stopped, took a breath and went on, "We thought she had a disease or something. She insisted she was fine. Didn't even bother inviting us inside. That was not our daughter. She was polite and mannerly. We begged her to come with us, but she insisted that she was fine. We asked where Dennis was. We'd only met him a couple of times, as I said, and he seemed decent enough."

She knew where this story was headed. And it broke her heart.

"Pamela said he was out of town on business. He was a supervisor at the post office, supposedly at a union workers' conference. Pamela told us that. But I knew she wasn't telling the truth. We left because she was upset, and we could see that our prying wasn't helping. I gave her the hotel's address and told her we'd be there for a couple of days if she wanted to see us."

James shook his head. "That was the last time I saw my daughter alive."

"I am so very sorry." And she was. How tragic and sad for them.

"Dennis wasn't at a conference. He was in jail for hitting her. I'll never know all the details except for what her neighbor told me. Dennis was a drinker. Pamela wasn't. They would argue about his drinking, and he would get loud and carry on; her neighbor called the police a few times. They would come, tell him to tone it down. I guess one night, he'd had one too many. He and Pamela argued, and he beat her. This happened three days after he was released from jail. He blamed her—this is all according to police reports and her neighbor. I'll never know for sure. We called several times, and no one answered. Lana was frantic; we both were. I called the Durham police and explained the situation. They offered to do a wellness check. Three hours later, I received a call from a detective telling me that Pamela was dead. Had been for a couple of days. He had beaten her to death."

This was not the happily-ever-after visit Joy had hoped for. She'd led a charmed life, in a sense. It was such a tragic story, and its being about a girl she knew made it so much worse. She kept thinking of that red-plaid lunch box.

"He was tried and found guilty. Life in prison. Not good enough, as far as I'm concerned, but Lana and I, well, we are God-fearing folk, and we forgave him; it's our way. I had all this money just sitting in the bank. In Pamela's honor, and for all those gals who are abused, we decided to do everything in our power to help women like Pamela."

"I don't know what to say." Joy was truly at a loss for words. These decent people did not deserve this. No one deserved this. A renewed sense of urgency to do what she could for as many shelters as possible was added to the top of her "get them done" list. This wasn't about nail polish and sparkly colors. This was life and death. While she couldn't help Pamela, she could use her connections in the business world to help these women have a chance.

"I probably shouldn't have told you that, but you kind of remind me of her. She was tiny, like you. Had that long blond hair."

"She used to wear it in one of those fancy braids," Joy told him.

"Yeah, Lana could hardly get her to sit still for those." He gave a wan smile. "Funny how all the little things come back to you, things that at the time seemed so unimportant."

"What you're doing now is remarkably important. I feel foolish bringing bottles of nail polish."

"No, no, don't feel foolish. These women need some normalcy in their day-to-day lives, even something a little bit frivolous to occupy their time. Here, they're safe, but frankly, a lot of them are bored out of their minds. We do our best to keep them occupied, but we're not always successful. Gals like pretty nails, so don't underestimate the value of what you're doing."

She couldn't help it. Her eyes gushed with tears. Perhaps it was his kind words of encouragement, despite the fact that he had just told the story of what happened to Pamela, and maybe she was saddened for all the Pamelas of the world. She blinked, hoping to keep her tears at bay, but she simply could not stop the flow.

"Let's get those boxes," James said.

Sniffing and wiping her eyes with the sleeve of her black sweater, she took the key fob from her pocket. "Sure thing," she said, and stepped outside.

James carried two of the boxes, and she took the lightest one inside. It was not enough. There had to be more that she could do.

"Could you do me a favor?" she asked. "It's silly, but I'd like to know if the women like the nail polish. I just want to know if this brightens their day in some small way."

"I'll do that, Miss Joy."

She shook his offered hand and returned to her car.

Chapter 17

On her way back from the shelter, Joy stopped at the supermarket to pick up some coffee pods. Inside, Christmas music was playing in the background, and colored lights were strung in the front windows. An artificial tree decorated with food labels made her laugh out loud. She needed something to ease the sorrow she was now feeling. Trying to focus on all the women James and his wife were helping increased her desire to reach out immediately. She'd e-mail Jessica and see how she was progressing.

She found the coffee pods on aisle four, next to the aisle where she'd found the pecans. It made her happy because it reminded her of Will. When he'd left last night, he hadn't committed to calling her, stopping by, or going for coffee. He did have Rex now, and he was either going to find his owners or become a pet parent, which reminded her of the chew toy she'd promised. In the pet aisle, she found a large bone, a plush raccoon, and a ball with a rope attached to it. This should be enough to keep him entertained. If Will found the owner, they could take the stuff, too. She liked Rex and secretly hoped he'd stick around. She couldn't imagine losing a dog, but she didn't have any idea of the circumstances that led the dog to Will's welcome mat, so there was no point in second-guessing and what-ifs.

She pushed her cart to the checkout, paid for her items, and was back in the car in twenty minutes. As she drove by, she saw that the town center was still packed. She loved the vibes of this place. Who, exactly, was she kidding? Yes, she liked Denver, and yes, her business was located there, but she was having serious thoughts of relocating to Spruce City. There was no way she would tell this to anyone just yet, but she realized that the possibility of not returning to Denver was there, simmering along. Just being at the B&B with her mom and Izzie and the rest of the crew made her realize there was more to life than running a successful business and making money, whatever the uses she put that money to. And there was nothing to say that she could not run her successful business here, on the East Coast, in North Carolina, in Spruce City.

Not that she had a bad life in Colorado—she had a great life there. A beautiful condo, a brand-new SUV, more money than she could spend, plus Hayley and Jessica, her two best friends. She was content. But there was that little something; she couldn't put her finger on it, but it was there, and she had to figure out exactly what it was that was missing in her life.

She parked in her usual parking spot behind the house. Of course, Izzie's Cadillac was there, which meant she was here and had not taken the afternoon off. Joy was going to have to play boss and force her to take some time off.

She carried the bags inside, and still, the place was quiet. Too quiet for a houseful of people. She put the coffee away but kept the dog toys in the bag to give to Will.

"Mom? Izz?" She went to the dining area—not a soul in sight. Except for all the giant Christmas trees, the formal living room was empty. The trees made everything look so cheerful that it made her happy. Pure and simple happiness. Her heart swelled with love for all that she'd shared with the people in this old house. Not many would refer to it as an old house; it was more like a mansion, but when you lived in such a place, no matter the size, at least in her opinion, it was still home.

Joy returned to the kitchen. She made herself a turkey sandwich, poured a glass of sweet tea, and sat down at the table where they'd constructed the gingerbread house, which had since been very carefully moved into the formal dining room. Once the judges had had their look, it would be edible history. All that work for only five minutes.

Joy heard footsteps at the front entrance, then voices. It was the couple staying in the Santa Suite. She didn't want to bother them, so she remained in the kitchen. This was the part of the B&B business that she did not like. Nana lived here. She had a small bedroom, which had yet to be cleaned out; they would get to that after the holidays. The pain of her death was still too fresh. The upside of their loss, if you could even call it an upside, was the B&B. Life continued, people still took vacations, and they had to eat, to be entertained. Spruce City and Heart and Soul played a big role in that. But Joy still couldn't wrap her head around the idea of living here. In the house. That had always been her biggest complaint. Even as a teenager, when she helped out, she felt like she was also a guest. Joy had always valued her privacy. Living here, you had to give that up. You had virtual strangers in and out of your house, day and night. You couldn't run through the house butt naked if you chose or play music as loud as you wanted. There were a lot of negatives. Did they outweigh the positives? She had no answer to that question, but she acknowledged that she was enjoying the time she was spending here, despite the unexpected loss of Nana.

She cleaned up her dishes and decided to plow into her e-mails. When Mom and Izzie returned from wherever they were, she'd come downstairs and do whatever they needed her to do.

Upstairs, she booted up her laptop, read through thirty-eight business e-mails, three jokes, and half a dozen ads for shoes, makeup, and furniture. She sent an e-mail to Jessica, stressing that it was urgent that she get the contacts for the shelters ASAP. When she finished, she ate another cookie and drank another bottle of water.

Another hour passed, and still there was no sign of her mother, Izzie, or Lou. Robert, Marie, and Chandra were gone for the day. Jeanette and Laticia were gone until tomorrow, mid-morning, as they didn't start cleaning the rooms until noon. Cheryl and Angie were part-time, so there was no reason for them to be here now. They'd all worked like troopers preparing Thanksgiving, then stripping the place to its bare bones in order for the decorators to do their thing. Most likely they were sleeping.

It was too late to drive to town to check out the Black Friday sales. She couldn't think of anything she needed, and most of the shops were probably preparing to close. It was after six, and the festivities in the town center would start soon. She hadn't looked at the evening schedule, so she wasn't sure what was happening, but whatever they had going on, it certainly was keeping the guests out of the house.

She'd no more than had that thought when she heard the front door open. She recognized her mother's voice and Izzie's boisterous one. "Mom, Izzie?" Hurrying downstairs, she met them as they made their way to the kitchen. *The heart and soul of Heart and Soul*, she thought.

"Where is everyone? This place is empty. Where have you two been? Izz, you were supposed to take the rest of the day off with Lou," Joy said, her voice a notch too high.

"Slow down, Joy. We were at the Santa look-alike festival. It's more of a Santa's beard competition. It's on the whiteboard. You should've gone. There were six Santas this year. I think they started growing those beards last year. Roy Kinley won. He had the thickest, longest, and whitest beard. Since we had a little lull, we were able to go. I'm guessing people are shopping, going to the theater. We do have all kinds of entertainment here." Her mother looked peaceful for the first time in days. Losing her mother and her husband had to be the saddest losses there were, yet she was still living her life. Then she thought of James and Lana Albert. Losing a child might be worse.

"I know. I took my gift bags to the shelter," Joy said, her tone somber. "I am so in awe of James and Lana Albert. I knew Pamela, sort of. We rode the bus together in fifth or sixth grade."

Izzie spoke up. "That worthless thing she was married to should've been shot."

"Izzie!" her mother said. "That's not right, though it wasn't right to take a life. I don't know how Lana gets through the day. She is such a sweetheart, and James, too. I try to donate as much as possible to them. Clothes, shoes, that sort of thing. They're not financially strapped in any way, but what they do is so admirable."

"I sent Jessica an e-mail. I want to get the ball rolling with shelters across the country. I'll donate funds, do whatever we can. This is so tragic. I hate to even talk about it, with Nana being gone. Dad, too. Loss has been a big part of our lives lately, but I think we're okay. What do you think?"

Her mother poured a glass of tea and sat across from her. "I'm terribly sad, and a little bit lost. I have been since your dad died. He was too young. I . . . I never expected—well, no one expects to die at forty-seven. A cardiologist. He took care of himself, too. You know that. Always running those marathons, visiting the gym. In the summer, he'd swim in the river. Some days, I have trouble believing that he's really gone. And now your grandmother is gone, too; it's all so surreal. I don't know if I'm okay now, sweetie, but I will be."

"Listen up, girls," Izzie said, inserting herself into their conversation. "We've got too much to do around here to be sad. Anna would have a hissy fit if she knew you two were as maudlin as an old dog. We can grieve, but we can't stop living our lives. We've got that Parade of Homes coming up, and you know we'll have to be on our toes for that. Then those two days of open house, or whatever you all are calling it now. Two days of hard work is what it is, but my Lordy, it is fun to see the looks on people's faces when they see all these trees and how fancy the outside is. Joy, you need to step outside the minute it's dark and look at those lights. Your grandmother would be so excited."

"It's dark enough. Flip the switch, and I'll have a peep now," Joy said. Knowing Izzie was doing her best to lighten the atmosphere, she picked up on it, and said, "Come on, you two, let's have a peep together."

Her mother clicked a few keys on her laptop, then they stepped out onto the front lawn. Taking several steps back in order to view the entire house, Joy could not believe this had been done in less than twenty-four hours.

The theme was snowmen! How like Nana to take a simple thing and turn it into a winter wonderland. Thousands of white lights lit up the lawn, and it looked like it was covered in snow and ice. Snow people—giant, mechanical snow people—moved about; it looked as though they were walking, pulling a sleigh with their snow children. A merry-go-round was lit up, and instead of horses, there were sleighs and more snow kids. Mechanical snowmen, snowwomen, and even a snowbaby.

"How did she come up with this? It's fantastic! They look real, like they're gliding across the snow! They did all of this last night? Unbelievable," Joy said, in awe of the display.

"This took almost a year to design and build. Mom spared no expense. She knew what she wanted, and the people she hires are the best in the business. So, what do you think our chances are of winning the parade this year?" her mother asked.

"If I said one hundred percent, it would show my partiality. Instead, I'd give it a ninety-nine-percent chance of winning. Now I get the snowman Christmas tree in the entryway. It is my favorite."

"I think it's mine, too. Mother had a talent for taking something simple and taking it to the next level. The mechanical snow family is controlled from my laptop. It's super easy to use. I wish Mom could see the end results of all of her and the team's hard work."

"Yep, she'd be hooting it up, big-time," Izzie said.

"What are they actually gliding across? I see all the little twinkle lights, but there has to be something . . . I don't know, solid?" Joy questioned.

"You can't tell, but the lights are *under* a made-to-order floor, sort of like clear wood planks. A movable dance floor she saw somewhere gave Mother the idea. She was worried that this wouldn't fit the front lawn smoothly; she had a variety of reasons, but as you can see, she worried for nothing. Our snow people look like they're gliding across an icy path. They're magnetized to the floor, too. Don't ask me how this is possible because I'm as amazed as you are. Mom was up on everything new and modern, all the technical stuff, but she didn't apply any of that modernization to the B&B, except during Christmas. Whatever gadget or gizmo would enhance her décor, she would spend hours researching it with her design team. Even though she still slid written updates under the door and posted the local activities on a whiteboard, she was up on all the latest in technology."

"I didn't know that about her. She was always super smart, though. She'd help me with algebra when I was in high school. She told me once that she'd never studied it in school, but she could figure out anything involving any form of numbers in her head. That still amazes me." Recalling that about her grandmother, Joy was even more in awe of her than before.

"I always thought Mother was a bit of a genius. Problem solving, of any kind, came natural to her. She was patient, took her time, when she wanted to learn something new. Like the wine room," Elizabeth said. "Izzie, how long did she contemplate that idea?"

"Actually, she helped draw up the plans, at least the first batch, just to give the guys an idea of what she saw in her head. You know, once she had her mind set on doing something, she didn't stop until it was complete. She was a brilliant woman and, back in her day, way ahead of most women. It was an honor to know her," Izzie said. "She treated me like her second daughter. Always said I was the child she never had."

"You are. She talked about that to me. She truly felt as though you were hers. And I feel the same way," her mother added.

They laughed together at the memory.

"Mother thought everyone should be hers. She was a caretaker for sure. I guess it only makes sense that she spent most of her life taking care of the needs of strangers. In her own home, too. Now we're very well-known across the state, and this is all because she had a vision and worked toward it. She told me that once. To find something you like and stick to it. It didn't matter what it was, but be the best you can be. If you love what you do, then it's really not work. I can't tell you how many times she said this to me during my first year in college, long before I had any idea of what I really wanted to do, career-wise," Elizabeth said. "I can't believe she's gone."

Joy looked at Izzie and shook her head, indicating that she should just let Mom be. Izzie winked.

Grief was like a heavy cloak. It could wrap itself around you. She knew this because she'd felt that way when her father died, and it could choke the life out of you if you let it. Joy had gone through a few rough months and talked to Stephanie Littleton, a counselor who had an office in the same building as Simply Joy. They'd said hi in passing all the time. When Joy stopped saying hello, Stephanie asked her if there was something going on that was causing her to be unhappy. All of this because she didn't respond to a simple hello. Joy had been amazed that someone with whom she had such a casual relationship had picked up on her emotions. When Stephanie suggested she might want to talk to her, Joy had scheduled an appointment for the very next day. While her depression did not end overnight, a few weekly sessions with Stephanie lifted the weight of guilt from her, and in its place came acceptance. It had been a bit of a struggle at first, but she'd followed her counselor's advice, and she still felt sad when she thought about her father, but the edges of the sharp, hard, painful, cutting grief had been softened by time and the techniques she learned during their sessions. With Nana, she'd already put those techniques into use, and this time she wasn't so totally engulfed in the blackness of grief. Nana would not approve of anyone's feeling unhappy over her passing; she'd want them to throw a party or hang out in the wine room.

"Mom, we'll get through this. You remember how Nana said that while we couldn't always control what happens in life, we can control our reactions. I didn't really understand that for a long time, and it's so simple—just common sense. Like Nana." The more they discussed Nana's attributes, the more Joy admired her.

"I know we will, Joy. I do believe that there is more than just this"—she waved her hand around—"and that I'll see Mother again, but it's still a bit of a shock. When I wake up, sometimes I'll think of something I need to ask her; then it dawns on me that she isn't here. I still do this at the house."

"Let's go inside. I'm making hot toddies. Right now, you two," Izzie ordered, and they followed her back inside.

They sat at their usual table in the prep kitchen while Izzie made turkey sandwiches and placed them on plates with dollops of stuffing, mashed potatoes, and cranberry relish. "Eat. Both of you," she ordered. "I've got to find that apple brandy Anna ordered if we're gonna have those toddies."

"Nana ordered brandy?" Joy shook her head. "Online?"

"Yes, and yep," Izzie said. "I'll be right back."

A few minutes later, Izzie returned, carrying a bottle of apple brandy and three glasses. "Anna said if you're gonna drink, you had better do it properly. By that she meant you'd best use the right style of glass. Always got on me when I'd have a bit of wine in a coffee cup." Izzie took a large pot from the rack and added water and a lot of honey. She cut up a lemon, squeezed that into the mixture, then took the pot off the stove and added a very, *very* generous amount of apple brandy. She removed a jar from the spice cabinet and put a fragrant cinnamon stick in each of the glasses.

"That's a lot of work for a drink," Joy said when Izzie joined them at the table.

"Eat some of that sandwich first. Then you can decide if those five minutes are worth the effort," Izzie told her.

Joy munched on the sandwich, enjoying every single bite. She dug into the stuffing, cranberry relish, and potatoes. Her favorite part of Thanksgiving. A good old cold turkey sandwich with cold everything else. It might be unappealing to some, but she loved it. No frills. Right out of the fridge. She took a sip of her toddy.

The hot drink went down the wrong way, and she began to cough and sputter. Her eyes watered, and she knew her face was beet red. "What in the hell, pardon me, did you do to that?"

Izzie and her mother both burst out laughing. "I believe our girl hasn't acquired our tolerance for alcohol."

Joy's eyes watered, and she used the hem of her black sweater to blot them. "Tolerance! There's enough brandy in there to kill a cow!"

"You're exactly right. That's why we're eating first," her mother added.

Joy choked out the words, "Gee, thanks for telling me, Mom." Joy hadn't regained her voice yet, but she watched her mother trying to hold back more laughter and decided that almost choking was worth it if only to see that old spark in her eyes, even for only a few minutes.

"Did Nana drink this stuff?" Joy asked when she had regained her voice. Her throat still burned from the hot alcohol.

"Mom liked hot toddies, mint juleps, strawberry daiquiris—all the foo-foo drinks, she called them. Not often, but when she drank, it was like watching a show on the Food Channel. She'd explain what she was doing, tell you the exact measurements, and make it out to be much more difficult than it was, but that was her way. I had many a laugh watching her," Izzie said.

Joy yawned, reminding herself that she'd had only three hours of sleep in more than twenty-four hours. "I'm going to *try* to finish this drink, then I'm calling it a night. I'll be ready to help out for breakfast."

"Tomorrow is Saturday, when we don't start serving until seven, so you can sleep in. I'll be here at four to get the biscuits made. Elizabeth, we can teach her how to make omelets. That will test her patience for sure," Izzie said.

Joy sipped at her drink. "I'm taking this upstairs. I'll see you two in the morning." She gave them each a quick hug, tossed what was left of her sandwich and sides in the disposal, and put her plate in the dishwasher before going upstairs. Busing after eating had been ingrained in her since childhood. You did not leave dirty dishes lying around.

"Night, Joy. I'll see you in the morning," Izzie said.

"I'm right behind you," her mom called out.

Upstairs, Joy decided she'd use the soaker tub again. She filled it with hot water, added a dollop of the cranberry bath salts, and eased herself into the tub. This was such a luxury for her. Work kept her busy and did not allow time for long, hot baths. The hot water eased the tension in her back, and the magnesium in the bath salts would rejuvenate her muscles. She had a Jacuzzi tub in her condo. Joy could count on one hand the times she'd used it. In the future, she would make time for this little luxury. When she returned to Denver, she was going to slow down and make some changes in her life. She was going to appreciate the fruits of her labor, and more than anything, she couldn't wait to start funding shelters across the country. She'd check her e-mail to see if Jessica had had any luck with working up a contact list.

For now, she just wanted to think. Not about work, or Nana, or the B&B. She needed to think about Will Drake. About her feelings for him. She'd known him for barely three weeks, hadn't really had a normal date other than their rendezvous at Uncommon Grounds. She didn't consider that a proper date, and before Will, she'd had a few of them. Some were great fun, while others had been either boring or downright weird. Will seemed different from all the other men she'd dated. He wasn't conceited, though he had every right to be. Then, he was movie-star handsome. And that voice—he could melt steel with that deep, low, and *sexy* voice. She could imagine him in a courtroom, mesmerizing a jury, a witness, a crazed client. Whatever he did, he seemed at ease. He'd found Rex, and it wasn't a bother to him. Actually, she could sense that he wanted to keep the dog, and she hoped he could, too. Maybe they could go to the shelter together? Pick out a dog for her, a pal for Rex. They could take long walks beside the river. Toss bones. Compare brands of dog food.

Wait! Wait! Wait!

She instantly stood up in the tub. Grabbing the towel from the heated rack, she decided that if it were physically possible, she would kick her own rear end. *What am I thinking?*

Yes, she was in a little bit of an alcohol haze, but in no way was she drunk. In a relaxed state, she'd let her mind wander, and where it led her was . . . was . . . could it be what she really wanted? Deep down? Was she ready to . . . what? Get married, have three kids, a house with a white picket fence, two cars, a boat? Joy had never had thoughts like this about any of her past dates. There were a couple of guys she had really liked, and she had enjoyed their company, but marriage? Never even entered her mind. She liked her life the way it was. It had been all about her, and it worked. She had created this life, and she was happy.

She dried off, put on her nightshirt, brushed her teeth, and globbed some cream on her face. Once she was back in her room, she opened her laptop and checked her e-mail. She needed to refocus her thoughts. Where thoughts of Will Drake led her was just . . . childish. Taking a deep breath, she clicked through her e-mail until she found a reply from Jessica. She skimmed through it, then read it again, slowly.

Yes, they were going to make this happen. There was a list of twenty-eight shelters that had agreed to work with Simply Joy. She hadn't doubted that they would, but she wanted to do this the right way. Jessica explained the specific needs of each shelter, and Joy could help. Write a check, Jessica said. The shelters ran off donations, and, simply put, what they needed most was money.

Okay, she thought. How easy. She could write checks. Looking at the list, she'd have to get some checks at the local branch as she'd left her checkbook at the office. No, she'd have Jessica overnight the checks. That would be much faster. She explained this in her reply. Feeling that giving money was too easy, she decided she needed to do more. Maybe she could talk with James and Lana Albert again, see if they were willing to share their story on how they actually put the word out that their home was now a shelter for battered women. She knew that these kinds of shelters had to be very discreet, given the threat of potential violence, especially because the women were running from a violent life. They shouldn't have to fear when they

were protected in these shelters. It would take a bit of fi-
nesse to keep such a place out of the public eye. She
closed the laptop and leaned against the bed.

There was a light tap at the door, and her mom came
in. "I thought you'd be asleep."

"No, just thinking about life stuff." Joy laughed, but
she was very serious.

Her mother sat on the bed. "What kind of life stuff?
We've talked more tonight than we have in years. Is there
anything you want to tell me?"

Sighing, Joy said, "I don't know. I've got a few issues
bouncing around, and I'm sure that only one of those 'issues' is right for me."

"Does this have anything to do with staying here in
Spruce City?"

Joy knew her mother was being patient with her, trying not to force her to make a decision based on guilt and
sympathy. "Yes, it does." There, it was out in the open.
Her mother could now have hope that she'd pick up her
life and return to the place it had begun.

"Okay," her mom coaxed. "Talk to me if you think that
will help."

"Being here has opened my eyes about a lot of things,
and not just grief. Sorry if that sounds insensitive. I don't
mean it that way. I guess what I'm trying to do is look beyond the grief and go back to happier times, but I know
that's not possible. I've grown since I've been out of college, and I'm almost thirty, there's that." She grinned at
her mom. "I like being here now. I'm having fun. I see the
B&B and the town in a different light, and I like what I
see. I'm afraid if . . . if, and this is a very big *if*, if I were
to move back to Spruce City, will I still be a professional
businesswoman, or will I just be Nana's granddaughter in

the second chair at a B&B? I have no clue if I could even run this place on my own and still give a hundred percent to a business I've worked my butt off for. Most of all, I don't understand why Nana would do this to me. She knew I was happy.

"Mom, do you think she might've been a little senile? Maybe she was at the beginning stages of Alzheimer's? This is just . . . I hate to use the word in context with Nana, but it's stupid. A stupid stipulation. I'll never understand this. Why me? Why not you? You love this. You can do everything and then some, and still, Nana is calling the shots for me. I don't think it's fair at all."

Her mother nodded. "That's quite a mouthful. First, Joy, it doesn't matter where you live; nothing can take away your accomplishments unless you allow it to. I know . . . before you say anything, just hear me out. You said you could run the business from anywhere, right? I think you're afraid that if you do make a change, allowing yourself to have more than one profession, hobby, whatever, you'll lose yourself, as you've wrapped so much of your identity in Simply Joy. It's a huge success. I am very proud of you, but you have to decide how to divide your time. You can do more than one thing and still give whatever it is, even one hundred percent, of yourself. It's like being a parent in a sense. The life you had before children will never be the same, but it's still your life; you've just enhanced it with a change. This is what I did when I found out I was pregnant with you. Your father and I had dreams, too. We wanted to open a clinic, where people could get free medical treatment. Anyone. Off the street, a transient, a young mother, just anyone who was in need. We knew we'd have to fund this ourselves, but it was our dream to be able to care for so many who, for whatever reason, couldn't afford decent medical care."

Joy soaked in this new information about her parents. She'd had no idea. It seemed there were many things she didn't know about them. "Why didn't you or Dad tell me any of this?"

"By the time you were born, your dad's practice was well established, I'd cut back on my hours, and I wanted to spend as much time with you as I could, but I still wanted to keep my hand in the medical field. I compromised, and it all worked out as it was meant to."

"What about now? Do you ever think about returning to work? Does it feel like a part of you is . . . missing?" Joy asked.

"I am sad now, Joy, for obvious reasons. I'll always carry this sadness with me. And you will, too, but it's not going to change the way I feel about my accomplishments, or your father's or your Nana's. I don't feel as though I've missed out on anything in the sense that you're asking. I was content to be a wife and a mother and a part-time nurse. We had a good life, Joy. I still have a good life, despite losing two of the people I loved."

"You're amazing, Mom," Joy said.

Laughing, her mother plumped her pillow and leaned against it. "I don't feel very amazing right now, but I know that I will feel that way again, so that gives me hope."

"What do you think about my seeing Will Drake? He's super nice." And super sexy, but she'd leave that part out. "And fun. He's fun to be around."

"Will is a gentleman, just like his father. I'm excited you two are interested in each other. He makes you smile, and I like that. He is a handsome man, looks exactly like his father. I didn't know the family until Mother started using the firm to handle some of her business affairs, and I've liked everything about both of them. Will is good for you."

Mom's seal of approval? A hint? Or just Mom telling the truth? Definitely the latter. "I do like Will." Here she goes. "He's . . . important to me." She said more than she should've, but they were baring their souls in a way, and Joy owed it to her mother to be as honest as she was being with her.

"Then he's important to me, too."

"What about Izzie and Lou? Do you think they'll get married, or at least move in together?"

"I know you're trying to take my attention off you, but to answer your question, Izzie and Lou have been living together for ten years."

Joy leaned up and turned to face her mom. "Are you serious? They actually live under the same roof? Izz? Living with her boyfriend." She started to laugh, and the more she thought about Izzie and Lou, the harder she laughed. "I can't believe she . . . they . . ." Joy could not control her laughter. Too tired and too wound up to calm herself, she cackled for a few more minutes, then calmed herself enough to talk. "She's always said she'd never get married again. I've been hearing that out of her since I was old enough to understand what a divorce was. Unreal. The things I'm learning about my family and friends are just unreal."

"They don't openly discuss this while they're working together, but most of the others know. It's okay. I don't judge her. She and Lou are happy. Izzie thinks a marriage certificate is a noose. Her ex-husband was controlling. Not violent, but demanding, and you know Izz. I can't see her with a man like that, but she wised up before her kids were affected, and that decision brought her to us. I can't imagine life without her. She's the sister I never had."

"More power to Izz. I'm glad she's happy. You know, the first day I was here I made some comment about Lou's being old. That white hair. Izzie ragged me a bit. More of me saying the first thing that comes into my mind."

"She told me, and we both had a good laugh."

"Shame on me, I know. Mom, if we're going to wake up with the chickens, we should probably get some sleep," Joy said, stifling a yawn.

"Let me get into my pajamas, and we'll call it a night," her mother said. She stepped into the en suite bathroom, and Joy turned off the light.

"Night, Mom," she called out, then sunk into the soft pillow, pulled the covers up, and drifted off.

Chapter 18

Joy was certain that if she ever saw another egg, she would get sick. When she'd offered to help, she hadn't planned on making omelets, nonstop, for two solid hours. For some reason, today of all days, every guest wanted an omelet. Izzie showed her the ropes, and Joy had no trouble flipping the omelets. She made cheese omelets, mushroom-and-cheese omelets, red-pepper omelets, green-pepper omelets, spinach, kale, onion, and sausage omelets—so many different kinds of omelets. But the kicker, the omelet that sent her coffee roiling was for the old guy, Mr. Wallace. It was the first time that he had appeared for breakfast. Why he'd chosen today of all days to show up, who knew? But he was the last guest in line for a specialty omelet.

"What would you like this morning?" Joy had asked in her most cheerful voice.

"I will have one of your omelets, but I do not want any of that," he said, pointing to the bowls of peppers, onions, spinach, sausages, and the like.

"Okay, you just want a plain omelet. I can do that," Joy said, then cracked three eggs into the metal mixing bowl, whisked them into a sunny fluff, sprayed her skillet with cooking spray, and poured the egg mixture into the pan.

Mr. Wallace reached for her arm. Before she knew what had happened, the pan was flying off the portable gas burner, and the eggs were slicing through the air. The skillet, thankfully, landed at her feet.

"See? I said I didn't want that stuff! I want an omelet, but you never let me tell you what kind of omelet I want. Where is Izzie? I think you should be fired!"

Joy whirled around so fast, she almost knocked one of the bowls off the table. A deep breath. In and out. "Is there something special you want in your omelet?" Her shoe, she thought, grinning.

"I want some of those mashed potatoes you had on Thanksgiving. I want them in my omelet. Izzie puts whatever I want in the omelet. I want Izzie, now!" The old man, while quite frail, had an excellent set of lungs.

"I'll go find her, Mr. Wallace. Why don't you have a seat over there with Miss Betty? She looks lonely," Joy said.

"Hmm, she's crazy, you know. Talks to her dead husband."

Joy's eyes bulged, and she excused herself and went in search of Izzie or her mom. Marie was helping Chandra in the kitchen, but there was no sign of Izzie or Elizabeth. "Have either of you seen Izz around?"

"She's out in the front lawn with your mom," Chandra said.

"Thanks," Joy said, and hurled out the kitchen door, racing around to see the two women, her mother with her laptop and Izzie with a wooden spoon in her hand. She didn't need to know what they were doing. No, she didn't.

"Izzie, I need your help, ASAP!" She knew that if she acted as if she were really in need of help, Izzie and her mother would follow her, no questions asked.

Inside the prep kitchen, Joy turned to them. "That Mr. Wallace is a real piece of work. He wants mashed potatoes in his omelet, so he grabbed me, the skillet went flying off the burner, and I almost knocked the bowls off the table. Could you just go out there and see to him?" Joy was frazzled. How, she wondered, did Nana ever manage all of this?

They both laughed at her.

"He's a lively old coot, but a sweetheart once you get to know him," her mother said.

"Who could get past the mashed potato omelet to even want to know the old guy?" Joy asked. She felt sorry for him. A little.

"He's been coming here for at least ten years. He's like Miss Betty, swears he sees his wife during the Christmas season. We know he's a bit ornery, but he's really quite friendly."

"I'm sure he is," Joy said sarcastically, but she was smiling. Her mother grinned.

"I have to say, Mr. Wallace and Miss Betty keep us on our toes. They didn't mess with Mom too much since she refused to treat them any differently than the other guests.

Izzie, on the other hand, caters to both of them. They know this, too."

Joy looked at the clock. It was almost ten, time to end today's breakfast at the B&B. She was ready for a break.

"I don't know if I'm cut out for this, Mom. Seriously. I like people, and I'm all for making the best of any situation, but I'm not making omelets for the next six months. If we need to hire a chef and prep cook, a whole team of pros, then let's do that. The fact of the matter is that if I have to even *look* at another egg, I am going to get sick. No eggs," Joy said, her frustration and aggravation evident. She wasn't smiling.

Izzie chose that moment to blast into the kitchen. "I swear I will kill that old coot! He drives me up the wall. Do we have any mashed potatoes left? He really wants an omelet with mashed potatoes. Well, do we or not?" Izzie asked.

Her mother searched the inside of the small fridge, and, fortunately, there was a plastic container with mashed potatoes inside. "Here, and throw it out when you're finished. If there's any left. They're okay to eat, but I don't want to reheat any more of them. Tell Mr. Wallace that after today, we won't be having potatoes of any kind."

Izzie took the container of potatoes and raced back to the omelet station.

"Let's watch," Joy said to her mother. "I need something humorous in my life right now."

"Let's do it."

They peered through the hallway that led to the main dining room, where Izzie stood behind the tables, smiling, and laughing, but as soon as she turned her back, she would make a face. Joy busted a gut. "Okay, that's enough. We're sneaky, and that's not a good trait to have."

"Do you have plans this afternoon? I thought maybe you and I could walk to the town center. We can take in the sights. Look at the decorations."

Joy wanted to say that she had plans with Will, but she hadn't made any when she had last seen him. "That's a great idea, Mom. I'm free."

"Will noon work for you?"

"Unless I have any new cooking lessons, noon should be fine." Joy was not cooking omelets ever again. Period.

Izzie whirled through the door again. "Mr. Wallace has his omelet, and I have had enough of Mr. Wallace. I explained that we weren't having mashed potatoes again, and he said fine. Just fine. Then he told me he was going to the supermarket for a bag of potatoes. Said he knew how to use a microwave! Can you imagine? He'll forget about the potatoes, Joy, so you can get that shocked look off your face right this minute!"

Joy looked at her mother, who was gaping at Izzie, then they all broke out in a fit of giggles.

"I think I understand. No, I'm lying, I don't understand," Joy said, then, once again, she busted a gut laughing. "I'm sorry, but this morning has seemed like we're in a TV sitcom."

"It really has. People are excited, Christmas coming up, all these beautiful trees, the decorations. I'm sure it's wound up some of the guests."

"Mother, please. Though there is a little excitement in the air today, don't you think?" And there was. Joy felt a tingle run from the top of her head all the way down to the tips of her toes.

For a minute, she could've sworn she heard Nana whispering.

Chapter 19

They went to every single store that was open. Joy bought coin purses in the shape of Christmas trees for Hayley and Jessica. They'd get a laugh out of them, if anything. She bought three magnets for Izzie: a fried egg, a potato, and a skillet. When they finished shopping, Joy insisted they stop at Uncommon Grounds on their way home. She craved a cup of their coffee, and it was possible Will Drake would be craving a cup as well.

"You don't like the coffee at the B&B?"

"No, not really. Sorry, Mom. I like the strong stuff," Joy said. "It's the brand you're using. It's cheap."

"What? Cheap?"

"Was Nana counting pennies, maybe?" Joy asked.

"Coffee would be something she would skimp on. I'm guessing whatever we're drinking is not premium at all. She never drank too much coffee; she was a tea drinker."

"Contact the supplier and change the order," Joy said. "Can you do that?"

"Of course. I've got all the information. You can talk with them and see what other brands they have, decide what's best."

Joy opened the door for her mother. Inside the coffee shop, Joy breathed in the scent of rich, bold, *good* coffee. She missed her special brew. Uncommon Grounds was a good substitute, though. "You want a pastry with your coffee?" Joy asked her mom. "I think they get them from Mary Jane."

"I'll have one, thanks. I'll get that table, Joy, over there."

She casually looked in her mother's direction, then did a double take. Just as she'd thought. Will Drake, in the flesh. She quickly placed their order, then followed her mother to the table. "Look," Joy half whispered, "it's him." Scrunching her brows, she tried to direct her mother's gaze to Will.

"Mr. Drake, Will, how are you?" Her mother walked right up to his table.

"I'm well, thanks. I just had the strangest sensation come over me earlier. I felt like . . . like someone walked on my grave. The shivers, whatever they call it. I just dropped Rex off at the vet; he's getting his nails clipped. I was planning on going to the office but didn't make it. I was so overwhelmed by a coffee craving. Hi, Joy. You look, like, pretty," he said, then laughed. "I bet you hear that all the time."

Her heart raced. "Daily." She smiled. "So, no news on Rex yet?"

"Not a word. I'm having him checked for a chip while

he's there. If he belongs to someone, I want to take him home. I'm already attached to the big fur ball, so I can't imagine what they're feeling."

She nodded. Will was acting strange. Very strange. "Are you feeling okay?" She had to ask.

"Mom, does he look odd?" she whispered in her mother's ear.

"Will, have you been sick?" Elizabeth asked.

"No, not at all. I just got a flu shot a few weeks ago, and a checkup. I'm fine. Thanks, though," he said.

"Are you sure?" Joy asked. "You seem a bit off your game. Are you worried about losing Rex?"

"Would you both join me? Your order is ready, and I need another cup. Sit tight—I'll be right back."

They sat down. In minutes, Will put the tray of coffee and two pastries in front of them. "Okay now, back to Rex. No, I don't want to lose him, but if there is someone out there searching for him, I know how they must feel."

"Absolutely," her mother agreed with Will.

"Whatever happens, I have a bag of toys for him. I promised him a chew toy the other night," Joy said, hoping to nudge his memory of that night. That *kiss*.

"Seems like I do recall your saying that, right after we—"

"Said our good-byes," Joy interrupted.

"You're a gem, you know that?" Will told her. His dark eyes gleamed with amusement.

"Me?"

"Yes, you. Do you want to have dinner with me tonight? We can drive to Raleigh if you want," Will asked her.

"Are you serious?" Joy knew she sounded strange, but he did, too.

"I'm *very* serious, Joy Preston. Very."

She thought she was going to pass out right in the middle of the coffee shop. What was wrong with her? She felt a whirl of air pass in front of her face, but there was no air blowing inside. Or outside. It was a perfect winter day.

"I . . . uh, I'm not sure. Mother, is there anything exciting happening tonight? In town?" Joy asked, trying to focus on the conversation.

"It's not official, but the homes that are participating in the parade usually have their decorations up. People around here like to be the first to see the start of what's going to be a nightmare. Just the competition."

"That's exciting. Why don't you and I pack up a dinner and take an evening walk so we can see the houses, too. I can bring Rex, unless I find he has a home." Will seemed to realize the dilemma. "I guess I'm jumping the gun a bit, but I'll have to see about Rex before we can make any plans. I'm sorry. I don't know what I'm thinking. Can I call you?"

Joy felt like Dorothy in *The Wizard of Oz*. Or that she'd been sucked down a rabbit hole into the land of oddballs. Either way, this was the weirdest day she'd had in a while. Was it the toddies they'd had last night? They were strong, but she hadn't felt this way when she woke up. Strange.

"Joy, Will wants to know if he can have your cell number," her mother practically shouted in her ear.

"Sorry, uh"—Joy took out her cell phone—"let me have your phone."

Will gave her his iPhone, and she added her number to his contact list. "It's under Joy."

She wanted his number, too, but he'd have to offer it to

her—she wasn't going to ask. If he called, then she'd save his number to her own contact list.

They drank cold coffee and ate the pastries. Will's phone beeped as he received a text message.

"It's the vet. I'd better go. As soon as I know what's happening with Rex, I'll call. If that's okay?"

Joy smiled because her heart was kicking in her chest, and she was about to tell him to hurry because she didn't think she could stand it if she didn't get to see him tonight. "Yes, I'll wait for the call." *Am I coming off as desperate?*

"Good. Elizabeth, nice seeing you," he said, then waved on his way out.

Her mother stared at her. Intensely.

"You're in love, Joy Preston, and don't tell me you're not."

What did she just say? In love?

"Well, are you?" her mother persisted.

Maybe. I don't know. Joy had never truly been in love before. Her heart rate increased again. A deep breath. In and out.

"I'm not sure how it feels to be in love," she said, and it was true.

"Your heart is beating incredibly fast. I can see the veins in your neck. Not once did you take your eyes off Mr. Drake. Will. He couldn't keep his eyes off you either, just so you know. I'm sure he's in love with you as well."

Her mother talked about her and Will as though she were reciting her corn bread recipe. A factual event. Real.

"Let's just go back to the house. I'm tired, and I don't really feel well."

"I'll check your pulse," her mother offered.

"No, I'm fine, just a little disoriented. When I was standing next to the table, yes, I was staring at Will, but it was like I was being forced to. Not in a bad way, though. My eyes felt like they were magnets and he was this mountain of iron. Then a swirl of air, almost like a mini whirlwind, blew around my head. I'm a true airhead, I guess. I'll feel better after a hot shower. Then, if you want, we'll take an evening walk to scope out our competition."

"If Will calls you, you're going with him. Understand?"

Joy laughed at her mother. She didn't need to be persuaded. "I understand."

When they reached the B&B, there was a crowd gathered by the gate. "It's starting already. Let's go in the back door," her mother suggested. "I'll peep at them when we're inside."

"Mother, that's being nosy. If this Parade of Homes competition is as vicious as I've been told, I wouldn't do anything to give the widows something to talk about. They've probably sent friends to take pictures. Let's go inside."

As usual, the kitchen was buzzing with life. Robert had gone home for the day. Chandra and Marie were preparing to leave when Elizabeth and Joy arrived. Izzie was at the stove, stirring a pot of something that smelled delicious.

"You were gone long enough," Izzie said without turning around.

"I always knew you had eyes in the back of your

head," Joy said. She looked at her cell phone, checking to see if Will had sent a text message. Maybe he'd do that instead of calling her.

"Are you expecting a call, young lady?" Izzie asked, her eyes glowing like a star on a clear winter night.

"If I am, it's not any of your business. You've been up to something, I can tell. Your eyes are sparkling," Joy shot right back.

"Izzie, we have quite the crowd gathered outside. They're waiting to see the snowmen. And women."

"Thank you, Mom," Joy said. She was trying to keep Izzie from prying. How well she knew these two. It was really sweet, though. She loved the way they all bickered back and forth, interrupting one another, giggling when it wasn't really appropriate. These two women meant so much to her. Joy felt lucky to be here.

"I know what she's doing. It isn't going to stop me from asking who you're expecting a call from. If it was business, you'd tell us. But it's personal. I'll bet it's that Mr. Drake. You two are gaga over each other; you just don't know it yet," Izzie said. All the while, she continued to stir the contents in the pot.

"Okay, we're all adults here. Yes, I'm hoping for a call or a text from Will. He's at the vet having Rex checked for a chip. If he finds the owner, he'll take Rex home. No dinner date. However, if Rex doesn't have a chip, then we're going to pack up something for dinner and drive around to see all the homes we're up against. Is there anything else you'd like to know?"

"That just about covers it," Izzie said.

"I'm going upstairs for a shower. You two stay out of trouble while I'm gone," Joy told them, then went upstairs. She put her phone on the charger just to make sure her battery didn't run out. She didn't want to miss Will's call. If he called. One way or the other. Hadn't he said he'd call either way?

This was ridiculous. She was acting like a teenage girl. It was so silly, but she could not help herself. She might be just a teeny bit in love.

She took the charger into the en suite bathroom, plugged it in, then stripped off her clothes as fast as she could and took a hot shower. She washed her hair and shaved her legs, just in case. Not going there just yet, but freshly shaved legs were a good thing. As soon as she'd wrapped up in a towel, her cell phone rang.

"Hello." She sounded out of breath, like she was about to have an asthma attack, and she didn't have asthma.

"Rex doesn't have a chip." Will sounded pumped.

"Oh, that's good news. I think." She did think it was good news. But she still wondered if he belonged to someone out there.

"We took a picture of him at the vet's office. He's sending a mass e-mail to his patients, hoping someone will recognize him."

"I didn't think of that, but it's smart."

"Do you still want to have dinner? Do the scenic drive?"

"I think it'll be fun. There is quite a crowd gathered in front of our place now. Come around to the back, and just come on in through the prep kitchen. The door is rarely locked."

"Don't go around telling people that. You don't want just anyone coming through your back door." He chuckled.

Joy could listen to him talk all day. His voice was un-like that of any man she'd ever heard speak. At least she thought so.

"I'll remember that. I'm wearing a towel and a mop of wet hair. I'll see you as soon as I'm decent."

"You don't have to go to all that trouble on my ac-count," he said. "But it's probably a good idea to get dressed. It's pretty chilly out tonight."

"Okay, I'm hanging up to do just that." Joy smiled, and hit the END button. Never in a million years had she expected to flip over a hometown guy, though it didn't matter where he came from. She really was knee deep in the smitten department.

Focusing on drying her hair, she flipped her head up-side down, fluffed her hair until it was dry, then smoothed it down. She quickly applied mascara and lipstick. Her face was pink from being outside, so she didn't need blush. In her room, she took her last clean pair of jeans from the closet and her last clean top, a chambray shirt that was one of her favorites. It was soft and comfortable, and she wanted to be comfortable if she was going to be riding in a car all evening. She found a red T-shirt—she assumed it was her mother's—and slipped it over her head, then put her chambray shirt over that. She wore her Uggs, then remembered that her ski jacket was down-stairs.

She hurried down so she could be waiting when Will arrived. If she left him alone with her mother and Izzie, who knew what damage those two would cause?

Elizabeth was slicing bread, and Izzie was pouring soup into a thermos. "What are you doing?"

"We're fixing you and your boyfriend a picnic, that's

what we're doing, but you're welcome to do it yourself. Maybe you could make some egg salad sandwiches. Perhaps mashed-potato omelets on hamburger buns."

Laughing, Joy said, "You're not getting me anywhere near an egg, Isobel. Never again, and I am serious. I'll help, but no eggs." Joy wasn't sure if Izzie and her mother thought she was just teasing them. "As one adult to another, I'm very serious. I won't cook eggs, and don't ask me to." This was her Simply Joy voice. Professional. Adamant. Confident.

"Well, listen to you, Miss Smarty Pants," Izzie said.

"Izz, can you just stop? Please. I know you and Mother believe I'm still a girl, but I'm an adult. I don't want to argue, but you need to listen to me. I'm not joking or playing our silly games—which I like, don't get me wrong—but you two need to stop hovering over me like helicopter parents. Will is on his way over, and I'd appreciate it if you two would treat him like a grown man. I'm having a fantastic time here, but there's only so much I'm willing to tolerate." Joy took a deep breath, waited for some smart-aleck response.

"Joy, we know you're a grown woman," her mother said. "You're free to go home, to Denver, anytime. I don't care if Mother's will says we have to sell this place to the state. If we do, then we'll cross that bridge when we get there. You do not have to stay here."

"I know, and thanks for that. I made a commitment, and I plan to keep it. You know my word is good."

"She ain't cooking eggs. End of story." Izzie roared.

It was hard to keep a straight face with Izzie, and Joy burst out laughing with her. "See," she spurted out, "you do this to me every time." She bent over and laughed so hard that her stomach hurt. Tears of laughter rolled down her face. "Is my mascara smeared?" She thumbed the tears from her cheeks.

"You look just fine," her mother said, then took a paper towel, dampened it, and handed it to her. "Just one little bit is smeared." She wiped under Joy's left eye. "There. All fixed."

"See? You're treating me like a teenager again," Joy said. "I can wipe my own mascara off. You two need grandkids."

"Carl said he was working on it the last time we spoke," Izzie said. "Caroline is content being single in Seattle. I do wish they could've made it home this year, but they have their lives, and I respect that."

"Exactly! Same with me. I think I'm older than Carl and Caroline, too. Remember that?"

"I do."

Where is Will? Did he change his mind?

They continued packing containers, jars, and, from the looks of it, anything with a lid. Joy wasn't sure how they'd eat soup in a car with a dog, but she wouldn't dare mention this because they—*Izzie*—would insist on making something else. Then she'd have to wait because Joy was that kind of woman, and she owed much of this to her mother and Izzie.

A knock on the back door sent her heart soaring. She'd have a heart attack before all was said and done if she didn't get control of herself. She inwardly giggled. Just like a little girl.

"Come on in," she said, and walked across the kitchen to the door. She didn't know if she should give him a kiss on the cheek or shake his hand. Knowing how she felt now made her feel a little awkward. What if? No! She planned to enjoy this and not start her overthinking process again.

"Something smells good," he said, then leaned down and kissed her on the cheek as if it were the most natural thing in the world.

She stepped back, removed her coat from the back of the chair, along with the bag of toys she'd bought for Rex. "That's our picnic. Speaking of food, where is Rex?"

"He's in the car. I wasn't sure if you'd want him in the kitchen. Public health laws and all."

"I didn't even think of that. Is there really a law?"

"There really is. No animals allowed in areas where food is prepared unless it's a specially trained animal. Personally, I think it's a useless law, but I have seen it enforced a couple of times in my career. A waste of taxpayers' money."

"Next time you come over, use the front entrance and bring Rex inside. It's too cold for him to be outside," Elizabeth said to Will. "I don't even mind if he's in the kitchen, but I don't want to break the law." She winked at Joy. Their little code.

"Take this." Izzie gave Will a picnic hamper the size of a laundry basket. From the looks of it, they'd have enough food to get them through the rest of the holidays.

"Thank you, Izzie, Elizabeth. Joy, if you're ready?"

"You're most welcome, but you two have to come in and give us the full report on the widows, no matter how late it is."

"You're spending the night?" Joy asked.

"I am. I'll stay in Anna's room," Izzie said somberly.

"We need to clean the room, wash the linens. While you're out enjoying yourselves, your mother and I will be doing laundry."

"Oh, I need a huge favor. I'm out of clean everything. My laundry is in the basket in the room. If you wouldn't mind tossing my jeans in the wash. I'd appreciate it; if not, no worries."

"Consider it done, now get out of here before Rex pees in the car," her mother commanded.

"Bye," Joy said, and she practically pushed Will out the door.

Chapter 20

Rex went crazy when Joy emptied the bag of toys in the back of Will's SUV. "I'll need to get him a seat belt if I get to keep him. A dog his size jumping around in the car could be dangerous."

"Is there a law that says animals have to be in a safety belt? I've never heard of that, but I suppose it makes sense. By the way, I really like your ride. I have a matching one in long-term parking at Denver International."

"Whoa, now you've really scored. You're serious?"

"Yes, I just bought it a couple months ago. I don't drive a lot, as I live a few blocks from my office building. In the summer, I walk to work. I really don't even need a vehicle unless we're going to the mountains, and then the four-wheel drive comes in handy."

Why are we talking about cars?

"I've never been to Colorado. You love it there, don't you?"

Joy had wondered when he'd ask about her home. He knew she planned to stay the required six months. She'd made it quite clear that day on the phone. "I wouldn't use the word 'love.' Maybe when I first moved out there. It was such a different lifestyle than what I was used to. I fell in love with the place in high school on a trip with the family. I couldn't ski enough when I moved. I was in college, but I made decent grades and didn't always spend the weekends cramming for a test, so I skied, and partied, and skied some more. The partying stopped my junior year. I was a little more mature by then and had no clue what my future held, but as you know, I had this idea for nail polish, and it took off. I haven't looked back on those college years in a while. We're so busy trying to stay one step ahead of all the competition, it's not unusual for me to work a sixteen-hour day."

"A workaholic, I see. I was a bit of a slave to my profession before Dad asked me to take over the law office. I was getting burned out; one criminal was as bad as the next. My fight for justice wasn't there anymore. I'd given thought to traveling for a year or two, and that's when Dad called. I've always felt this was my true home. And I wouldn't want to live anyplace else."

Is he trying to tell me something?

"Let's go to The Golden Bear first. It's where we found Rex."

"Ah ha, the poo house," he said, then took his right hand off the steering wheel and placed it on her leg. He gave it a slight squeeze, and she practically shuddered at his touch. If things were to progress to an intimate level, she would be in deep poo.

"The one and only."

Traffic was at a standstill when they turned onto Airport Road. "It looks like the entire town had the same idea we did."

"It's what some of these folks have been looking forward to all year."

Rex gnawed on his new bone in the back of the SUV, content as ever. "I guess it is. I can't believe our place, how fantastic those floating snow people look. Izz said Nana worked all year having those mechanical snow people built. I couldn't even think of a theme for one Christmas tree, let alone, I think we have seven different themes on the trees inside the house now, not to mention those outside. I'm not the one who'll continue with all this." She pointed to the home with reindeer on the roof, plastic Santas leading a plastic Rudolph to the North Pole. "Nana knew Christmas was, is, my favorite time of year, but she also knew I wasn't the most creative member of the family."

"I find that hard to believe. You've created your company, you're extremely successful, plus you have to come up with all those names for the colors."

"And you know this how?" Joy asked, and couldn't help but laugh.

"I admit I looked you up online. I saw some of the names of the polishes, and frankly, I didn't realize the size of your company. You're all over the world."

Joy felt a sense of pride at his praise. "Thanks, we're trying our best. I couldn't do it without Hayley and Jessica. I have four other girls who work for me, but they're in sales and rarely come into the office. We use a lab in New York City. There is a process we go through, and it's fast-moving, but I do like what I do. I'm thinking of branching out, maybe opening a day spa or two. I'll stay in the pampering business. Women love to be pampered." She wouldn't mind a bit of pampering herself, but not by way of a manicure.

"Here we are," Will said, as they slowly followed the line of cars to The Golden Bear.

Joy took out her cell phone, made sure the settings were accurate, then started snapping pictures. Thousands of yellow-gold lights wrapped the entire house in a golden flame. "This is it? Where are the decorations? The lawn, stuff, whatever they call it! This is excellent for Mom and Izzie. Odd, but good for Heart and Soul."

"I don't understand all of this, but I do hear a lot of talk. This place is your family's number one competitor, isn't it? I guess she's tired of competing. A bit of a disappointment for me."

"Really? You're not cheering for us to win? What about the gingerbread house? Do you think there's a chance we lost? There's just so much pettiness over this 'who's got the best this or that?' that it's almost borderline crazy. I'm falling into the same trap, though. There's a huge competitive streak in our family. If we lose this year, according to Izzie, we'll get bumped off the list of the top ten places to stay during the holidays. I haven't involved myself in that aspect yet, and I really don't want to. I need to call the accountant, look at Nana's books, but it just feels so personal, like I'm invading her private space. I don't like this at all. Will, do you know when Nana amended her will, added these changes? I hate to talk shop, but I thought it was so out of character, I wondered if there might've been any signs she was suffering from dementia, or maybe Alzheimer's."

"Dad took care of Anna's will long before I came into the picture. I'll look at the dates and call Dad, see what his take is. He knew your grandmother for years. He'd know if she was acting unusual. Wouldn't Izzie know, too? She spent every day with her. Why haven't you asked her, or have you?"

They'd just passed The Golden Bear yet were still tied up in a traffic jam, which allowed them to talk freely.

"I haven't exactly come out and asked her. Izzie, being Izzie, would've noticed, I would think. Not much escapes her ever-watchful eyes. Mom wouldn't know, what with her traveling the world. I think this is the longest span of time she's stayed in Spruce City since my dad died. I don't know. I think I'm searching for a reason, anything, that would explain why she did this to me. She of all people, too. She begged me to stay here and go to college in North Carolina but accepted my decision. I know she was proud of my success, and she knew I was happy. But there's a side of me that can't help but think she was selfish and wanted me to come back to Spruce City just to keep the B&B in the family.

"Did she really think I'd walk away from all that she'd worked for? She had some strange notion in her head, and I'm simply at a loss as to what she really wanted to accomplish by having me here for six months. There's no reasonable answer." Joy was talking too much, but he seemed to be a good listener. He was an attorney; they had to be good at listening to people. "At least that I know of."

The traffic started moving at a normal pace once they were away from the riverfront. "Where to next?" Will asked. "This is your night."

"And all I'm doing is complaining. I'm sorry, Will. I

don't mean to be such a whiner. Let's try the Swanson House, since we're going to pass the street if we keep heading this way."

"You're fine. I like listening to you. You've got a legitimate complaint, I'll agree with that. I didn't know your grandmother, but she had to have had a good reason. You know what? I have a cell phone. I'll call Dad now. What the heck?"

"Okay," Joy said, unsure that it really was a good time, but she'd asked, and now she was receiving.

Will pulled into a service-station parking lot. Good idea, she thought. She'd get the picnic supplies out after he finished his phone call.

He scrolled through his phone, then hit the bright green SEND button. "Dad, hey, what's happening in the Sunshine State?

"No way! You're telling me a fish story. I can tell by the sound of your voice." Will laughed. "I'll make sure to ask Bill next time I see him. I have a serious question to ask. You remember Heart and Soul, the bed-and-breakfast? Anna—yes, that's her. This is going to sound crazy, but that codicil you did for her, do you remember offhand when, and was she in her right frame of mind?" He looked at Joy and mouthed the word "sorry."

She remained quiet while he discussed her grandmother's state of mind. When she took a container from the hamper, Rex sniffed it, then went back to his bone.

"I see. Then you've answered my questions. I'm going to lean on the no side for now, but if that changes, I'll call and let you know before you take off again. Thanks, Dad." He clicked the END button and turned to look at her. "My dad says your grandmother added the codicil a couple of years ago. He said she knew what she was doing. He advised against it, said it was, and I quote, 'a crock of shit,' but she insisted. Apparently, she had her reasons and told no one. I can't believe your mother didn't know about this. I've gathered that you're a tight-knit family, but this you may never have an answer to. My advice, as a friend, is, do the six months and sign the place over to your mother. She doesn't seem to have a problem with the place. Hasn't she put her house on the market?"

"She has. The place is a castle, way too big for her. It was too big for a family of three, but they had to build their dream home, as most couples do. Mom had been talking about putting the place on the market for a while. I'm glad she did. I assume she'll stay at the B&B when the house sells. She's been going over to it for clothes and things, but she doesn't seem to have any real attachment to the place. It never felt like home to me when I lived there, and I think Mom felt the same way. We spent so much time at Nana's that that was home. At least it was to me."

"Sometimes you think you know someone, and they turn out to be completely the opposite. Maybe your Nana had another side that you didn't see."

Joy thought about that. Maybe, but it wouldn't matter because she was gone, and she was getting her final wish fulfilled. As much as she disliked Nana's controlling her from the hereafter, she had to admit that she'd enjoyed these three weeks way more than she'd expected.

"Let's forget about this for tonight and enjoy the sights. I, for one, am getting a kick out of the widows, but I haven't seen a trace of this so-called feud between them. Maybe it's just the gossip; that's sometimes worse than a good old-fashioned knock-down, drag-out fight. I'm teasing. I am totally against violence of any kind." She thought of the shelter and wondered if she should share her vision with Will. Why not?

"I've seen a lot of it in my career. There are no winners, believe me."

"Turn here. It's the last house on the right."

Along with a smaller caravan of vehicles, they slowly drove past Swanson House, owned by Amanda Swanson, who was a cheapskate, according to Izzie. The three-story house was lit up like a carnival. Red, green, blue, yellow, and orange lights covered the roof and windows. And all of the trees in the front had green lights on the branches and gold lights on the trunk. "Not bad," Joy said. "I'm hoping she hasn't decorated the lawn. Izz says she's beyond frugal."

Slowly, they inched down the street. When they passed the giant home, Joy was surprised to see a Santa fantasyland. The centerpiece was a mechanical Santa, with a little one on his lap and a puppy at his feet. The puppy's mechanical tail wagged back and forth. "It's cute," Joy said as she took in the rest of the scene. Another Santa was in a sleigh packed with gifts; the sleigh was placed to make it look as though it had just lifted off, and it looked very good. One more Santa on the front porch faced the street, and his white-gloved mechanical hand waved back and forth. "That's a bit creepy. All in all, I think Amanda Swanson did a terrific job. It's cute, but not over the top."

Will followed the traffic back onto the main road. "Where to next?"

"Do you want to eat this feast they packed? I'm a little hungry."

"I thought you'd never ask. Want to go to the river? I can let Rex have a break while we eat."

"Perfect."

As soon as they reached the river and found a parking spot, Will let Rex out through the door in the back and had a death grip on his leash. "Hang on, and I'll help with the hamper. Here, take this." He put the leash in her hand. "Hold tight."

She bent down and rubbed Rex between his ears. "You've been a very good boy. I think there might be an extra treat in the hamper for you," Joy said in a high-pitched voice.

"He likes it when you talk that way," Will said as he hefted the hamper onto the hood of the SUV. "Let me help you up." Before she knew what he was doing, he held her high in the air, then set her on the hood.

"I have to say, this is a first. A picnic on the top of the hood. Good going, Mr. Drake."

He easily climbed onto the hood and sat as close to her as he could without knocking her off the vehicle. "My first, too. A redneck picnic is what I'd call this."

"So let's see what's inside," Joy suggested.

For the next twenty minutes, they ate ham, biscuits, dill pickles, and tomato soup from a thermos. "This is delicious," Will said. "You're lucky you're from a family of cooks. Dad didn't know how to cook; we either had takeout or a TV dinner. Though we would go out often, and always to a fancy restaurant. I think Dad tried to make up for his lack of culinary skills."

"Poor guy, it's not something everyone knows how to do. I can't cook worth a hoot, but I have learned how to make piecrusts, corn bread, and crêpes. I don't know that I'll ever make them when I go back home, but it's good to know how."

Rex sat on the ground beside the truck, unaware of anything except the container of ham and cottage cheese

Elizabeth had fixed for him. "I didn't know dogs ate cottage cheese," Will said.

"Me, either. I never had a dog growing up, but I wanted one. I'm going to get a cat when I go home. They're easy, and they won't need me to be there to take them on walks, toss a ball, all the other stuff that comes with having a dog. Maybe when I move into a house with a big yard, I'll get a dog."

"Tell me if I'm out of line, but I need to know. You're obviously planning on returning to Colorado when the mandatory six months is up. I get that, but . . . this is going to sound like I'm weird, and please feel free to express that if that's what you feel. It's been a little over three weeks since we met, and I know this is fast; in fact, it's blowing my mind." He tossed a piece of bread crust to a flock of some unknown type of bird. "I have feelings for you."

Her mind went blank for a few seconds. She didn't respond because she needed to organize her thoughts, her reply. She'd been raised to be honest. Lately, she'd been telling more than her share of lies where Will Drake was concerned, but she couldn't sleep comfortably at night knowing she'd lied to him.

"You're shocked, right? You think I'm some kind of stalker." He said this to her, his voice sounding rough, hurt.

"Will, it's not that at all," she finally managed to say. "You're not a weirdo or a stalker. In this town, I'd already know that if it were true."

He didn't say anything.

It was her turn to fess up. She couldn't, *wouldn't* let him suffer another minute. "I'm glad you said it. First. I didn't want to be one of those women who needs a commitment after the first date, but I honestly thought about it. I . . . I have, I think I have very strong feelings for you, too." She wanted to add that long-distance relationships weren't for her, but that he might have the power to change her mind.

Will reached over and pulled her close to him, tilting her head back so he could kiss her. His lips touched hers. A shiver went down and up her spine, and back down again, settling in regions of her that were for a later time. She pulled away and looked into his eyes, shocked at the physical sensations passing through her. Heavy and warm, she leaned in, and this time, she kissed him, moving her mouth over his, teasing him with her tongue, in a slow, almost drugged manner. She kissed him with a hunger that contradicted her outward calm.

"Joy." Will said her name while their kiss lingered, lightly now, with a teasing flair. His mouth was soft yet firm. She could not believe this handsome, intelligent man was attracted to her. Just knowing he wanted her, had feelings for her, made her want him even more, but she eased back, then touched his cheek with her fingertip, tracing the outline of the sharp bone, the angle of his jaw. He was perfect for her. She knew this as surely as she knew the sun was going to rise in the morning. There was no point trying to shake this off as a passing fling because it wasn't. This, she finally admitted to herself, was love.

Having been ignored for the biggest part of an hour, Rex started barking, reminding them he was there.

Joy took a shaky breath. "Poor guy, we didn't mean to ignore you." She said this in that baby voice that Rex liked so much.

"Yes, we did," Will teased as he lifted her off the hood. "You're a tiny little bundle of fire, aren't you?" He held her close, kissed her on the neck, then gently lowered her to the ground.

"I've never been called a bundle of fire—tiny, yes. If you could've seen Nana, you'd understand. I definitely took after her side of the family. Mom is tall and takes after her dad. He died right after I was born." She was getting maudlin again. "That's in the past."

"You'll have to show me her picture sometime. I'd like to see this old gal, get an image of her so that when you're talking about her, I'll know her face. Is that okay with you?"

"I'd love to introduce you to the family album. Nana was a stickler for keeping the albums organized. There are at least ten or so. I don't know where she found the time to do all that she did, but somehow she managed." At this very moment, she thought Nana's amendment to her will was the best gift she'd ever had. Now, she just had to do something that she swore she'd never do.

Rex started barking, reminding them it was time to float back to earth. "Let's take a ride by the B&Bs we missed. I think we told Elizabeth and Izzie we'd tell them every detail."

Joy smiled at him. "They're probably watching the clock, just waiting, so we'd better get a move on." Will opened her door, then took Rex to the back, where he opened the wide door and helped Rex leap into the SUV.

"Hey, boy, did you have a good time? I know it wasn't that exciting for you, but there'll be other times," she cooed to Rex like a baby.

"He's not going to hear that baby talk out of me, I can tell you that. He does seem to like it. Maybe whoever had him talked to him that way. I don't know, but I am attached to the furry guy," he said, then pulled out of the parking place back onto the main road. "Where to next?"

"I think Waterside is just a few blocks from here. It faces the river, I know that. Edna Blakely was widowed about the same time as Nana. She's the biggest gossip— all of this is according to Izzie and Mom—so I don't have firsthand knowledge about any of it, but Mom's honest, and Izzie is, too. According to them, she's mad at the world; they just haven't figured out why."

"Good to know," he said, a grin a mile wide on his handsome face.

"Here, take this road. There it is." Joy pointed to a large Victorian home. Odd that it faced the river, but that was part of the attraction. "Nice to see she went all out," Joy said in a mocking tone of voice. She saw nothing but blue lights.

"Let's go around to the front. She has to have more than this. It's pitiful."

Will parked the SUV on the side of the road, opened the rear hatch, and let Rex out, with his leash wrapped around his hand. "What if we get caught?"

"This is what the locals do. We're not trespassing. It's expected."

"You're right. I can't get Helen Lockwood out of my head, though. I'll never look at that place again without thinking of it as the poo house."

"She would love that, no doubt," Joy said. There was a small path between Waterside and the neighbor's house that was exclusive to Waterside guests. That memory came out of nowhere.

They rounded the side of the house to the front, which faced the river. "Oh, wow," was all Joy could say. The front lawn, if you could even call it a lawn, was covered in dancing ice faeries. They were silver, with wings that sparkled like diamonds. Blue faeries flew high, then low, repeating that pattern over and over. White faeries were made to appear as though they were dancing across the light. It was stunning, Joy thought. "This is the competition, no doubt about it." She was surprised at the tug of irritation she felt.

"Pretty amazing," Will said. "Not perfect, though. Look." He pointed to the ladderlike stand where the blue faeries flew up, then down. "See how that one hesitates."

"I do." She breathed a sigh of relief. "It could break," she said to Will to confirm what they'd seen.

"It could. Now, one more stop, and we're going to go back, and I'll let you have the rest of the night with your mom."

Fifteen minutes later, they were passing The Green Way. "The owner here is very eco-minded. Recycles dirt, according to Mom and Izz. She renamed the place a few years back when she started her clean, green life." Joy laughed, but she respected the woman for her part in saving their planet.

"There, drive a little slower if you don't mind. She has a composting area in her front yard." She made a face at him, and they laughed.

"That's a bit odd, but to each his own," Will told her. "I need to be more conscientious myself."

As they drove by Juanita Howard's eco-B&B, Joy was surprised to find another lawn filled with golden angels. "They really do take this seriously."

Angels with flashing wings drifted back and forth, swooping up and down, somewhat like the faeries but more graceful. White twinkle lights were everywhere—

so much so that they overpowered the angels. Still, this was an awesome presentation.

"This is nice. I like this one."

She nodded. "They're all really nice—no, they're all beautiful in their own unique way. I never asked, but who judges the Parade of Homes?"

"The people who buy tickets," Will said. "I think it's another ballot-in-a-box deal."

"Then I should ask, who counts the votes?"

"Mayor Harper. I picked this up from the guys at Cherry Suds, so take that for what it's worth, but they tell me the votes are counted in the town center, with Judge Thatcher. He's a decent fellow."

"That seems fair," Joy said. "I think Izzie and Mom are making more of this whole vicious-widow thing than necessary."

"Time will tell," Will replied.

They were quiet on the short drive home. Joy had a million and one thoughts drumming in her head. She had someone else to consider when she made her decision. She would keep things to herself for now.

When the Christmas season was over, then she would decide. Or not. She wasn't going to commit to anything just yet.

Chapter 21

December 20, 2018

"After the lies that Juanita Howard spewed, we'll be lucky to sell even one ticket," Izzie said. "She went around telling anyone who would listen that we have a health code violation. Can you believe that? Us?"

"You put too much stock in those gossipmongers, Izzie," Elizabeth said. "People know better. She's making herself look bad by spreading those ridiculous stories."

"We'll know tonight," Izzie said. "Mary Jane and I baked ourselves into the ground for this. I hope we've got some visitors with a sweet tooth."

Izzie had spent two afternoons at the bakery, helping Mary Jane and baking the goodies for the Parade of Homes, which began tonight at seven o'clock.

"Let's just enjoy this; it only happens once a year. It's my first Christmas without Mother. I know she wouldn't want us bickering and carrying on over a holiday theme."

Elizabeth was excited about the next two nights. It might be hard getting through the next few days, but she could do this. She came from hardy stock, as her mother used to tell her. She would get through this just fine.

For three weeks, Elizabeth had shared a room with Joy, and now it was permanent since she'd sold her house—aka her castle—last week. After Christmas, the movers would pack away all the things she wanted to keep. She sold the furniture with the house because she'd never really cared for it. Too stark and modern—Joseph's taste—but she'd lived with it just fine. She would have to decide what she would do when Joy left. They all knew it was going to happen but ignored it. She would get the B&B, she knew that, and she would take over for her mother. She and Izzie, and Lou, and the rest of the crew. They were like family to her. She'd given each one a very hefty Christmas bonus. They worked so hard to keep the place going, and she knew it was in all their best interests to keep her people happy. Happy people, happy guests.

Miss Betty and Mr. Wallace were having breakfast together every morning now at promptly seven o'clock. A few times, she'd eavesdropped on their conversations, and not once did she hear any mention of their dearly departeds' ghosts. Who knew? Elizabeth knew what she knew, and she'd keep that to herself. This place didn't have a reputation as being a little bit haunted for nothing. And that was enough.

"I hear you, but I don't agree. She's just downright mean. I've never seen such a scowl. I bet if the woman smiled, her entire face would explode."

Elizabeth cackled. "Don't get me started. I've giggled so much lately, my stomach muscles are sore."

"It's a good workout then," Izzie said.

"I never thought of it that way, but I swear my abs are looking pretty good for an old woman."

"I'm older than you, so watch what you're saying. I'll be fifty-three, and I don't feel a day over forty-nine."

"Are you two at it again?" Joy asked. "You're worse than two teenage girls with a crush on the same boy."

"Are you going to the shelter today? Lana called, wanted you to know that the shipment arrived. Mind if I ask what it is?"

"It's the Valentine's Day color kits, plus a few girly items. Hayley keeps coming up with all these ideas, and we're working with three other shelters in Colorado now. We're trying our best to give these women a little pampering. We added gift cards that are good for a massage, a manicure, and a pedicure. Plus a new complete makeover, if they choose, at Serenity Spas; they're nationwide, and they've agreed to work with us. Jessica is over the moon since this was one of her contacts."

"You, my dear daughter, are a good egg."

They all chuckled.

"Don't say the word 'egg' around me. After that morning trying to make omelets, those old slimy eggs aren't going to be in my diet for a very long time."

"I am headed over to the shelter, but just for a few minutes. I'm meeting Will at Uncommon Grounds for lunch, then I'll be home."

She hadn't told her mother or Izzie that her friendship with Will was more than friendship, but since they weren't blind, the older women knew that the two of them were attached before they did. She just had yet to acknowledge it verbally. She would when the time was right.

"Tell him hello and enjoy yourself."

"Will do, Mom. Thanks."

Ten minutes later, Joy was at the shelter. She and Lana had become fast friends, despite their age difference. Joy suspected Lana thought of her as a younger sister. She was in her early fifties, and life had left her a bit worse for the wear. Joy taught her a few makeup tips, and she'd taken at least five years off her face.

She knocked on the door according to the shelter's unbreakable rule. James had installed an alarm on the door. If one so much as touched the door handle, the police would be on them like a fly on candy.

"Joy, what a nice surprise. I didn't know you were stopping over today," James said. "Come in and have a coffee. Lana just made a fresh pot."

"Thanks, I'll take you up on that. We ordered a new brand of coffee from our suppliers, but they're still sending us that watered-down garbage, so a good cup of coffee is much appreciated." By now the Alberts knew that Joy was a coffee addict. It was her only vice, and she realized that too much caffeine wasn't healthy, but who knew, it might be deemed good for her tomorrow, so she didn't obsess over her indulgence.

She went into the kitchen and sat at the table, one that was similar to the one in Heart and Soul's prep kitchen. "I take it the Christmas gifts arrived," Joy stated. She didn't want these women and their children to wake up Christmas morning without gifts to open. Lana had helped out tremendously, getting sizes and color choices from the women, who had no clue why they were being asked for that information. Then she and Hayley went online together—the beauty of the Internet—and they shopped. And shopped. New tops and bottoms, shoes, boots, underclothes. Then there were toys—lots and lots of toys. Plus three iPads, two laptop computers, cell phones, anything she could think that these women and their children needed. She and Hayley did their best to make sure they had it all.

Money wasn't an object, and Joy liked to share the rewards of her hard work with others. People were supposed to give back. There was no question in her mind that she was doing good things for the shelter's occupants. Her feelings of guilt were assuaged because she'd learned that financial help was what they needed the most. She'd keep pushing her polishes all over the world, and she would help as many women as she could. She would never forget Pamela and her plaid lunch box.

"I couldn't believe it when FedEx arrived. It took that man more than four trips to bring all the boxes to the door. You're going to give a few women and children a very happy Christmas morning. I can't thank you enough." Lana's eyes filled with tears. "You're a Santa in disguise."

"I like that," Joy said. Finishing her coffee, she said her good-byes to the Alberts. It was time to meet Will at the coffee shop, and her heart raced at the thought of setting eyes on his handsome face. She'd told Hayley and Jessica about him, and they ragged on her a bit, but they came around when she told them that this was probably *the one*.

She arrived ten minutes early, ordered her new special blend of coffee, and saw that their favorite table was open. She took her coffee, inhaled the aromatic blend, then sipped. Five minutes later, Will walked in, and she just knew. This was the man for her. Nothing else mattered as long as she had this beautiful, funny, kind man by her side.

"Hey," he said, planting a kiss on her cheek. "I'll get a coffee."

"Sure."

Joy had asked Will to meet her here today. She was about to make a life-changing decision, and it included him.

He sat across from her, taking her hand in his, just as he had the first time they'd shared this very same table. "So, tell me your big secret. I couldn't concentrate on work today. Do I have a reason to worry?"

Joy was shocked. "Why would you even think that?"

"You were so serious over the phone."

"Because what I have to tell you is serious. Will, this is my life. I'm about to make a decision, and I need to know if this decision I'm about to make is worth making." She gave him a minute to absorb her words.

"Anything you choose to do is worth doing if it's important to you," Will said.

He wasn't catching her drift, hint, whatever. She didn't want to just blurt it out. "This is very important to me. One of the biggest personal and professional decisions I've made since I started Simply Joy."

"What?"

She couldn't help but laugh. Men didn't get it sometimes, and now was one of those times. "Will Drake, I am moving the headquarters of Simply Joy to Spruce City." She gave him a few seconds to absorb that.

She watched him as her words sunk in. Surprise, uncertainty, then total joy.

"Wait, don't say anything." She quickly typed a note into her cell phone for future reference.

Total Joy.

It had a nice ring to it. And she was making drastic changes. Why not add a new line while she was rearranging her life?

"Okay, give me a minute." He looked at his Rolex. "Okay, it's been a minute." He stood up, walked two steps to where she sat, then got down on one knee, took her hand in his, and said, "Marry me?"

Never in a million years had she been prepared for this!

"Joy?" Will said.

"Yes, yes!" Happy tears rolled down her face, and she let them. This was the most outlandish, craziest, spontaneous, exciting, awesome, and . . . she couldn't think of another word to describe what she was feeling. This man, this hunk, wanted to marry her!

"You will?" he said again. "You'll marry me, have my babies, and take Rex for walks and meet me for coffee?"

"I will." She laughed. "I probably need to ask you this, and maybe I should have earlier, but is your name really just Will? Are you a William, a Wilson? If we're going to get married, I'll want to know this." She knew she was being silly, but she felt silly, giddy, happy, and witty, and her heart was racing, her eyes damp with love tears. This was a shock. But it was the charge of her life.

"It's just Will Drake. No middle name, I'm a 'what you see is what you get' type of guy. No frills—that's the word I'm looking for. Joy, you've been, you are my future, my destiny. If I believed in faery tales, I'd say your Nana was a faery godmother and arranged this."

"I know it's crazy, but I think she did. We both had that strange day here in the coffee shop, remember? And a couple of times—I know you'll think I'm loopy—but I could've sworn I heard Nana whispering. It happened one day not too long ago while I was alone in my room. I told Mom about it. The same day, while I was here, I had a gush of air whirl around my head, but there was no physical source, no air vents, fans, or anything. I'm not so sure Nana didn't have a hand in this, but if she did, then

I'd kiss her if I could, but instead, I'm going to kiss my . . . fiancé!" Joy pulled Will close, then proceeded to kiss his soft, oh-so-sexy lips, which sent shivers throughout her body.

"What would you think about making a trip to the jewelry shop in Charlotte?"

"I would think I'd like to be surprised."

"That's my girl." Will kissed her so hard, she was sure her lips would be bruised, but it was heavenly.

"Should we keep this a secret until—I don't know! I've never been proposed to."

"I think we should wait until Christmas Eve. That will only add to the excitement of the day."

"Agreed," Joy said. "I love you, Will Drake."

"I love you, Joy Elizabeth Preston of Spruce City."

"Okay, I hate to propose and run, but I've got a client in fifteen minutes. Kristabelle will have a conniption fit if I'm not there. She runs the office like a drill sergeant."

"I'll talk to you later?"

"You will. I love you, and don't you forget that, okay?" He led her to the door. Outside, the December air was freezing. A cold front had moved in yesterday, and if the weathermen were right, they'd have a little bit of snow on Christmas Day.

"I promise I won't forget. Now get to work, time's a-wasting." She smiled. "I'll see you." She walked away first because she knew he'd linger another ten minutes telling her how much he loved her, and that would be just fine with her—but with his client, not so much.

As she drove the few blocks to the B&B, she hoped she could keep her new fiancée status secret. She was good at keeping secrets. Today was a big day at the B&B—it

would be the first official night when anyone who paid a dollar for a ticket could walk through the rooms Nana and her team of pros had decorated. Izz and Mom would think she was just excited about the evening. She was, but she was much more excited about the fact that she and Will were getting married.

As was becoming normal, she parked her rental car next to Izzie's Caddy, which she'd recently learned was a classic. She wasn't into old cars, but this old car was pretty darn fancy for its time.

She took a few minutes to gather herself before going inside, as she needed to kick her plans into high gear. She'd called the rental agency the first week she was here to see if she could get out of her lease without causing too much hassle. Of course, she had to pay a large fee, but she had expected that. Then she'd need to tell Hayley and Jessica. She knew they were up for the move, as she'd discussed it with both of them. Jessica had family in Colorado but saw them only on holidays, so she was tickled pink. The sales team could work from anyplace they chose. They had a FaceTime conference once a week, and she didn't see that moving the office headquarters would make any difference to them. They each had territories, and with the new Total Joy idea dancing around in her head, she would have to hire a bigger staff, but that was good. The company's sales records were beyond excellent this year, and she would make next year even better.

Now, if she could get inside without being bombarded with a zillion and one questions, go upstairs, and get on her computer for a couple hours, she would put a dent in what she needed to do to relocate the business to Spruce City. She'd already decided she wasn't telling Mom or Izzie until Christmas Eve. This would be her gift to them—the two women she most adored, loved, and respected. Okay, it was time to go inside. If she didn't, it was a certainty that one or the other of them, possibly both, would see her sitting in the car. And they'd rush right out the door thinking she'd had another low-sugar attack. Thankfully, she'd kept that problem at bay by doing what her doctor told her to do. It still embarrassed her when she recalled all the hateful things she'd said that afternoon, but that was the past, and the past was prologue.

She entered the prep kitchen to the smells and sounds she was becoming accustomed to. "Izz, Mom, I'm back."

She hurried upstairs before either of the two had a chance to drag her into the kitchen to taste another pot of Izzie's soup. That really warmed her up, but she didn't need anything to warm her now. Will's love was enough warmth for her. The image of him getting down on his knee in the coffee shop was burned into her memory forever, and she would cherish this date for the rest of her life.

She went inside her room, the Scrooge Room, which she'd spiffed up a bit with two new chairs and fluffy pillows. She'd had Lou remove the old plank-style desk, and she'd ordered a mini desk to use while she was here. Joy thought about putting her condo on the market, then rejected the idea. As much as she loved to ski, she was keeping it. Hayley and Jessica could use it when they needed to. She wanted to take Will to Colorado to show him the majestic mountains, the giant evergreens that ribboned up the slopes, her favorite ski resort in Vail. She had so much to do, and here she was daydreaming about the future.

She booted up her computer and proceeded to write

formal letters to the manager of her office building, the condo association, and her suppliers in New York. She was sure there would be a dozen other things she needed to do before all was said and done. An hour later, she had the letters written and saved to a flash drive. She would see if Will could have Kristabelle print them out for her. She didn't dare use the printer here. Mom or Izzie always seemed to be lurking around the corner, just when she needed a few minutes of privacy.

She'd contact a local realtor after Christmas when things settled down. While she enjoyed the B&B, she would need her own home. She'd been on her own for so long, it was only natural for her to buy a house. Will lived in his childhood home, and he had told her he couldn't sell it because it belonged to his father, but he was in the market for a place of his own, too. Maybe they could wait, and they'd purchase a house together once they were married.

It dawned on her they hadn't even discussed a wedding date, but it was too soon. She'd only been a fiancée for two hours. They would work the details out soon enough. Joy was super organized. All this work of relocating would be a nightmare for some, but it was just a challenge for her.

She finished what she needed to do without any interruptions—a miracle around here. She thought it might have been more than a little miracle that had led her to Will, but she couldn't prove it. It was a nice thought, one she could tell her grandchildren about someday.

That was pushing it, she thought. They hadn't even told anyone they were engaged, and she was thinking about grandchildren.

Downstairs, the atmosphere was full of holiday cheer.

"Where have you been? I was starting to worry about you," her mother said, and gave her a hug.

"I went to the shelter. Lana and James were tickled pink with all the Christmas gifts we sent. They're moving forward, I think. Lana looks like a new woman since I taught her those little makeup tricks. She has a glint in her eyes now that wasn't there the first time I met her. James does, too. Though they're still devastated, they're accepting and forgiving people. I'm so glad I met them even if I dislike the reason why."

"Well, that's quite an interesting day for you and for them. I'm sure those poor women and children will have their best Christmas ever. It's still sad, and I'm planning on getting involved as soon as all these seasonal activities are out of the way. Mom would have my neck if she knew I said that. Not that I don't enjoy all the hoopla. I do, but it's a little bit silly, these competitions with the other B&Bs. It's what brings the tourists here, so I'd best not complain too much."

"It doesn't make you a bad person if you have a complaint now and then. It seems I remember Nana telling me this not too long after I started Simply Joy. I'd call her and ask for advice, and she'd give it to me straight. No sugarcoating at all, just hard facts. I miss her so much, and I know it's hard for you and for Izzie. You've got to allow yourself to grieve. I went through a bad phase after Dad died. I talked to someone regularly. It helped, too. Mom, if you need a shoulder, I'm available."

"I'm getting there. We'll never stop missing Mother and your dad, but we're dealing with it pretty well, if you ask me."

"I think so, too."

"You met Will for coffee. How did that go? Has he decided if he's going to go to Florida for Christmas? He mentioned it, but I've never asked, as it's none of my business. I'm afraid I'll turn into a nosy old woman. If I keep nibbling into your private life, you're going to stop talking to me."

"Mother, please! You know me better than that. I'd never cut you out of my life, and you're not nosy or old. Now tell me what you're wearing tonight. I've got the navy dress, and that's it. I don't want to wear jeans."

"I thought I'd wear that red dress you seem to like so much. Red is such a vibrant, lively color. It's my favorite. And I think someone stole a red T-shirt from me. Wonder who that could be?"

"I'll return it, I promise. I didn't plan on staying this long, and I haven't taken the time to buy anything new. I should have Hayley pack up a few things and send them to me."

"I'm teasing. You can have it."

"Thanks."

"So tell me about coffee with Will. He's coming over tonight, I hope."

"He is, and he said he couldn't wait until they tallied up the votes. He and I both think we're the winner, hands down, though our competitors are going to give us a run for our money. I can't wait to eat the desserts. Izzie won't let me have even a cookie."

"I heard what you said, girl. I told you that after tomorrow night, whatever is left is yours. We could have a thousand people in this house, and we've got to give them what they want. Desserts are part of that, so don't you two start sneaking. I know you both." Izzie grinned the entire time she gave her little dessert spiel.

"I can't wait. If you don't need me, I'm going to use that soaker tub and relax. My body is craving hot water and cranberry bath salts." Joy laughed, but it was true. She loved hot baths now more than showers, and the tangy sweet smell of the cranberry salts Nana had made for the B&B made them special.

She was going to think about her future husband. Life was good.

Chapter 22

At promptly seven o'clock, they would open the doors. A line trailed all the way down the sidewalk and across their neighbor's driveway.

"Would you just look at this? I told you we'd need all those desserts," Izzie said. "Now, here's the routine again. Elizabeth, you greet them, walk them through the house, as quickly as humanly possible, then lead them to the dessert table. From there, Joy, you take them into the front hall, where the voting box is. People fill out a score sheet. Most of these people are just starting the tour, so we want to make the best impression possible. Are we all clear?"

"As clear as the crystal in the wine room," Joy said. "At least, I'd guess some of those glasses are crystal."

"What time did you tell Will to be here? He's late, and

we can't have that. He's going to charm all the old ladies, remember?"

They heard the back door open, and in walked Will. When Joy saw him, he literally took her breath away. He was wearing a black suit with a white shirt and a red tie. With his longish hair, he looked like one of those sexy guys on the cover of a romance novel, only he was the real deal. "Look at all of you—you're stunning. How did I get so lucky to meet such a gorgeous group of women? Don't answer that."

"If everyone is ready, let's open the doors," Elizabeth announced. "You all know how punctual Mother was."

"Mom, open the doors," Joy said.

She smiled at Will, and he winked, then mouthed the words "I love you," and she mouthed, "Me too."

As soon as Elizabeth opened the doors, she set the computer to start the snow people. *Oohs* and *ahhs* came from the crowd. One by one, Elizabeth led the people of Spruce City through the formal living room, then the formal dining room to view the trees, then on to the dessert table, where they could choose from cookies, fudge, mini pies, cupcakes, and hot cocoa, coffee, or hot cider. The cups were embossed with HEART AND SOUL. The idea was to lead the guests out while they still had that cup in their hand, so that when they toured the next B&B, they would remember who had fed them and plied them with dessert. On their way out, Joy stepped in and led them to the little voting table, with the forms and the box the mayor had provided. It was a simple scoring system, using a one-to-ten scale for the various categories, which included the obvious: design of lights, lawn décor, style of trees, et cetera.

The open house lasted for only two hours, but Joy did her best to keep track of how many people voted. In all, over seven hundred visitors had filled out the form.

When they led the last person out, an older woman who'd attached herself to Will—and who could blame her—it took a few minutes to move her on to the next B&B.

"I think we deserve a drink after this," Izzie said.

"I'll drink to that," Joy's mother said. "A few of those little old ladies from the church wanted to fix me up with their sons, two of the kids kicked me in the shin, one man tried to pinch my rear, and an adorable little girl wiped her chocolate cupcake icing on my dress." She pointed to the hem on her dress. "It's all good, though. This is what I remember. Mother would love knowing how many people walked through this mini wonderland. I'm dead on my feet, I have to admit."

"I had a few little old gals trying to hook me up with their daughters, a couple of them wanted me for themselves, and one girl—she couldn't have been a day over twelve—blew me a kiss. I guess it's good for the old ego," Will teased, then led Joy to a chair.

"I didn't have any troubles, really. I think we got plenty of votes, though I have no clue how they marked the score sheets. But we'll know in four days. I can't believe Christmas is here so quickly. It's been a blast. Add all the guests, and we've had a mini Biltmore celebration."

Some of the guests had come downstairs for the tour and dessert. Miss Betty and Mr. Wallace had so much dessert, Joy was sure that Jeanette would be cleaning up barf tomorrow. She had noticed that they were holding each other's hands, and that was just too sweet. Two little old souls meeting while visiting the ghosts of their mates.

"Who wants an apple toddy?" Izzie called out.

"I'll try one," Will said.

"Be prepared to get a little woozy," Joy said. "Izz adds so much booze to the mix, you'll be flying high in no time. I had one the other day, and it made me so woozy I could hardly walk. But they are tasty if you like apple brandy. I'm going to have a cup of tea since I'm not in the mood for booze tonight." She didn't want any substance to diminish the excitement of this day. She'd probably lie awake all night, just thinking about her and Will's future. What a good way to spend her night, she thought.

"I think I can handle one, but easy on the booze. I'm driving," Will said.

"Okay, you lightweights, I'll skimp tonight, but you don't know what you're missing, Mr. Drake," Izzie said.

"Izzie, you don't have to call me Mr. Drake. I'm Will. Mr. Drake is my father, and calling me that makes me feel like I'm a hundred years old," Will said, and they laughed.

They spent the next hour rehashing the night, recalling the people they'd met, and wondering what tomorrow would bring. When they'd tired themselves out, Izzie went to Nana's room, Elizabeth went to the room she shared with Joy, and Will gave her a soft kiss and whispered, "I love you" in her ear before he left.

Joy went upstairs as soon as Will left. She was quiet when she came into the room so as not to disturb her mom.

"I'm awake," Elizabeth said in the darkness.

"Oh good, then I can turn on a light," Joy said. "I've been dying all evening to get out of these heels."

"You looked beautiful tonight, and Will was quite the showstopper. He's such a nice man, don't you think?"

Joy knew her mother was on a fishing expedition, but she and Will were keeping their news to themselves until Christmas Eve. "I do think he's a great guy. I enjoy his company, plus he's almost as big a coffee addict as I am. We're good friends." They were that, to be sure, so she was not lying, but now they were so much more. It was only a few more days before she could shout to the world that she was totally, completely, madly in love with her Nana's attorney.

"You look like more than friends, Joy. I see the way you two look at one another. If you're just friends, then I'm losing my mother's intuition."

"You'll never lose your touch, because you're a mom, and moms know things, right?" Joy had hoped to crawl into bed and dream about Will, but her mother was wide-awake.

Joy changed out of her dress into her nightshirt, then, in the en suite bathroom, she removed her makeup, added a glob of cream to her face, and brushed her teeth. She slid into bed and was glad to see that her mother was sound asleep.

She turned off the bedside light and let her mind wander where it would.

Would Will want a big wedding? Would she? She knew she wanted to get married in the church downtown, but she'd compromise, as long as it was a church. No clerk of courts or running off to Las Vegas. Ever since she was old enough to think about marriage, she'd dreamed of getting married in a church. It seemed to her that it sanctified the event. She didn't know why; maybe it was her upbringing, but she would insist on that.

Where would they go for their honeymoon? Colorado? No, she wouldn't take Will out west for a honeymoon, nor would she suggest it. How silly, she thought as she lay in bed contemplating everything.

What about kids? How many would they have? She knew Will wanted children because they'd talked about that a few times, and she thought three would be a good number. Maybe four. Since they were both only children, they agreed that they didn't want to raise one child without a brother or sister. Joy had missed having a sibling, but Nana, Izzie, and Mom were a close second because they had spent their lives making her happy. She'd raise her children this way, too. Lots of love, no doubt about it, but they'd also learn to respect people and not judge them. That wasn't her way, as she was a bit of a critic now and then. She'd keep that to herself, however. Kids didn't need to know every single detail of their parents' lives. She'd learned so many things about her mother that she had never known. Her and Dad's dream of opening a clinic, her mother's putting that gingerbread house together like a pro. She was a pro. Joy wondered whether she would work when she had children? Probably, because her job could be done from anywhere in the world.

She hadn't met Will's father yet. Would he like her? Think her silly because she ran a nail polish company? If he was like his son, he'd respect her, regardless of her chosen profession. She was anxious to meet him and hoped he would fit in with her family. He had known Nana, and if her grandmother had thought he was good enough to handle her personal affairs, then he already had the family seal of approval as far as Joy was concerned.

She lay there for hours, thanking the heavens above that she'd met Will, though the circumstances were less than desirable, and there was still a part of her that resented the commitment she had to make to keep Heart and Soul in the Preston family, but it was as if it was meant to be. She would always believe that Nana's spirit had played a role in putting her where Will Drake could enter her life.

She looked at the bedside clock. It was after two in the morning. She had to be up at four-thirty to help Mom and Izzie with breakfast. Joy was content to stay in the kitchen. She'd washed dishes, scrubbed pots, and mopped the floor a few times. This was fine. She'd do whatever was needed except make omelets. Someday, she'd look back on this and laugh, and maybe she'd even have an egg, but that wasn't happening in her near future.

Trying to shut out her thoughts so she could get a little bit of sleep, she stared at the red digital numbers on the bedside clock. Scrooge didn't have a digital clock in his room, she thought.

Good grief, she should've taken a Tylenol PM, but she didn't think even that would have shut her mind off and allowed her to fall into a drug-induced sleep. She was getting married! She was supposed to lose sleep. With that thought in mind, she turned away from the garish red numbers and closed her eyes.

The loud buzz from her phone alarm jolted her out of a dead sleep. "Mom," she muttered. "It's time." She opened one eye, saw that her mother's side of the bed was empty, then heard the shower running.

Beyond tired, she forced herself out of bed, did a few stretches, then a yoga pose that was supposed to get the blood flowing. She needed coffee; she could smell it wafting up the stairs. She'd have to settle for that weak brew, but at least it was caffeine.

Her mom came out of the en suite bathroom, followed by a gush of warm steam.

"Morning, sweetie. Were you able to get any sleep?"

If only, she thought. "A little, but not enough. How about you?"

"I fell asleep as soon as my head hit the pillow. I had a long day, and we're about to have another. Between us, I'll be glad when today is over. It's quite stressful, especially with the added chores of cooking and taking care of the people, our guests, who love this home during the holidays. You can't blame them for wanting to stay here, though. It's just beautiful here, don't you think?"

Her mother definitely hadn't had enough sleep. She was talking too much, and Joy thought this was because she was trying to appear wide-awake. She laughed to herself. No need to fake it—if you're tired, you're tired.

"I do think our B&B is beautiful. It's hectic now, but that's what it's all about for the tourists. It's mind-boggling, the amount of work that goes into the day-to-day operations. Do you think we should hire more help during the season?"

"We do sometimes, but for obvious reasons, we didn't this year. We can handle it. Now, I need to get downstairs before Izzie comes up and drags me down. Get a shower, and I'll see you in the kitchen."

Joy took a hot shower, then adjusted the water temperature to as cold as it would go and stepped under the spray. "Whoa!" she said when the icy cold water hit her. "Just what I needed to wake up."

She went through her usual morning routine, then hurried downstairs for her caffeine fix.

"Morning," Izzie said. She was working on a giant baking sheet of biscuits again.

"Hey, Izz," Joy said as she filled a mug with the weak coffee. She drank it black because if she added cream, the drink would become nothing more than coffee-flavored cream. "Are we going to get that other coffee? I'd be ashamed to serve this to our guests."

"They're old, and most of them drink decaffeinated tea," Izzie said. "Get on that supplier's tail; you're a sharp woman. Tell them you want the coffee you asked for or we'll take our business elsewhere."

"I'll do that first thing Monday," Joy said, knowing full well that she'd most likely forget and end up grabbing a large cup to go from the coffee shop.

Joy inhaled the weak coffee and poured another cup before offering to help. She felt bad, but she was tired and happy and wanted to see Will and ask him all the questions she'd come up with last night. She would, soon. "What's my duty today?" Joy asked Izzie.

"You can start frying the bacon," Izzie told her. "Everything's ready to go on the stove."

"Okay, I can do bacon." For the next half hour, she fried the thick, smoky bacon, snatched a couple slices for herself, then, when she had enough cooked for twenty or so, she filled the silver serving dish.

"Bacon's ready."

"Where's Mom?" She hadn't seen her since she'd left their room earlier.

"Someone had a total upchuck fest. She's helping Jeannette strip the beds in a certain person's room."

"Ugh, I knew that was going to happen when I saw all that dessert they were gorging themselves on. Was it Mr. Wallace or Miss Betty?'

"Both."

"We need to keep an eye on those two. When are they leaving?"

"After the New Year, they'll return to their lives, and we'll resume a bit of normalcy. Not so many guests once the holiday is over. That gives us time to make repairs, replace linens, that kind of stuff."

Joy had the sudden urge to blurt out her news to Izzie. She'd promised Will they would wait until Christmas Eve, but it was not going to be easy.

"Joy, what's on your mind? You've been acting strange. You're still planning on staying the full six months?"

"Of course. I said I would, didn't I? I don't know why you think I'd do otherwise. My word is good, you know that."

"I guess I keep thinking about how difficult this was on you. I admire you for doing what Anna asked, but for the life of me, I can't understand why she did what she did."

"It's all good, Izz. Seriously, I'm fine. I'm running my business—rather, Hayley and Jess are. They know as much as I do, and I trust them. I wasn't too pleased when I heard this, as you know, but it's a change, and I'm embracing it. Who knows when I'll get to do this again?"

"That's true. Now, I've got to get the omelet station set up. If you could grab the veggies out of the walk-in freezer, I'd appreciate it. Robert chopped everything before he left yesterday. That man is practically a saint."

"I'll get the veggies." Joy feared another egg adventure. She went to the freezer, found what she had come for, and put it on the counter for the veggies to thaw.

For the next three hours, Joy washed pans, cleaned the stove, wiped out the freezer, and mopped the floor. Chandra and Marie were off today, and Joy didn't mind the physical work at all. She actually preferred it over cooking. She'd done all of this when she worked here as a teenager, so she knew the routine.

Joy cleaned everything in sight. She should go help her mother with the linens. She'd no more had the thought than her mother appeared. "That was the nastiest mess I've seen since you were a baby."

"Izz told me what happened. We knew it was coming. Is there anything I can do? I've scrubbed every pot and pan in the kitchen, mopped the floors, and wiped out the freezer. All those health-code violations," Joy said, and they both laughed.

"Juanita is a gossip, just like I said. I wish she weren't so unhappy with herself. She's not that old; she could have another life. If she'd just get that sour look off her face, she might attract a nice gentleman."

"Mother, please! You don't have one bit of room to talk. You are young, *you* could have another thirty, forty years ahead, and I know Dad wouldn't have wanted you to spend the rest of your life alone."

"You're right, he wouldn't, but the time isn't right for me yet. Losing Mom was, *is*, devastating. As I said, the time isn't right, but someday I'm bound to meet someone, and hopefully I'll fall in love again. It's hard to imagine, but I certainly haven't ruled it out."

"Good, because there is someone out there for everyone." Joy didn't want to sound too perky; it might make her mother suspicious, and until Christmas Eve, her lips were sealed.

"Thanks, Joy. I want the same for you. Someday you'll meet someone who blows your socks off, and trust me, you will know when it happens."

She certainly had.

"I've had a couple of semi-serious relationships, though I wasn't deeply or madly in love. They were more friends than . . . anything." She was not going to speak of the two immature relationships she'd had in college. She'd been young and inexperienced, and too eager. Now she realized that. For with Will Drake, she knew a love just like her mother described.

"I remember. You were young and inexperienced," her mother repeated her exact thoughts. Joy needed to sleep. She was beginning to feel loopy.

"I was, and I'd like to forget that part of my life. Crazy college days."

"Yes, we all had those days, Joy. I wasn't a saint by any means. We had our booze and boys, and did you know, I smoked when I was in nursing school?"

"No, I didn't know, but I've learned so much about you in the past few weeks. I think it's because I'm older, and you know I'm not going to judge you," Joy said, but she had to chuckle. This was another silly conversation, but it was fun getting to know this side of her mother.

"I suppose. Our relationship has changed—for the better, I might add—though we've always been best friends, haven't we?"

"Yep, we have, and that's never going to change.

Mom, I need to lie down, if you don't mind. I'm practically falling asleep on my feet."

"Go on, there isn't anything left to do. Rest. We have one more night of our parade, then we'll calm down a bit."

"Then I'll see you later."

Joy ran to her room, shocked that she actually had the strength to make it up the stairs. She saw the bed and crawled beneath the covers, clothes and all.

Chapter 23

Joy slept like a rock for seven hours. She couldn't believe it when she saw what time it was, but her body needed the rest. She took her time getting ready for the parading through the houses tonight. It wasn't quite as fun as she'd remembered, but she was sure something would happen that would make for an enjoyable evening. Will was coming again tonight to entertain the ladies, and maybe another woman would've been jealous, but she truly did not have a jealous bone in her body. Never had. For Joy, jealousy was a totally useless emotion that only led to trouble.

Joy used the round brush to dry her hair, giving it a bit of bounce. She wore brown shadow, with winged-out eyeliner. She borrowed her mother's tube of red lipstick and swiped it across her lips. She blotted her lips with a tissue, then added another layer. This would keep her lipstick in place. Of course, if Will kissed her the way she wanted him to, her lipstick wouldn't last through one kiss.

She wore her black jeans tonight because she didn't really need to dress too fancy. She wore a red cashmere sweater and her black ballet flats. Her outfit wasn't knock-down, drag-out, but it's all she had. She needed to go shopping or see if Hayley would go to her condo, pack a few things, and ship them to her. Even if she was moving to Spruce City for good, she would still need some clothes before she got the chance to return to Denver and pack her things for the move.

She checked the time and went downstairs early, so she could eat something before duty called. Fear of another sugar episode kept her on her best behavior. She made a peanut butter and jelly sandwich and poured herself a glass of milk. So much for the red lipstick, she thought, when she saw her lip prints on the glass.

"You're looking awfully sexy," came that now familiar voice.

"I didn't hear you come in," she said, wiping the milk off her mouth, along with a little more red lipstick. "I just had a peanut butter sandwich. You want one?" she asked. "We do fantastic breakfasts here, but for the rest of the meals, we're on our own. Though Izz is a terrific soup maker, we're all out. So it's peanut butter or nothing."

"Thanks, but I had a late lunch. I had a lengthy meeting with a client this afternoon. She was kind enough to bring lunch."

"Good. Now, are you ready to entertain the ladies tonight?" She eyed him, giving him the once-over. He wore a dark pair of slacks with that black turtleneck sweater and a jacket. Straight out of *GQ*. Better than *GQ*, she thought.

"I am," he said, then pulled her in for a quick kiss.

"Mmm," she sighed.

"What do you two think you're doing in my kitchen?" Izzie came storming through the door like a hurricane. Her usual graceful self.

"What did it look like to you?" Joy asked.

"You two were sucking face."

Will laughed. "Do they still call kissing sucking face?"

"I do," Izzie said.

They all laughed.

"Then I'm telling your mother you're not just coffee pals. That is, if you don't tell her first."

"Don't be so nosy, Izz. I don't spy on you and Lou when he just happens to be in the freezer, and suddenly, *you're* in the freezer with him. I've seen you more than once, too."

"We heat it up in there, too," Izzie said. "Look, you know I'm just razzing you, it's my way. Now, Will, you'll have to remember this because if you think I'm trying to offend you in any way, I probably am, but you can sling it right back at me."

"I'll keep that in mind," Will told her with a smile on his face.

"It's almost seven o'clock," her mother said as she entered the kitchen. "Good, we're all here. Izz, you need to guard Miss Betty and Mr. Wallace tonight. Do not let them near the desserts under any circumstances. Jeannette and I ended up tossing their bed linens. I don't want to go through that disgusting mess again. I'm too old for that."

"Mother, more power to you," Joy cheered her on. "I wouldn't tolerate that either, even though it's not their fault. I think they're too old to be here on their own, without a family member."

"I do, too, but Anna refused to tell them they couldn't stay. I think the family doesn't realize what their physical and mental state is, but I'll make sure to let them know when they come and get them in January. Or one of you can have the pleasure," Izzie said. "I'll keep an eye on them tonight, for their own good."

"There's a crowd of people. I can hear them," Joy said, and went to the front entrance to peep out the door. She ran back to the kitchen. "There are more here tonight than there were last night. Do we have enough desserts left?"

"We do. Now go on and get in place, and I'll get ready to flip the icon on this laptop," Izzie said. "Go!"

Will took her hand and led her to the front, where her mother was already standing. Elizabeth was wearing a dark green wrap dress with black heels, and her hair was pulled up in another sophisticated topknot. "Okay, Izz, turn on the lights."

As soon as the lights went on and the snow people began their show, *oohs* and *aahs* came from outside.

Her mother opened the front door and allowed the public inside once again. She smiled, directing them in and out of the rooms to see the trees, then to the dessert room. Everyone came out with a smile on their face. Joy made sure to be extra cheerful when she handed out the score sheets. They needed this win. For Nana.

At half past nine, the last group left, telling them their trees were as beautiful as those at the Biltmore Estate. And they were.

Closing the door, her mother leaned against it as though she were trying to keep the crowds out. "I had a great time tonight. Much better than last night. I had some great feedback, too. We're the only ones serving dessert and drinks. That should count for something." She sighed. "I'm wiped out.

"I'm going to call it a night, if you all don't mind. I didn't rest enough last night. Good night," her mother said, then headed upstairs.

"I've got a big day in court tomorrow. I should get out of your hair and get some sleep myself. I have not been sleeping well lately." Will did look tired.

"Go on, and I'll talk to you tomorrow. I need to take care of some business tonight anyway."

Will pulled her close and gave her a fairly chaste kiss since Izzie was watching. "I'll see you later." He winked and let himself out through the kitchen door.

"Y'all are definitely a thing, maybe more than a casual thing. Are you serious about him, Joy?"

She was getting tired of talking about her personal life. It wasn't their business, yet she hadn't told Will she wouldn't say anything about them being in a relationship, only that she wouldn't discuss their engagement.

"I think we're getting serious."

"What's he going to do when you up and leave? Have you thought about that?"

"Yes, I have. We both have. What about you and Lou? Are you planning on a wedding anytime in the next ten years? Dammit, I don't like you prying into my personal life. I've asked you on more than one occasion to stop treating me like a thirteen-year-old! I know this is all fun and games for you, but find someone else's life to nose into, okay!" Joy was ticked off and didn't give a crap if Izzie liked what she'd said or not. This was almost—no, it *was*—coming to the point where she was going to toss the guests out of one of the cottages and stay there. At least she would have some privacy. "I'm going to take to my bed. You really need to back off, Izz. I am beyond ticked." Without saying another word, she headed to the room with her mother. She actually didn't mind sharing a room with her mother, but tonight she wanted to be alone.

Instead, she took her laptop into the en suite bathroom, plopped down on the floor, and locked the door. If her mother needed to use the facilities, they had three downstairs.

She sent Hayley and Jessica the e-mails they'd been expecting. She thought she would have a heavy heart when she made this move, but she felt as light as a feather. Step one was in place. Joy answered a few business-related e-mails forwarded to her from Jessica. They'd just picked up two more shelters in Texas. Woo-hoo! This was going to be a good project to get involved in. After she replied to a couple of e-mails from friends, she turned the computer off. She was tired, even after spending the afternoon sleeping.

She hung her jeans in the bathroom and wrapped herself in her mother's robe. She slid in beside her, happy and elated, and ticked.

"Mom, are you awake?" She poked her with her elbow.

"Now I am, but I was just dozing. What's going on?"

"It's Izzie. She's driving me insane. She's still treating me like I'm twelve. She stood in the freezer earlier and watched Will and me share a kiss. She's nosy, and it's really starting to piss me off!"

"She means well. I'll talk to her. She doesn't get that people like their privacy. She's spent almost half her life here at the B&B, so she's used to not having any privacy. I'm not sure how she is at home with Lou, but I'll say something to her. She needs to respect you. As another adult."

"Thanks. I feel like I need to go and apologize."

"No. You don't need to. Let her stew a bit; she needs to stop this. You stay right here, and we'll take care of this in the morning."

"Good, because I'm too tired to deal with her now."

"Izzie will be just fine, trust me—she's made of rocks and steel."

"Okay, then I'll see you in the morning," Joy said. She switched off the light and was asleep before her head hit the pillow.

Tomorrow was another day.

Christmas Eve

Joy woke up early so she could help Izzie in the kitchen. Her mother had gotten up even earlier and was already out of the room, her bed neatly made. Joy lay in bed for a few minutes before starting her day, half-dozing and appreciating the quiet.

Out of the corner of her eye, she thought she glimpsed something moving. She half-turned her head on her pillow. Silhouetted against the gray morning light coming through the window was a hazy figure. It almost looked like light itself, but in a sort of shape. The form drifted over to the Christmas tree in the corner, and then, for an instant, Joy saw her grandmother. Saw her fully, looking as she always remembered her best, with her apron on. She locked eyes with Joy and smiled, the lights from the Christmas tree shining behind her.

And then she was gone.

Joy sat bolt upright in bed, her heart racing. She stared

intently at the corner of the room where the Christmas tree sat. The Christmas tree, and nothing else. Slowly, she lowered herself back onto her pillow, and her heart quickly resumed its normal pace. Sometimes, she knew, a dream would linger into waking hours; sometimes the light could play tricks on your eyes. Sometimes you saw what—or someone—you desperately wanted to see, even just once more.

Whatever had just happened, Joy felt grateful and confident in a way she hadn't felt since she first came back to Spruce City. She felt ready to face not only the day, but whatever else came next.

Three big events were happening today—well, four, if you counted the announcement of Joy's personal news. "I've made three pots of good coffee for all the tea drinkers," Izzie announced. Since they'd changed to a new, more robust roast, almost all the guests had stopped drinking tea. "I noticed that the new coffee has been a success. I guess I had drunk so much of that old cheap stuff Anna bought that I got used to it."

"What do you think will happen today? Any gossip on who's picked to win that crazy gingerbread-house contest?" Joy inquired. She knew Izzie had an ear in just about every corner of town, and then some.

"Not a word. They're usually tight-lipped about this. Don't want to spoil the fun. Plus, I think the judges— minus Will—like to see the girls squirm." Joy didn't know what her mother had said to Izzie, but she was more like her old self.

"Speaking of girls, I've arranged a luncheon after the New Year. It's for the widows. I called them myself. I said we wanted to host lunch and make nice. I can't make nice for them, but I can at least get them in a room together."

"Does your mother know about this?"

"She does, and she agrees that it's time for the childish bickering among them to stop. They can still compete, but they don't have to gossip about one another. I really haven't seen or heard anyone coming down on each other. Maybe they've mellowed since last year. I hope so, because we need friends." She almost spilled her secret but caught herself. Her gray matter filtration system was functioning properly today.

"Okay, then I'm all for it. If it will put a stop to the gossip, at least the stuff I hear, then more power to you for taking the bull by the horns and doing something about it. I can't imagine all those gals in the same room together, but I do believe in miracles. I've seen a few in my day."

"I'm a believer, too. I know that many people are not too hip on faith these days, but I just say a little prayer and hope they'll understand."

"You really are on a roll! You've got your Nana's spirit, for sure. She's probably looking down on us right this very minute and giving us the thumbs-up sign and a wink. She was a winker, just like you and your mom." Izzie popped herself on the head. "Duh. Your mother comes by it naturally. Now we've gabbed enough. It's Christmas Eve, and I've made a breakfast casserole and a big bowl of fruit, and I picked up a zillion pastries from Mary Jane's. We are not slaving in the kitchen today. I think the whiteboard says, 'A light breakfast will be served on Christmas Eve.' This is light enough for me."

They spent the next half hour setting out the food and

plates. It seemed strange not to have the full buffet and the omelet station set up. Joy was glad she didn't have to see or smell eggs.

"You're up bright and early," her mom said. "I thought you'd sleep in, given it's a holiday, and we're serving just a light breakfast."

"It's an exciting day. I couldn't sleep."

"Aren't you excited, Mom? Today you'll find out if we're going to be on the top ten list of the best B&Bs to visit during the holidays."

"I am a little excited, I have to admit. I'm good if we don't win. Give someone else a chance. Maybe if the widows felt like they had half a chance, they'd mellow out."

"I told Izz about the luncheon. She thinks it's a good idea, too."

"If it will stop the gossip, which I've heard, too, then it's worth it. Spruce City is too special to have all this bickering among the B&Bs. We need to act more like a team instead of lone players. There have been countless times when we needed extra rooms, and Mom called a couple of them—I can't remember who—but they would not take our guests. That's spiteful, but we're going to do our best to put an end to all this silliness."

"Agreed," Joy said.

For the next two hours, they cleaned the kitchen until it sparkled. The judging results were set to be announced in the town center at two o'clock. That seemed like an odd time, but it is what it is, Joy thought as she wiped down the same counter she'd wiped down three times already.

"I don't think we can clean anymore. We're going to wear out the counters," her mom said. "I want to get to the town center a few minutes early so we can find a place to sit.

"I'm leaving in an hour, if anyone wants to walk with me. I need the fresh air and exercise."

"I'll go with you," Joy said. "Will is going to meet us there. He's spending the morning in the park with Rex, so he can play for a while before he leaves."

"Makes sense."

"Izz, you want to tag along with us?"

"No, I'm going with Lou, and we're driving. He just bought a beefed-up Mustang and wants to show it off, said he's wanted a cherry-red Mustang since he was old enough to drive. His Christmas gift to himself. I'm giving him a year of free car washes because I know he'll use them. So, thanks, but I'll look for you two there."

Upstairs, Joy and her mother shared the en suite bathroom, bumping into each other, dropping hairbrushes, lipsticks, and face creams. "We're worse than teenagers," Joy said.

"I know, but it's fun. We didn't get to do this much after you left for college. Well, you left, and now you're here for a few months, so I don't want to miss a thing. I'm dreading the day you leave, and it's still months away."

"Don't do that to yourself. It will all work out. I'm a plane ride away. You could come and visit me. We could ski, and you could meet Hayley and Jess." Joy was really playing this up. "You can come to the office, see how we run things."

"That's a fantastic idea. Izzie and Lou will be here, with all the others, so that will give me something to look forward to."

"It'll be fun. Mom, I know I've asked you this a dozen times, but why do you think Nana added this to her will when we both know this place is yours as soon as my six months are up. It's never going to make sense. I need a 'why' answer."

"We'll never know, sweetie, but mom had a reason for everything she did. She wasn't a foolish woman."

"I know, but it's okay. Really. Now let's go. By the time we walk to the town center, we will only have ten minutes to find a seat."

"Yes, we'd better go."

They left through the back door as usual. The guests were free to roam the house and do as they pleased, but they knew where the Prestons and Izzie would be if an emergency arose. Miss Betty and Mr. Wallace were going with the Moore family.

It was below freezing, the sky was overcast, and snow was predicted. They didn't get a lot of snow in Spruce City, so everyone in town seemed to be excited at the prospect of the first white Christmas in forty years.

As soon as they arrived, Joy saw Will in the crowd gathered around the stage that had been set up for today. He waved at her, and she waved back and hurried through the throngs of people, practically dragging her mother behind her.

As soon as Will saw her, he kissed her. "My two favorite ladies. Merry Christmas. Come on. I've managed to save a few seats."

On the bottom steps of the portable bleachers, too. "This is perfect," Joy said. He was perfect—well, almost. Life was good, and she was going to work on making so many more lives have a chance, but most of all, she was about to embark on the biggest change in her life. She was ready for this.

The high squeal of the microphone hushed the folks who'd gathered to hear the results of the voting.

Joy sat in the middle between her mother and Will, holding their hands. Almost there, she thought, and smiled.

"I want to welcome you all to the town center on this beautiful Christmas Eve. Can you believe we might have a white one this year?" Mayor Harper asked. "Amazing. We've already tallied the votes because of the weather, so we won't have to keep you folks out in the cold and away from your families. George, give me a drumroll." George was a member of a local band. He'd set his drums up just for this purpose.

The sound of drums started out low, then got faster and louder. Then, two minutes into his solo performance, he hit the cymbal. "Thanks for the show, George. Okay, it's now or never. Only our local bed-and-breakfasts participated in the gingerbread-house contest, and I'll announce the winner of that competition first." He opened a sealed envelope, and said, "The winner of the 2018 gingerbread house competition goes to . . . no drums, George"—the crowd laughed—"Heart and Soul."

"Oh my gosh. We did it!" Her mother stood up, turned, and gave a little wave to the crowd. There was no trophy, but there was a plaque. Her mother walked up to the stage and accepted the plaque. "Let's give Heart and Soul a big round of applause." The crowd clapped, and Will kissed her right there in the middle of town.

"There is one more winner to announce, and that's the winner of the Parade of Homes. This is judged by those who visited the bed-and-breakfasts that participated. So here we go again." Mayor Harper opened the envelope, and smiled. "And the Oscar goes to . . . I always wanted to say that, but you folks know I'm just messing with you." More chants from the crowd. "Okay, calm down. The winner of the 2018 Parade of Homes goes to . . . drumroll, George, and a short one this time. People are getting cold." The crowd laughed, and George tapped the cymbals again. "The winner is . . . Heart and Soul!"

Joy actually jumped off the bleachers, and her mother was laughing at Izzie, who was hooting at her. Her mom once again walked up to the stage and accepted the award. "Thank you to all the people who took the time to visit us and vote. I hope we'll see all of you next year!" A thunder of applause and whistles and foot stomping, then her mom sat down, and the noise from the crowd died down.

The mayor made a few more announcements, then wished them all a Merry Christmas.

As the crowd dispersed, Joy caught sight of Miss Betty and Mr. Wallace, once again hand in hand, talking animatedly while people dodged around them. In the past, Joy's first instinct would have been to shake her head or maybe laugh at their antics. Now, she thought back to that morning, alone in her room. Her—dream? Vision? Whatever it was. She thought about how Miss Betty and Mr. Wallace both insisted that they had been visited by their loved ones at Heart and Soul. Suddenly she felt a kinship with the eccentric elderly couple, and a rush of happiness that they had found each other.

As the crowd milled about, Will and Joy motioned for Izzie and Lou to join their group.

"Mom, Izz, Lou, I've made a decision, and I wanted you all to be the first ones to hear it." She paused. "I'm moving Simply Joy's headquarters to Spruce City!"

"What? Are you serious? Really, Joy, this isn't some kind of silly joke you and Izz whipped up, is it?"

"No, it's something I whipped up, all by myself. Took a lot of deep thinking, but I want to be around my family, and I told you, Mom, I could work anywhere, so we'll be here after the New Year!"

"Now that's a true Christmas miracle!" Izzie said, and wrapped Joy in a bear hug. "You are one sneaky woman, but I love the dickens out of you!"

Joy kissed Izzie, kissed her mom, and even kissed Lou. "It's my gift to you all, the most important people in my life."

"Hey, what about me?" Will asked. "Doesn't your fiancé rate as one of the most important people in your life?"

Her mother, Izzie, and Lou all looked at Will.

"You said, 'fiancé,' am I right?" her mother asked.

"Look." Joy held out her left hand. A diamond glistened on her finger. "Will gave it to me when you were on the stage." Joy embraced her mother, hugged Izzie and Lou, then wrapped her arms around the man she would spend the rest of her life with. "Merry Christmas, Mr. Drake."

Don't miss
THE BRIGHTEST STAR,
the newest holiday story from Fern Michaels!

A special treat to warm your heart, just in time for the holidays—a sparkling new novel from **New York Times** *bestselling author Fern Michaels. . . .*

Christmas is more than just a celebration for Lauren Montgomery. For generations, it's been her family's livelihood. Their Christmas shop, Razzle Dazzle Décor, has seen seasonal fads come and go, but there's one trend they can't escape. Online superstores are swallowing their sales, and this Christmas season will need to be their best ever if the store is to stay in business.
To help keep the shop afloat, Lauren also has a sideline, writing biographies for business figures. She's thrilled when her literary agent contacts her with a new proposal—before learning that the subject will be none other than John Gerald Giompalo. He's the titan behind Globalgoods.com, the online retailer that has spelled doom for hundreds of small businesses just like Razzle Dazzle Décor. Despite her misgivings, Lauren travels to Seattle to confer with the mogul, and is caught off guard when his son, John Jr., attends the meeting too. Handsome, intelligent, and deeply kind, he's perfect—apart from the fact that he's part of the company threatening everything Lauren loves.

As her deadline, and Christmas, draw closer, Lauren knows that there's more than her family's shop at stake. Her heart is, too. But there's no better time than the holidays to make a secret wish on the brightest star you see—and let the season's magic take hold . . .

*Available now from Kensington Books
wherever books are sold!*

Connect with

Us

Visit us online at
KensingtonBooks.com
to read more from your favorite authors, see books
by series, view reading group guides, and more.

Join us on social media

for sneak peeks, chances to win books and prize packs,
and to share your thoughts with other readers.

facebook.com/kensingtonpublishing
twitter.com/kensingtonbooks

Tell us what you think!

To share your thoughts, submit a review,
or sign up for our eNewsletters, please visit:
KensingtonBooks.com/TellUs.

Books by Bestselling Author
Fern Michaels

More by Bestselling Author
Hannah Howell

More by Bestselling Author

Lori Foster

Bad Boys to Go	0-7582-0552-X	$6.99US/$9.99CAN
I Love Bad Boys	0-7582-0135-4	$6.99US/$9.99CAN
I'm Your Santa	0-7582-2860-0	$6.99US/$9.99CAN
Jamie	0-8217-7514-6	$6.99US/$9.99CAN
Jingle Bell Rock	0-7582-0570-8	$6.99US/$9.99CAN
Jude's Law	0-8217-7802-1	$6.99US/$9.99CAN
Murphy's Law	0-8217-7803-X	$6.99US/$9.99CAN
Never Too Much	1-4201-0656-2	$6.99US/$8.49CAN
The Night Before Christmas	0-7582-1215-1	$6.99US/$9.99CAN
Perfect for the Beach	0-7582-0773-5	$6.99US/$9.99CAN
Say No to Joe?	0-8217-7512-X	$6.99US/$9.99CAN
Star Quality	0-7582-1008-6	$4.99US/$5.99CAN
Too Much Temptation	1-4201-0431-4	$6.99US/$9.99CAN
Truth or Dare	0-8217-8054-9	$4.99US/$6.99CAN
Unexpected	0-7582-0549-X	$6.99US/$9.99CAN
A Very Merry Christmas	0-7582-1541-X	$6.99US/$9.99CAN
When Bruce Met Cyn	0-8217-7513-8	$6.99US/$9.99CAN

Available Wherever Books Are Sold!

Check out our website at **www.kensingtonbooks.com**